RED HERRING

RED HERRING

JONOTHAN CULLINANE

HarperCollins*Publishers*
New Zealand

HarperCollins*Publishers*

First published in 2016
by HarperCollins*Publishers* (New Zealand) Limited
Unit D1, 63 Apollo Drive, Rosedale, Auckland 0632, New Zealand
harpercollins.co.nz

HarperCollins*Publishers*
Unit D1, 63 Apollo Drive, Rosedale, Auckland 0632, New Zealand
Level 13, 201 Elizabeth Street, Sydney NSW 2000
A 53, Sector 57, Noida, UP, India
1 London Bridge Street, London, SE1 9GF, United Kingdom
2 Bloor Street East, 20th floor, Toronto, Ontario M4W 1A8, Canada
195 Broadway, New York NY 10007, USA

A catalogue record for this book is available from the National Library of New Zealand

ISBN 978 1 7755 4098 4 (pbk)
ISBN 978 1 7754 9136 1 (ebook)

Cover design by Darren Holt, HarperCollins Design Studio
Efforts have been made to trace and acknowledge copyright. Where the attempt has been unsuccessful, we would be pleased to hear from the copyright holder to rectify any omission or error.
Typeset in 11.5/17pt Bembo
Printed and bound in Australia by McPhersons Printing Group
The papers used by HarperCollins in the manufacture of this book are a natural, recyclable product made from wood grown in sustainable plantation forests. The fibre source and manufacturing processes meet recognised international environmental standards, and carry certification.

For the former Deb Lawrence

AUTHOR'S NOTE

Where the facts have interfered with the story I've changed the facts.

Not a single problem of the class struggle has ever been
solved in history except by violence.

— Lenin

Chinese Communists had won their civil war and created the People's Republic of China in 1949. That victory, coupled with the descent of an "iron curtain" across Eastern Europe after the Second World War, gave credence to the fear of communist expansion. When, in 1950, the New Zealand Government was asked by the United States to support American-led United Nations intervention in the Korean civil war, it agreed to do so.

Anxiety about the threat of communism lay behind the National Government's strategy for dealing with its second potential crisis, the waterfront dispute of 1951. National was worried about the power of the militant Trade Union Congress in opposition to the more moderate Federation of Labour. The TUC was led by Jock Barnes and Toby Hill of the Waterside Workers' Union. The FOL was dominated by the conservative and authoritarian Fintan Patrick Walsh, whom one historian has called "the nearest thing New Zealand had to an American-style industrial gangster".

— Michael King, *The Penguin History of New Zealand*

CHAPTER ONE

Auckland, New Zealand
February 1951

Johnny Molloy stood in the shade of a verandah at the bottom of Vulcan Lane and watched the wharfies marching up Queen Street. He was in his early thirties, not a bad-looking bloke, lean, with dark curly hair brushed back and a long Irish face that had been through the wringer. He wore a dark suit and a red tie. A cigarette was stuck to his bottom lip, smoke drifting up around the brim of a brown felt hat tipped back on his head. He was a private detective.

The wharfies tramped in loose formation behind a large canvas banner inscribed with the words "Waterside Workers' Union", the letters drawn like red and black coiled rope, looped at the end around baling hooks held in clenched fists. The banner was strung between two wooden poles. The WWU president, Jock Barnes, carried one and his offsider, Toby Hill, the other. Barnes did some drainlaying on the side and looked it, his big chest and broad shoulders squeezed into a bulging tweed jacket that seemed a size too small. Hill, with his Harold Lloyd glasses and knitted vest, could have been an insurance clerk. But Molloy knew they were tough roosters, both of them.

Molloy had an appointment with an American named Furst at half past twelve in the Hotel Auckland. He didn't mind Yanks, having met a few in Italy during the war. Not bad blokes for the most part. Thought they won the show on their own of course, but that was all right.

Queen Street was full of pedestrians. The shops were crowded. A Mt Eden tram was taking on passengers, the conductor reconnecting the pole to the overhead wire, the wheel arcing and spitting. The motorman leaned out of the cab, raised his cap to the passing wharfies, and shouted, "Good on you, boys!" A few spectators clapped their support. Some booed. An office boy in a white shirt a size too big called out, "Go back to Russia!" and his friend laughed and said, "Too right!" A uniformed policeman in a white summer helmet gave them a look and the boys turned sheepish and shut up. Molloy knew the cop. Pat Toomey, a sergeant at Newton Police Station in Ponsonby Road. They nodded to each other. Auckland was a small place.

The hotel foyer was dark and cool, with patterned carpet and a large painting of the Southern Alps along one wall. The dining room was busy and Molloy could smell roast meat and hear the clatter of cutlery. The receptionist was listening to an English couple complaining about the noise the previous night. They had been kept awake till twelve by someone belting out selections from *South Pacific* on the piano in the house bar, directly beneath their room. They insisted on talking to the manager. The receptionist tapped the office bell and turned to Molloy.

"Hello, stranger," she said.

"How are you, Esme? I'm here to see a guest named Al Furst. A Yank."

"Let me check," said Esme, opening the ledger. She ran a nail-polished finger slowly down a column. "Long time, no see, Johnny," she said, her voice lowering. "Missed you at the Orange. Have you put away your dancing shoes?"

"Oh, you know," said Molloy. "How's Mac?"

"Down Kaikoura," said Esme. "Crayfish." Her finger touched the edge of his hand. "Won't lay my eyes on him till March. You should pop round."

"You still in Point Chev?"

"Door's never locked," she said. "Mr Furst is in 309."

Molloy walked up the stairs to the third floor, straightened his tie, and knocked on Room 309. The door opened. Furst was in his late forties, barrel shaped, with short legs and a big chest. He had coarse grey hair parted in the middle and deep-set red-rimmed eyes. He was wearing a white shirt, unbuttoned at the neck and creased from travel. Chest hair poked over the frayed collar of a singlet. Braces held up his suit trousers, dark brown with a thin stripe, the sort a gangster in the pictures might wear.

"Yessir?" he said.

"Mr Furst? I'm Johnny Molloy. We've got an appointment."

"Oh, yeah, the private investigator," said Furst. "Damn, is that the time?" He stood back and opened the door wide. "Well, all right. Come on in."

CHAPTER TWO

Furst's room had two single beds and a narrow chest of drawers, a club chair and a writing desk. A leather suitcase was open on the spare bed. Sun was coming through venetian blinds.

"What time did you get in?" said Molloy.

"This morning," said Furst. "Not sure. Six? It was just getting light." He ran a hand over his scalp. "I don't know what the rules are here but my head's still in Pago Pago and I believe over there it's cocktail hour. Care to join me?"

"That'd be good," said Molloy.

Furst poured whisky from a small flask into two hotel cups and handed one to Molloy. "Your good health," he said. "Take the chair." He pulled a stool out from under the writing desk and sat down.

"You were recommended by the feller who runs the New Zealand Insurance Company office in San Francisco," said Furst. "Paul Lipscombe."

"He sent me a telegram," said Molloy.

"Smoke?" Furst shook two cigarettes from a pack. "What got you into this line of work, Molloy? Were you a cop?"

"No," said Molloy. "I sort of fell into it after the war. Yourself?"

"San Francisco Police Department," said Furst. "Twenty years. Twelve years robbery-homicide. Six years bunco — fraud, what-have-you. Last two as chief of detectives." He handed Molloy a business card.

"Now I run the Investigation Unit of the US Life & General Insurance Company of California." He lit a match. "You do missing persons?"

"I do industrial investigations, mostly," said Molloy, leaning in to the flame. "Fraud and theft. Some matrimonial. But I've found people, if that's what you mean."

"It is. I'll tell you the job. You tell me if you're interested." The American took a folder from the top of a pile on the desk, opened it, and passed an item to Molloy, an alien seaman's identification card, issued by the US Coast Guard, marked and worn.

"I'm looking for this gentleman," he said.

The photograph on the ID showed a man in his mid to late thirties wearing a leather jacket and an open-necked white shirt. He had a tough, handsome face, black wavy hair parted off-centre and pushed straight back, a cowlick sprung loose. He was staring into the camera with an expression halfway between a smile and a sneer. His details were typed below. **Name Francis Xavier O'PHELAN. Date of Birth 11/26/15. Place of Birth United Kingdom & Ireland.** His signature was scrawled along the bottom. The card had a red stamp through it, the word **DECEASED.**

Molloy took a notebook and pencil from his suitcoat pocket and thumbed for a clean page.

Furst tapped the card. "O'Phelan was an Irishman, second engineer on a coastal service freighter between San Diego and the Bering Sea," he said. "He was washed overboard during a storm in the Gulf of Alaska."

Furst handed Molloy a second seaman's card. "This feller witnessed the tragic event."

The photograph on the second ID showed a gaunt and pock-marked man around thirty with thinning fair hair and a bent nose, named — according to the particulars — **Hendrik Lech SUBRITSKY.**

Furst shook his head. "This guy saw something? Cross-eyed bastard would have been looking the other way his whole sorry life." Like the first card, Subritsky's had been stamped **DECEASED**.

"O'Phelan had a policy with US Life," said Furst. "On paper everything seemed in order. The claim was met."

He rested his cigarette on an ashtray. "In March last year we had an approach from an Oakland public defender acting for Subritsky. His client had shot a guy. He was looking at hard time. His girl was in the family way. He wanted to talk about O'Phelan. If he could show us the Irishman had faked his death, would there be something in it for him?

"I went to see him at California Correctional. He told me that O'Phelan had hidden in the hold during the storm and snuck off the ship in Juneau two days later. In return for providing a witness statement, O'Phelan promised Subritsky a percentage of the insurance money. Of course, Subritsky never saw a penny." Furst shrugged. "And a week after I talked to him, Subritsky was dead."

Molloy looked up. "O'Phelan?"

"Stabbed to death in the Yard," said Furst. "The Coloured section. There are rules. This was not a smart guy." He reached around for his hip flask. "Little more?"

Molloy shook his head. He checked his notebook. "There's no record of him coming ashore in Juneau?"

"It's US territory," said Furst. "You just step off."

"Who was O'Phelan's beneficiary?"

Furst produced another item from the stack on the desk. "This peach. His loving wife Valma. De facto wife, I should say."

He showed Molloy a mugshot, front and side views, a tough-looking woman in her twenties, black roots visible through peroxide, holding a sign with the name **Valerie Marie ROSEN**, and beneath

7

that a list of offences including the words "solicitation", "prostitution", "theft" and "narcotics".

"The insurance business has gone to hell," said Furst, taking back the photograph. "Before the war a broad like this could have no more succeeded in a claim than gone to the moon." He raised his hands in disgust.

"You think Subritsky was telling the truth about O'Phelan?" said Molloy. "That he faked his disappearance?"

"I do," said Furst. "Verified by Valma. He skipped out on her too. The scam was Valma's idea, dreamed up after watching *Double Indemnity*. You seen that damned picture? When it came out every mutt in America started planning." Furst shook his head at the fecklessness of Hollywood. "We made copies of his picture and sent them out with a request for information and a reward. We got sightings. Honolulu. Mexico. Nothing solid."

He picked up a folded magazine and passed it to Molloy. "But a month ago an operative in Sydney sent us this."

It was the Australian weekly magazine, *The Bulletin*, opened to an article about Communist infiltration of the union movement in the South Pacific. Furst offered a magnifying glass to the detective.

"Take a good look," said Furst. "The one in the circle."

There was a small photograph accompanying the story. Four men leaving the Trades Hall in Hobson Street in Auckland. The first two were Jock Barnes and Toby Hill; Barnes hatless, suit coat unbuttoned, a striped tie halfway down his front, Hill in a three-piece suit, holding a briefcase in one hand and a pipe in the other. The third was putting on his hat, his face in shadow, but Molloy recognised the curly hair of Dave Griffiths, a watersiders' delegate. A circle had been drawn around the fourth. He was wearing a white shirt and dark tie, jacket in the crook of his arm, looking past the camera.

8

Furst put O'Phelan's Merchant Marine ID next to the *Bulletin* photograph. Molloy bent forward and ran the magnifying glass over the picture, going in on the circled figure, comparing it with the ID. A tough, handsome face, black wavy hair parted off-centre and pushed back, a cowlick sprung loose.

He looked at Furst. "It's the same bloke," he said.

"That's what we think."

"And you want me to find him?"

"I do," said Furst. "If it turns out he's not our man, well, okay. If, on the other hand, it turns out he is, then we would be delighted."

Molloy stubbed out his cigarette. He pointed at Barnes and Hill.

"Look, Furst," he said. "Thanks for the offer but I think you're talking to the wrong bloke. I know these two. There's a big showdown coming on the waterfront. I don't want to get tied up in something that's going to cause them even more trouble."

"Okay," said Furst, sitting forward, one hand on his knee. "First thing, it's Al. Second, Lipscombe said you were a Commie. Doesn't bother me. My brother is a union big shot in New York. Garment Workers. Bright red. Been to Russia even. Worked in a factory over there showing them how to cut patterns. So what? He's a good man. I was a cop long enough to know that a feller's politics don't tell you an awful lot about him when all's said and done, not about the things that count. Third, US Life & General doesn't want the publicity. A case like this? It's an embarrassment." He nodded towards the *Bulletin* story. "And maybe, if *this* guy is *our* guy, it's something your pals would want to know? A grifter in the ranks?"

"Could be," said Molloy.

Furst stood and stretched. "And fourth? I've got to get some sleep."

"I charge a pound per day, plus expenses," said Molloy. "Five pound minimum."

"Company pays a generous closure bonus if a case is cleared," said Furst.

"Sounds good," said Molloy.

"When can you start?"

"Now, if you like."

"Glad to hear it," said Furst, taking a five-pound note from his wallet.

Molloy picked up the magazine. "Mind if I hang on to this?"

"It's yours."

Molloy wrote a number in his notebook, tore out the page, and handed it to Furst. "This is my landlady's telephone number," he said. "You can leave a message there if you need to get in touch. I'll phone you here at the hotel."

They shook hands.

"Welcome aboard," said the American.

CHAPTER THREE

Molloy caught the Mission Bay tram and got off in Quay Street. The road was lined with trucks along both sides, motors idling, drivers leaning against the mudguards smoking and passing the time. On the wharf, cranes were slinging freight into the holds of ships, wharfies standing on top of bales and pallets, swinging through the air. Men sat or squatted along the red wrought-iron railings in the sun, eating their lunch and drinking tea from Thermos flasks, reading *Truth* or making calculations in the margins of the *Friday Flash*. Hard to believe there was insurrection in the air.

He crossed the road and approached the barrier at the entrance to Queen's Wharf. Billy Burgess was leaning on a walking stick and counting out loud, using a pencil to point at wool bales stacked high on the tray of a Bedford idling in front of the traffic barrier, while the driver, a hard nut in a black singlet, Armoured Brigade beret pushed back on his head, made whistling noises.

"Whistle as much as ye like," said Billy. "It'll take as long as it takes."

"Och aye, I know," said the driver, in a Freemans Bay tough's idea of a Scottish lilt.

"Johnny," said Billy. "Seven, eight — you here to see me, son? — nine, ten."

"When you've got a minute," said Molloy.

"Go on inside," Billy said, tearing a duplicate from his tally book and handing it to the driver. "I won't be long. Put the kettle on."

Billy was a Glaswegian in his fifties, short and lean and angular, face like a knucklebone, skin dry and cracked, sharp eyes a watery green. He was a Harbour Board gatekeeper. A tattooed schooner disappeared into a fog of curly grey hair on one wiry forearm, the blurred outline of an anchor was faintly visible on the other. He had come to New Zealand as an engineer on the Union Company coalburner *Kent* in 1920, met a girl, bought himself out, got married. One child, a son named Graeme, a civilian radio operator with Post and Telegraph, seconded to a Coastwatch station in the Gilbert Islands in August 1942, captured two weeks later, and executed, aged twenty, his head lopped off by one of those big curved swords the Japs used, buried up there in the jungle somewhere. His last radio message was, "Japanese coming. Regards to all."

Billy's world was a quadrangular one. The Sailors' Mission where he lived, Queen's Wharf where he worked, the Grey Lynn Returned Services Club where he drank, and a weekly visit to Symonds Street Cemetery to tidy the ground around his wife's grave and enjoy a reflective smoke. He spent eight hours a day checking freight manifests and keeping the port traffic moving. If he had a soft spot it was his overweening belief in the Social Credit theories of Major Douglas, which he would promote at the drop of a hat. But he was well liked, and everyone coming on or going off the wharf — seagulls, sailors, shippies, watersiders — had to pass by his station. He knew them all. If anyone would know the bloke in the *Bulletin* picture and be able to keep his trap shut, Billy would. If it *was* O'Phelan, and word got out that someone was asking about him, he could go bush or be halfway across the Tasman before you could say Jack Robinson. And at a quid a day plus expenses it made sense to be cautious.

Billy's shed was a single man's hut, low-ceilinged, with a standing desk and a window on sliders cut into the west wall and opening onto the traffic barrier. Molloy turned on the Zip. There was tea in a willow-pattern tin, sugar in a glass jar, and a teapot and two stained cups on a shelf. A half bottle of milk sat in the corner out of the sun. Billy's brown dust-coat hung on a hook behind the door. There was a calendar and statutory regulations and weight lists on the wall, and a framed print of the HMS *Royal Oak*. Billy had won a DSM at the Battle of Jutland, "wounded by a shell splinter but continued to carry on" in the words of the citation which he kept in a drawer, along with the medal, in his room at the Mission. He had shown it to Molloy once in a sentimental moment after a few restorative whiskies at an Armistice Day breakfast.

Billy came in and shut the door, hanging his hat and his stick on the hook. Immediately, horns started tooting. "Toot away, you bastards," he said, taking a handkerchief from his pocket and wiping his forehead. He waved at the window. "Wool. Every day's like this. Trying to get the stuff out while they can. There's lorries and freight backed up to blasted Timbuktu."

"Think of all that overtime."

"Bugger the overtime," said Billy, taking an egg sandwich from a brown paper bag and offering half to Molloy. "Brave men fought for the eight-hour day and I don't need the money."

Molloy passed him a cup. "Could come to a screaming halt pretty soon," he said.

"For all the good it'll do them," said Billy. "I was on Clydeside after the war. The Great War, that is." He gestured with his sandwich. "You pansies never knew what a real war was. The Glasgow general strike. Soldiers everywhere, mounted policemen, machine guns, talk of Bolsheviks." He hooked a thumb over his shoulder. "Felt like this, if you know what I mean."

"How did that end up?"

"Not well for the boys. These things never do. They've been quietly moving lads to Papakura Camp all week, my pals on the railways tell me. Fellas in civvies were sneaking around here a few nights ago, getting the lay of the place. Had 'officer' written all over them."

A truck horn tooted. Billy put down his tea and slid open the window.

"I'm coming!" he said. "Let me finish my cuppa, for the love of God." He looked at Molloy. "What's it you need, son? I'd better get back to it."

Molloy opened the *Bulletin* and pointed to the photograph.

"Recognise either of these blokes with Barnes and Hill?" said Molloy. "On the QT."

Billy squinted.

"Can't tell for sure with his arm up like that," he said. "But I think it's Dave Griffiths."

Molloy pointed to the second figure. "What about him?"

"I've seen him around a bit. Watersider. Likes a drink."

"That narrows it down," said Molloy.

Burgess gave him a long look. "He takes his waters at the Grey Lynn RSC," he said. "His name's Frank O'Flynn."

CHAPTER FOUR

The Grey Lynn Returned Services Club was a two-storey brick building in Francis Street, just off Richmond Road. It had originally been the Grey Lynn School, then a picture theatre called the Galaxy, and, from 1947, a watering hole for merchant seamen, who — denied entry to the Returned Services Association because they were not considered to have been servicemen, as though manning unarmed freighters on the Murmansk run was a peacetime occupation — had taken over the lease and established a club of their own, one with more generous entry criteria.

Molloy went through the front door into the Public Bar. It was quiet and dark, with stained sunlight coming through high windows that wouldn't have had a decent clean since the place was the Galaxy. An elderly man was sitting at a table in front of two empty jugs, his yellow-stained fingers slowly turning a rollie, twisting both ends with the delicacy of a safe-cracker, a terrier keeping a furious lookout on the carpet at his feet.

"How are you, Davey?" said Molloy.

Davey Coulson didn't look up. "That you, Johnny?" he said. "How are you, son?"

"I'm good," said Molloy. "You all right?"

"Yes, I'm all right," said Coulson.

A man in the corner was picking out a tune on the upright, stumbling over notes.

"Bloody hell, stop that flamin' racket!" someone yelled.

"Get stuffed," said the tunesmith.

"Come on, gents. Language, please," said the barman, Bones Harrington. He was leaning against the back bar, tea towel over one shoulder, wiggling a tooth. "G'day, Johnny," he said, straightening up and tossing off a salute.

"G'day, Bones," said Molloy. He took some coins from his pocket and put them on the bar. "Give us an eight, will you?"

Molloy and Bones had been in Greece in 1941 with the 27th (Machine Gun) Battalion, dug in near Katerini at the base of Mt Olympus. They'd watched as an endless column of German trucks, tanks, mobile artillery and sidecars mounted with machine guns, came straight at them, grinding and clanking, the worst kind of dream — an army that had never lost a battle advancing on soldiers who had yet to fire a shot. But sappers had mined the approach with naval depth charges "obtained in an irregular manner" by Colonel Clifton, CO 6th Brigade, who had learned of their unconventional use in Norway the previous year. Without any authority whatsoever, he had commandeered forty from the Royal Navy in Alexandria and talked the captain of his transport into taking them to Greece. Not for nothing were the New Zealanders known as the 40,000 thieves. The explosion blew a tank sideways, the advance guard piled up, and the Brigade's zeroed-in mortars and machine guns gave them a stonking. The Div's first combined exercise was a battle and they did pretty well. The German advance was held up for a day and a night before the New Zealanders were ordered to fall back.

In the confusion of the withdrawal, Bones' convoy drove straight into a motorised brigade of the *Leibstandarte SS Adolf*

Hitler, an SS formation of singular and ferocious reputation whose command was later prosecuted *en masse* for war crimes at Nuremberg. Bones spent the next four years in prisoner-of-war camps in Italy and Austria. Molloy got to the embarkation point at Porto Rafti, near Athens, one of five thousand men rescued by the Royal Navy and taken, not to Egypt, but to Crete. Out of the frying pan into the frying pan.

Bones wiped his hands on the tea towel and took an eight-ounce glass from a tray.

"Me teeth are playing up," he said, pouring beer from a rubber hose. "You still got your own gnashers?"

"Most of them," said Molloy. "Couple of the back ones wobble a bit, now you mention it."

"I'm thinking of having the whole blimmin' lot pulled out. Get some dentures." He slid the beer over. "Here you are, Johnny," he said. "Get that down your rotten guts."

"Cheers, Bones," said Molloy, drinking the top inch.

The barman made a sucking sound. "This one, for instance," he said. He took a white handkerchief from his pocket, carefully unfolded it, and showed Molloy a bloody bicuspid. "I was wriggling it a bit and next thing, I'm holding the bugger in me hand."

"That's no good."

"It's not." Bones poked round with his tongue. "My brother had all his taken out," he said, returning the handkerchief to his pocket and wiping his hand on his strides. "Last time he come to town he went to old Mr Geddes there and he said, 'no, bugger it, I'm sick of this. Take the bloody lot out'. Had uppers and lowers fitted. Cost a packet but he can afford it. You ever considered that, Johnny? Deer culling? Not a bad life for a single bloke, out there in the bush with a rifle, all that dough and nowhere to spend it."

"That's a thought," said Molloy. "Is Tim working today?"

Bones' tone changed. He leaned in. "Jeez, poor bloody Tim. You heard what happened?"

Molloy shook his head.

"Remember Paddy?" said Bones. He hooked a thumb in the direction of Asia. "Copped it over there in Korea."

"You're joking," said Molloy, putting his glass down.

"No," said Bones. "He come in yesterday and told me. His mum just got the telegram. He's taken a couple of days off he's so cut up."

"What was Paddy doing in Korea?"

"Kayforce. Lance bombardier with one of the batteries up there," said Bones. "He volunteered."

"Oh, you never volunteer."

Bones raised his shoulders. "Fundamental rule," he said.

"Kayforce?" said Molloy, trying to make sense of it. "He was too old for the bloody army."

Bones snorted. "You didn't know his missus. Actually, you probably did. Mary Kelly? Remember? This high? From St Joseph's? Grew up in Paget Street? Father was a plumber?"

Molloy remembered her. "Even so," he said.

"What a bastard," said Bones. He counted them off. "Of the five O'Connor boys you got Vincent killed in North Africa, Barney killed in the Pacific, and now Paddy. Just Tim and Peter left."

"Not good."

"One more?" said Bones, straightening up.

"I better," said Molloy. "Bloody Paddy, eh."

Bones took his glass.

"What's Peter up to these days?" said Molloy.

"Wellington. Got a good job with the Dairy Board. He studied for his accountancy papers while he was in the bag."

"Did he now? Good on him," said Molloy. "What did you study?"

Bones laughed. "Oh, cripes. Tunnelling, I suppose. I was on the escape committee. Wandered round with me hands in me pockets most of the time. Beady-eyed Huns, it's all you could do."

"I should drop round to Mrs O'Connor's. Offer my condolences," said Molloy.

"Good idea. I should too." Bones filled a glass with lemonade. "Here's to a good little bugger. May he rest in peace."

"To Paddy," said Molloy. They clinked glasses and drank. Molloy pointed to the lemonade bottle. "You off the plonk?"

"Just for a bit."

"I wanted to ask Tim something, but you might know," said Molloy.

"Fire away."

"Under your hat?"

"My word."

"I'm looking for a wharfie called O'Flynn," said Molloy. "Irishman. Billy Burgess said he's seen him up here."

"Well, there's an Irish joker called O'Flynn who comes in here with Barnes and that mob a bit," said Bones. "Loudmouth? That the one? Why? What's he done?"

Molloy shrugged. "Behind on a lay-by. Nothing much."

"Oh, yeah?" said Bones, looking straight at Molloy. "Actually, doesn't surprise me. He puts his drinks on the slate half the time and we always have to chase him up."

"Does this O'Flynn stay around here, do you know?"

"Think he might, as a matter of fact." Bones banged the till and took an old school exercise book from under the cash drawer. "If a

member has a big night we sometimes get him home in a taxi."
He slowly turned the pages, running his finger down the columns.
"Here we are."

Molloy took out his notebook.

"Number 3 Chamberlain Street," said Bones, pointing over
Molloy's shoulder. "It's a big boarding house near the top of
Richmond Road there."

CHAPTER FIVE

A black 1938 Chrysler Plymouth turned the corner into Princes Street and stopped in front of the Northern Club. The passenger got out. He was a solid man, in his fifties, face like a Belfast bricklayer, small mouth, black hair, thick eyebrows that curled up at the ends. He wore a brown double-breasted suit, the trousers belted high over his stomach, and a green tie.

"I'll be half an hour, Sunny," he said, wiping his hatliner. "Wait here."

"Right-o, Mr Walsh," said the driver, reaching into the glovebox for tobacco.

Fintan Patrick Walsh put his handkerchief back in his pocket. He looked up at the elegant sandstone building, Union Jack hanging above the entrance, thick green carpet of Virginia creeper shining in the sun, dark recessed windows giving off "the wealthy yellow light" that Mark Twain had noticed when he stayed there in 1895.

It was a long way from Patutahi in Poverty Bay, where Walsh had grown up. Not that he cared tuppence. He doubted there was a puffed-up member of this foolish piece of transplanted Englishness that he couldn't buy or sell or put out of business or run out of town.

The doorman, Barrett, thought about asking the driver to move his motorcar, and then, realising who the passenger was, thought again. Walsh was the most powerful union man in the country. Most powerful anything, a lot of people said, the uncrowned king, someone around whom violent rumour swirled, a union official in the sense that the American gangster Vito Corleone was an importer of olive oil.

In 1912, aged eighteen, Walsh was one of a handful of armed men guarding the Miners & Workers Union Hall in Waihi from an assault by strikebreakers and police. During the mêlée, a scab was shot in the knee and a constable in the stomach "by a person or persons unknown". Walsh was spirited out of Waihi that night, left New Zealand soon after on a four-master from Napier, wound up in California, worked on oilers in the Gulf of Mexico and freighters on the South American run, jumped ship in San Francisco, spent two years as an organiser and enforcer for the Wobblies in Idaho and Montana.

He was a founding member, in 1921, of the Communist Party of New Zealand. He had bent the ears and twisted the arms of prime ministers from George Forbes to Sid Holland. He was the *éminence grise* of the Federation of Labour. He was said to own more land in the Wairarapa than the Riddifords. He was a riddle, wrapped in an enigma, holding a gun.

Why cross him?

Which is not to say that the doorman was windy, or lacked moral fibre. Far from it. Barrett had lost a leg at Gallipoli, shot out from under him during the charge up Rhododendron Ridge, the Auckland Battalion heading straight into the sun, Turkish bullets thick as bees, in the opening assault on Chunuk Bair. Three hundred boys were killed or wounded in less than twenty minutes.

He had lain all day in the heat, no water, flies in his mouth, lads around him crying out for stretcher-bearers, for shade, for their mothers, to die.

The CO of the Wellingtons, Colonel Malone, had refused to allow his men to follow in daylight. Now *there* was an officer and a gentleman, Barrett thought. Could have taught some of the newer members a thing or two.

Malone was killed next day on the summit, careless rounds from a British destroyer. Or possibly the Turks. Barrett preferred to blame the Poms. What a cock-up. "When I think of Chunuk Bair," a cobber of his had said once, in the RSC after an Anzac Day do, "I think of reddish-brown. And that was blood."

What was left of Barrett's leg was amputated above the knee on the New Zealand hospital ship *Maheno* in Suvla Bay, and he returned home to a job at the club arranged by the Battalion 2IC, Major Campbell-Stevenson, whose father was on the committee.

Barrett was used to opening the door for powerful men, and men who thought they were powerful, had done it now for more than thirty years, and wasn't bothered by it. Part of the job.

But Walsh was Walsh. His war was the class war.

Both sides.

The doorman brought up his arm in a polite salute. "Morning, Mr Walsh," he said, with a deference he usually reserved for judges of the Supreme Court. "Another beauty."

Walsh gave his name and hat to the duty manager and said he was there to see Henderson. The manager rang an electric bell and a maid in a black uniform and white apron appeared. He told her to show the gentleman to the library. She bobbed and glanced at Walsh. Pretty, he noticed. On the plump side, which he liked.

He followed her up stairs hung with portraits of long-faced Englishmen, governors-general and the like, club patrons since 1869. She had a behind that Walsh could have grabbed with both hands. Her buttocks rolled like two Tahitians dancing in a sack. Was she sending him a message or was she simply climbing the stairs? She reminded him of a girl he'd kept in the Arundel Private Hotel, along the road in Waterloo Quadrant, before the war. Jane something. Or Julia.

At the top of the stairway was a wide wood-panelled corridor lined with prints from the Maori Wars. A faded blue and green Persian runner, held in place with polished rods, led to a set of tall double doors halfway along. The girl stopped. "This is the library," she said. "Would you like me to knock, sir?"

"In a minute," said Walsh. "What's your name?"

"My name?" She looked around. "It's Brenda."

"You're an attractive wee thing, aren't you, Brenda."

"Oh yeah? Mum warned me about fellers like you in the big city. Men of the world. All hands."

"A wise woman. Where are you from?"

She rolled her eyes. "Otorohanga, I'm embarrassed to say."

"But you got out. Which shows you have ambition."

"Ambition! No one's ever said that to me before!"

"Here's another thing I bet no one's said. How would you like to go for a ride in an American motorcar? Bet you've never been in one of them."

"American? Not American. Lots of ordinary ones though. I like going in cars."

"I bet you do. Tell you what. Be waiting out the front at nine tomorrow morning. I'll take you for a drive in a Plymouth. That's a real car."

"Oh, love to, but can't, sorry. Working." She pointed at the floor. "He's put me in the laundry the whole day. I'm 'on probation' according to him."

"That ponce downstairs? Don't worry about him."

"I'm not. Have to pay the bills though."

"How much do you get here?"

"Cheeky!" She paused. "A pound a week with room and board."

"You live on the premises?"

"Eight girls in the attic. Gets so hot at night." She fanned herself.

"Tell you what. Come and work for me. I'll give you thirty bob a week for starters and find you a nice place to live. On your own? With another girl? Whatever you like."

She was unsure. "What'll I do? For a job and that?"

"Not sure yet. This is not the place for a girl who wants to get ahead in the world, I know that much."

She thought about it.

"Nine o'clock?"

"Out the front with your suitcase packed."

"All right." She winked. "Sir."

Good girl.

"Now you can knock."

They heard a chair scrape, and footsteps.

The door opened. A man about Walsh's age, wearing a dark suit of some expensive London weave. Tight-mouthed. Rimless glasses. Thinning hair parted well to the side and brushed back with a light layer of Brilliantine. He had the look of the late Prime Minister, Peter Fraser, but with none of Fraser's warmth.

"Walsh," said David Henderson.

"Henderson," said Walsh.

Brenda curtsied.

For a moment both men watched her go, then Henderson showed Walsh into the library, a dark, high-ceilinged room with bookshelves lining one wall, and along the other, large double-hung windows looking out onto an enormous oak at the top of Victoria

Street. A large map of the world was open on a wooden stand at the head of a boardroom table, around which sat half a dozen men of a similar ilk to Henderson, though probably not as well-heeled.

Very few New Zealanders were.

Walsh was one of them.

"Gentlemen," said Henderson. "Allow me to present Fintan Patrick Walsh. The face of responsible unionism in this country." He smiled. "I think we're all agreed. If there have to be unions, they might as well be responsible."

"Well said!" said one of the men to general laughter.

"Right-o," said Henderson. "Introductions. How do you like to be known? Fintan? Pat? Jack? Quite a choice."

"Walsh. Or Mr Walsh. I'm not bothered."

"Walsh it is," said Henderson. "Good Irish name."

Good Taig name you mean, you bowler-hatted bastard, thought Walsh.

"Over there, Stuart Hoar," said Henderson. "The Pacific Steamship Company."

Hoar nodded graciously.

"To his right, in more ways than one, Sir John Newton. Federated Farmers."

Newton acknowledged the laughter.

"S. T. Marsh. City Council."

"We met during the war when I was on the Stabilisation Commission," said Marsh.

Walsh nodded.

"Bruce Solomon. South British Insurance."

"D'you do," said Solomon, scraping the bowl of his pipe with a penknife.

"Keith Petrie. Dominion Brewing."

"Pleased to meet you," said Petrie.

"Last but not least, Roger Hall. A working stiff, much like yourself." Henderson paused. "Bank of New South Wales."

The banker coughed out a polite laugh.

"Gents," said Walsh, taking a seat. He nodded towards a young man in a navy blue suit, one arm resting on the mantelpiece. "And who's the sharp-looking fella holding up the fireplace?" he said. "The butler?"

"That's Olivier," said Henderson. "He's with the Prime Minister's Department. Reason I asked you to join us. He addressed a small gathering last night regarding the present trouble on the waterfront. He was decent enough to delay his return to Wellington to talk to us here today."

"The trouble on the waterfront," said Walsh. "That's a grave topic. Is there whisky in the room?"

"You know, I think there is," said Henderson, looking at his wristwatch. "Keith?"

Petrie got a decanter and glasses from a cabinet.

"Right-o," said Henderson. "This is an informal meeting, no minutes, myself as chairman. Any objections?" There were none. "Carried. Now, I hardly need to tell you chaps that we have a very dangerous situation brewing on the wharves. Tons of goods piling up, mutton and butter and God knows what else, food for Britain—"

"Poor beggars," said Hoar.

"—and Jock Barnes and his cobbers threatening to shut down the whole show." Henderson glared. "Over my dead body."

"Hear, hear," said Marsh.

"Which is the ideal point to hand the floor to Olivier." Henderson leaned back in his seat. "Over to you, son."

Olivier straightened up and walked over to the map, buttoning his suit coat. Here he was, in the sanctum sanctorum, the library of the Northern Club, with the fabled Kelly Gang itself. A good performance in front of these fellows, a word from them in the right ear? My God, the possibilities. He wondered what his old Collegiate Housemaster would say if he could see him. Not such a ding-dong after all, eh, sir?

He placed his briefcase by the table, squared his glasses, picked up a wooden pointer, turned to the map, and tapped China.

CHAPTER SIX

"Gentlemen," said Olivier. "Last week I had the honour of attending a meeting in Wellington at which President Truman's personal representative, Mr John Foster Dulles, addressed the Cabinet on matters concerning the conflict in Korea and its links to the spread of Communism in the Free World."

He paused, and gave his audience what he hoped was a charming and self-deprecating smile. "Sitting quietly at the back of the room taking notes, I hasten to add."

The men chuckled. *Good lad.*

Olivier circled the Pacific with the pointer.

"Over the past several months there has been a series of strikes in ports from San Francisco to Singapore to Sydney."

He turned to the group. "It is the American view that these strikes have been engineered by local Communist-dominated waterfront unions acting on the orders of their political masters in Moscow, whose sole purpose" — he tapped the map — "is Soviet world domination.

"The Americans believe that these actions are designed to place a stranglehold on the flow of war matériel to United Nations forces fighting the Reds on the Korean Peninsula. Why? Because without supplies and ammunition, how can Korea hold? And if Korea falls, what's to stop the Reds from turning to Indo-China?"

Olivier's pointer zigzagged across the map. "Then Borneo. And the Philippines. Java. On and on, one country after another. Toppling like dominoes, as Mr Dulles said."

He traced the pointer down the Indonesian archipelago, across the Timor Sea, hesitating at Darwin. "Will they stop here, does anyone imagine?"

"Darwin?" said Henderson, winking at Walsh. "Hell's bells, I shouldn't think so."

"And from Darwin?" Olivier's baton continued its relentless journey south, tip grating on the parchment, the sound now a tear in the fabric of all that these men held dear, around Australia's east coast, marching south, overrunning the brave but outgunned defenders of Melbourne, across the Tasman, up the Waitemata, charging ashore at Queens Wharf.

There was silence. Olivier laid the pointer gently on the table.

"My God, what a thought," said Newton with a shudder, "Queen Street, teeming with Chinamen."

"You know what this reminds me of?" said Hoar. "The Japs in 1942. No sooner put *those* Orientals to bed and here comes the next lot."

"This is worse," said Newton. "Say what you like about the Jap. A brute no question, but at heart he was a soldier. With a code of honour. Bushido. You could reason with him." He reached for the decanter. "Your Red, on the other hand?" He shook his head. *Res ipsa loquitor.*

"This is happening already," said Henderson, waving a hand at the map. "Korea, of course, papers are full of it. You've got the French in Tonkin up there. You've got the British in Malaya. Dominoes is right."

"Barnes and Hill, the wharfies' bosses, both as red as they come," said Petrie.

"Whole damn lot of them," said Solomon.

"Taking their marching orders from Moscow," said Hall. "The swine."

"Shouldn't have stopped at Berlin," said Petrie. "That was the mistake. On to Moscow. Finished the damn thing then and there."

Hall nodded. "Bolshevism. Churchill was right. It's a bacillus."

"Right-o, gentlemen," said Henderson. "Any questions for Mr Olivier?"

"What's the American plan?" said Solomon.

"More important, what's *our* plan?" said Henderson, determined to keep the conversation local. "We're on the front line of this thing. Where's the Prime Minister stand?"

Olivier poked the bridge of his tortoise-shell glasses. "Well, Mr Holland is most concerned, of course," he said.

"Oh yes, I bet he is," said Henderson. "Soviet world domination and the possibility of a by-election in Whangarei. He's got a lot on his plate." He leaned forward. "But there are elements in Wellington — and I've got this right, haven't I, Olivier — who would applaud an initiative taken by responsible citizens?"

"Mr Dulles used a quote from *Julius Caesar*—" Olivier began.

"'*Et tu, Brute?*' you mean?" said Petrie, who could be a bit arch for Henderson's liking. "Good God, man. You're not suggesting a *coup d'état*, I hope? Daggers in the Forum, that sort of thing?"

"No, he's not," said Walsh. "'There is a tide in the affairs of men, when grabbed by the gonads, leads on to fortune.' That's the bit, isn't it, son? Words to that effect?"

"Well, along those lines, Mr Walsh," said Olivier.

Henderson stood. "Very good, young man," he said. "*Te salutant!* Most impressive presentation."

There was a round of applause.

"I'll take over from here, son," said Henderson.

"But ..." said Olivier. He indicated his briefcase. There were Special Branch reports. Diplomatic memoranda. Veiled evidence of foreign entanglements. He had barely begun!

"Be sure to give my best to your CO," said Henderson, putting a hand on Olivier's shoulder, indicating the library doors. "Spent the war in an office in Bowen Street with Mac." He turned to the others. "Alister McIntosh, that is. Big Chief of the Prime Minister's Department these days." He turned back to Olivier. "Still struggling with his rhododendrons?"

"Rhododendrons?" said Olivier, bewildered. "I'm really not—"

"Used to say to him, 'Karori's too damn windy for Ericaceae, Mac'," said Henderson. "But he'd be out there, every weekend, with his stakes and fertiliser and whatnot."

"Well. The southerly, I suppose," said Olivier, trying to keep up but knowing his cause was lost.

Henderson took Olivier by the elbow. "Have a spot of lunch downstairs," he said. "They'll take care of you. Then I'll get my chap to run you down to the station."

"I am a bit peckish, actually," said Olivier, in a small voice, as the doors closed in his face.

CHAPTER SEVEN

"Well, Walsh," said Henderson, returning to his seat. "What did you make of that?"

Walsh reached for the decanter and removed the stopper. "What did I make of it?" He poured a finger into his glass, returned the stopper, leaned back in his chair.

"What that young fella's saying, if I've got this right, is that Moscow is working with its flunkies in waterfront unions round the Pacific to help ensure a Chinese victory in Korea, and that'll lead to the spread of communism throughout the region. And the impending rumpus here in New Zealand's all part of it. That about sum it up?"

Henderson nodded.

"All right." Walsh scratched his chin. "What he says may well be true, though I have to say I don't share his faith in the Soviet Union. In my experience — and I've had a bit, I've dealt with the bastards — they couldn't organise a piss-up in a brewery. I'm going to speak frankly. Forget the map and the dominoes and that other business. That's the march of history. What *we* need to be concerned about is the goods sitting on the wharves. And when I say goods, I mean wool."

He leaned forward.

"Do you really think the Yanks are going to let an army of coolies chase them out of Korea? The chances of the Reds prevailing are non-existent. Non-existent. They'll drop an atom bomb on China before you can say Charlie Chan. Rather than Thailand and Malaya and the rest capitulating to communism the opposite will happen. The Yanks will go all the way to Peking. And they mightn't stop there. They might decide to go on to the Soviet Union and finish the job, who knows? And that's not going to happen overnight. It could take years. There's a lot of snow in that part of the world. And that means uniforms and blankets to keep their soldiers warm and dry. Those poor beggars are going to find out exactly why they're calling it the Cold War. Think about it. Millions of uniforms and blankets. Made from wool. *Our wool.* This is New Zealand's biggest opportunity since the gold rush."

He pointed to each man in turn, his finger underlying the importance of his words.

"With the Yanks paying record prices for every scrap, with the amount of money that's going to be sloshing around in this country soon, we, the fellas in this room, and the interests we represent, are faced with the sort of financial opportunity that comes along once in a lifetime."

He sipped his whisky.

"Which brings me to Jock Barnes and the Waterside Workers' Union. Those red wreckers cannot be allowed to close New Zealand's ports. Because if they do, and the wool can't be sent overseas, then our good friend Mr Dulles will pack up his dominoes and go somewhere else without so much as a backward glance. That's the way the Yanks are. I've dealt with *those* bastards too. It's hard to imagine how they could be less interested in this country were it not for our sheep."

He turned to Henderson. "You know this, Henderson. You've had dealings with them, I'm sure. The rest of you blokes too, for all I know." He looked around the table. "Let me repeat. This is a once-in-a-lifetime opportunity. Not just for us, but for New Zealand. Something else old Brutus told Cassius. 'We must take the current when it serves, or lose our ventures.'"

He turned his glass slowly on the table. It made a grinding, industrial sound in the captivated stillness of the room. The men were transfixed. Here was a muscularity with which they were largely unfamiliar.

"Do you have a proposal, Walsh?" said Marsh.

Walsh looked at him. "I do. If the wharfies don't pull their heads in, the Government will have to act. And if it won't act it'll have to be *made* to act. To come down on the Waterside Workers' Union like a ton of bricks. And if that means getting soldiers and sailors in to ensure the ports stay open and working, then so be it."

Hoar spoke for them all. "By God," he said, looking around. "Now *this* is responsible unionism."

"Quite agree," said Newton. "*Quite* agree."

"So you're saying, what?" Henderson said, stirring the pot. "That in the face of this anarchy we may need to force the Government's hand in some way?"

"Pretty much," said Walsh.

"Barnes and his red friends, now," said Hall. "Are they, shall we say, biddable?"

"Will they take a backhander, do you mean?" said Walsh. "Not a dog's show. Barnes is an honourable man. So are they all, all honourable men. They're not interested in money. They want to tear the whole show down."

"Then force the Government's hand how, exactly?" said Solomon.

Walsh looked at him. "You can leave that to me," he said.

35

The others paused.

Oh?

These were not men used to leaving things to someone else, especially to a roughneck like Walsh who deliberately threw such coarse locutions as "gonads" and "piss-up" and "bastards" into formal conversation.

"I see. We can leave that to you, can we?" said Solomon. He looked at the others and back at Walsh. "What's your game, Walsh? It's common knowledge you were a Red once yourself."

"I used to wear short pants," said Walsh. "But I grew out of them, too."

"Well put," said Henderson. "Now—"

"One moment please, David," said Hall, refusing to be intimidated. "But Bruce has a point. Walsh's position is, to say the least, unorthodox for someone with his background." He turned to Walsh. "What do you want out of this, sir, if you'll allow me to speak directly?"

"What's in it for me, do you mean?" said Walsh. He held up three stubby fingers and began ticking them off. "Firstly," he said. "Concessions in the area of wages and conditions from you people for my people. Nothing drastic. Just something that looks like progress to the rank and file."

There were no objections.

"Secondly," he said. "A guarantee that from now on the organisations you blokes represent will deal only with unions affiliated to the Federation of Labour. None of this Trade Union Congress malarkey."

No objections there either. The Federation of Labour was responsible and pragmatic. Its leadership, although it engaged in pro forma tub-thumping on occasion, could be relied on to agree that the interests of the working class were almost invariably in happy and coincidental alignment with the interests of the employing class. The Trade Union Congress, by contrast, was a recent breakaway body of bomb throwers and Reds. Let it burn.

"And thirdly." Walsh picked up his glass. "A thousand guineas, in cash, delivered to me, details to be worked out with Henderson."

He swirled the whisky round in his glass and knocked it back with a quick jerk, an epiglottal gulp the only sound in the now deathly silent room.

"Did I hear that correctly?" said Solomon, resting his pipe on the edge of his ashtray.

"A thousand guineas?" said Marsh. "Is that what he said?"

"What's he mean by cash?" said Hall. "Unmarked notes in non-sequential order, that sort of thing?"

"As though we're, what, negotiating on behalf of the *Lindbergh baby*?" said Newton.

"In the *Northern Club*?" said Petrie.

"Were you *aware* of this, David?" said Hoar.

Henderson brought his fist smashing down on the table, startling the men into silence.

"You're *damned right* I was aware of it!" He got to his feet and leaned forward, his hands on the table. "It's a *fee* for a *service*. Entirely proper too, given what's at stake. Business and destiny have converged in this room, gentlemen. It's no place for sissies."

CHAPTER EIGHT

The boarding house at 3 Chamberlain Street was a large white villa built in 1910. The roots of an old pohutukawa had cracked the concrete base of the iron railing that ran along the road frontage. Children were playing bullrush in the middle of the street. An elderly woman carrying shopping in two string bags got off the Ponsonby tram and began walking stiffly up Richmond Road. There were two other vehicles parked in the street: a red snub-nosed panel van with "G. Heap Esq. Butcher. Meat, Poultry, & Fresh Game" painted on the side, and a brown Baby Austin.

Molloy sat in his car watching the house. The sky was a royal blue and full of stars. The light above the outline of the Waitakeres was a faint lemon. It reminded Molloy of North Africa. Three people had arrived at the boarding house and two had left in the hour or so he had been there. None of them was O'Flynn, unless he had aged thirty years or put on a lot of weight. Molloy looked at his watch. He would give it another twenty minutes before declaring.

A match flared in the Austin. The driver's side window wound down a few inches and a waft of smoke caught the last of the evening light. Molloy waited. No movement other than the occasional glow of the cigarette. He got out of his car and walked quickly down Chamberlain Street, along Rose Road, up Dickens Street, past the shops in Richmond Road, and back down

Chamberlain Street, approaching the Austin from behind, keeping close to an overgrown hedge. He glanced at the number plate as he passed: J328. The occupant was female, her hair in a scarf. He returned to his car and wrote the number down in his notebook.

Molloy drove to Arch Hill and parked outside Sergeant Pat Toomey's cottage. The policeman's house was set close to the road in Home Street with the backyard dropping down to the Kingsland gully. Molloy kept a crate of Waitemata in the boot for emergencies. He carried it round to the back porch and knocked. Toomey opened the door. He was wearing his uniform trousers, braces unclipped, white shirt open at the throat. Molloy could see the remains of tea on the kitchen table. Chops and mashed potatoes and string beans. Toomey's wife, Brigid, was doing the dishes.

"I think you met my wife at the Christmas do," said Toomey.

"That's right," said Molloy, raising his hat. "How are you, Mrs Toomey?"

"Well, thank you," she said, into the sink, her voice a soft brogue.

Molloy and Brigid had danced together at a social at the Irish Hall in Great North Road a few weeks earlier. Toomey had spent most of the evening drinking whisky with his cobbers from the Hibernians, police and firemen mostly, while their bored wives partnered each other or sat around the walls, talking and waiting to go home. Brigid loved the reels. After a frenetic round of "The Walls of Limerick" and "The High Cauled Cap", and finally, "Mairi's Wedding", she said she was boiling and needed to go outside for some fresh air.

They had leaned against his car in the darkness and looked at the moon. Molloy offered her a flask. She took a sip and passed it back to him.

Their hips brushed.

A look passed between them of such intensity that two strong men could have carried a double bed across it.

Toomey came out of the hall and called for her from the steps.

"I have to go," she said.

"All right," said Molloy. Toomey was on the gaming squad and knew the bookies and the hard men who did their dirty work. He could be a nasty bastard.

The policeman turned on the porch light and closed the kitchen door. He knocked his pipe on a verandah post and pushed the ashes onto the path with his slippered feet. "What can I do for you, Johnny?" he said.

Molloy indicated the crate of beer. "I dropped something round for the Social Club," he said.

"Very good," said Toomey.

"Could you have a look and see if there's anything on a wharfie called Frank O'Flynn? Irishman. He lives in a boarding house in Grey Lynn. 3 Chamberlain Street," said Molloy. "Don't know much else about him."

Toomey took a notebook from his back pocket. "Any other names?" he asked.

"O'Phelan, possibly," said Molloy. He spelt it out. "Same Christian name."

"Anything in particular you're looking for?" asked Toomey.

"Nothing in particular," said Molloy.

"I'll let you know," said Toomey.

"One other thing," said Molloy. "I've got a number plate for a 1937 Baby Austin. J328. Can you look that up for me?"

Molloy called in to Furst's hotel, wrote a note for him, asked the night man to put it in the American's pigeon-hole, and drove home.

CHAPTER NINE

Molloy lived in a whare on the back section of a boarding house in Williamson Avenue. It was one of two ex-army huts. There was a single bed and a chest of drawers. He had a radio on a bookshelf, and an electric ring on the windowsill for cooking. There was a calendar on the wall and a mirror above the basin. He got his water from a tap in the washhouse and used the long drop behind the tool shed. The bath was inside the house. He had the use of the garage, and grew beans and tomatoes along the fence in the summer.

He had been there for three years and thought of moving from time to time, but the set-up was convenient. Mrs Philpott, the landlady, ran a tight ship, and the other tenants were pleasant and kept largely to themselves. There were the McGill sisters, two spinsters who shared what would have been the living room when the boarding house was a private home. They worked in the haberdashery department at Farmers, catching the tram to work each day. They were inseparable. The Misses McGill's familial resemblance was slight. Mrs Philpott did sometimes wonder about the exact nature of their relationship but was unable to get to grips with the physics. There was Jim, Mrs Philpott's nephew, a post office cadet. There was a shy Dutchman named Albert who lived in the other whare. He worked as a mechanic at Alder & Co in Ponsonby Road and was saving his money to go share-milking. There was always a copy of the *Weekly News*, turned to the farming pages, on the shelf in the long drop. He listened to the Dutch language broadcast of the BBC World Service on a shortwave radio at night. On payday he would buy a flagon and drink it in his room, occasionally asking Molloy to join him, an invitation Molloy did his best to avoid. The Dutchman's English, barely intelligible when he was sober, turned to mush by the time the flagon was at the halfway point, but that didn't stop him from talking. He would get worked up, reliving the war, reliving *something*, sitting on the edge of his bed, making a point with a stiff accusing finger, beer slopping, hands gesturing, tears running down his face, occasionally holding an imaginary tommy gun and firing into — what? Germans? Javanese? *Untermenschen*? There was Brian, a compositor at the *Herald* who had been a conchie and spent the war years in a prison camp in National Park. There was Mrs Baker, a widow whose husband was killed in Trieste in the last week of the war. She taught the piano to disinterested local children after school and cried in her room at night. There was Miss Perkins, a senior typist at Russell McVeagh & Co, a law firm in town.

Molloy filled a pot with water from the outside tap and lit the gas ring. He removed his shirt and singlet and gave himself a sponge bath. Old army habit. There was a gentle knock on the door. He opened it. Miss Perkins. She stepped out of her slippers and took off her dressing gown. She got into his bed, pulling the blankets up to her neck. Molloy turned out the light and took off his trousers and shoes in the dark, hung his greys on the back of a chair, and got in next to her. It was a narrow bed, but they made do.

Miss Perkins had grown up on a sheep station in the foothills of the Ruahines — 12,000 acres and a twenty-stand woolshed built in the days of blade shearing. There were six full-time shepherds, one of them a young Englishman named Cavendish, good with horses, a remittance man, third in line to something. Miss Perkins found herself pregnant, she couldn't remember the circumstances exactly — sixteen, home from Nga Tawa for the May school holidays, a party, a Western swing band from Ohakune, games, gin, the devilish Cavendish charm, morning sickness. Miss Perkins' family sent her to Auckland to stay with an aunt in Parnell. The last time she saw her father was from the platform of the railway station in Taihape. She was standing with her mother, both staring straight ahead, a suitcase at her feet, in her purse five ten-pound notes and a letter of introduction to the matron of St Helen's written by the family doctor. Her father waited in the car. She wanted him to get out and come over and put his arms around her, to tell her that things would be all right and not to be scared. But he didn't. He drowned two months later, fishing in the Rangitikei River. It was impossible for her to come home for the funeral in her condition. Still, years later, she would think she saw a flash of him in the distance, standing on the footpath looking at her, or driving past in a car.

Cavendish moved to Mt Peregrine, a South Island property owned by the Borthwick family, who were big in the frozen mutton trade and had Home connections. In 1940 he returned to England, took up a commission with the Tank Regiment, and was killed in a training accident.

Miss Perkins had the baby, a boy, whom the nurses let her hold briefly. She signed something but the line where the name of the adoptive parents was supposed to go was blank. A South Island couple, was all she knew. It was the best for everyone.

She became something of a remittee herself, her mother thinking it would be best for her to remain in Auckland under the circumstances, sending five pounds a week for board and lodgings and paying for her enrolment in a clerical college. She had a room in Mrs Philpott's boarding house, with good light and a bay window. She had brothers, Molloy knew that. He'd met one of them once, a big, gruff, sunburnt bloke named Richard, who ran the farm. He'd come to Auckland for the Easter Show and called round to see Miss Perkins and take her out to tea. He called her Gee. He'd been a navigator in 75 Squadron and had a burn mark up one side of his face and a chewed ear.

From time to time she would knock on Molloy's door and, without saying anything, get into his bed. She never stayed the night.

CHAPTER TEN

In April 1940, the body of the late Prime Minister Michael Joseph Savage arrived at Auckland Railway Station after a twenty-eight hour journey from Wellington. The casket, covered with feathered cloaks and the New Zealand ensign which had flown from the cruiser HMS *Achilles* during the Battle of the River Plate, was loaded onto a gun carriage. The cortège made its slow way up Queen Street, along Karangahape Road, across Grafton Bridge, down past the Captain Cook Brewery where Savage had worked as a cellarman when he first arrived in New Zealand in 1907, up Broadway and along the length of Remuera Road to the site of a never-completed artillery battery at Bastion Point overlooking the Waitemata. The procession was watched in silence by 200,000 people, half of the city's population at the time. In the harbour hundreds of pleasure craft rode at anchor, sails furled and pennants at half mast.

Bastion Point was the site of Fort Bastion, one of sixteen coastal defence installations built in response to emanations from the Panjdeh Incident in 1885, when Tsarist forces seized disputed territory south of the Oxus River in Afghanistan. It was the height of the Great Game and New Zealand played its part. Russian scares of one sort or another have been a consistent theme in New Zealand political life, one not easily explained in geographic terms. The installation was never completed. Changes in artillery elevations made it redundant. Savage's successor as prime minister, Peter Fraser, announced a competition for a suitable memorial to be erected on the site. The winning design was an obelisk and a mausoleum with a sunken garden and a reflective pool, designed by architects from the Auckland City Council, and built by the Fletcher Construction Company.

David Henderson was standing in front of the obelisk, hat tilted back, hands on his hips, suit coat in the crook of his arm, looking at a portrait of Savage, a cameo rendered in greening copper, the late prime minister's gentle face ringed by a wreath of concrete flowers, when Walsh joined him.

"Critiquing the stonework?" said Walsh.

"I was thinking about his state housing scheme," said Henderson. "Made us a fortune before the war."

"I bet."

"Quite the pantheon," said Henderson, gesturing. "For such a modest little fella."

"Fraser's idea," said Walsh. "He was a strange bugger, Peter. Loved funerals. Loved organising them, loved going to them. Pity his own was so damn long in coming."

"'There is no fame to rise above the crowning honour of a People's love'," Henderson read the inscription below the cameo. "My God."

"You'd find the next couplet more to your liking," said Walsh. "'So leave him to his rest who toiled for all, nor gave his life to pile ill-gotten gains'."

"You're quite the literary fella, aren't you?" said Henderson, after a moment. "All that time on boats, I suppose."

David Henderson had started his working life as a stonemason in Dunedin. He served as a transport officer with the New Zealand

Division in France. In 1919 a senior deacon at his lodge made sure
he got the commission to build a war memorial at Kapanui on the
West Coast. Soon he had four gangs of returned men on the go
across the South Island. No New Zealand country town considered
itself complete without a bespoke venue for the dawn parade. In
1922 he won a South Otago tender to build houses for the Railways
Department and set up D.A. Henderson & Co, Building &
Construction. With cheap housing loans the 1920s were boom years.
The Depression hardly touched him. He took leave from the
company in 1940 to help with the war effort, becoming chairman
of the Supply Board. Soon Henderson & Co was turning out army
huts by the thousand, built with Henderson lumber transported on
Henderson trucks. Conflicts of interest were subsumed to the
demands of central planning. In 1946, when the War Department
disposed of surplus bulldozers and machinery from the Pacific
theatre, Henderson & Co had the inside running. New Zealand is a
small place and it pays to know people.

Henderson's car, a dark-green Rover, was parked in the shade of
a line of pohutukawa up from the reflecting pool. Walsh's Plymouth
was nearby. Sunny Day, Walsh's driver, was leaning against the side of
the car, arms folded, smoking. Henderson's man, a wiry, fit-looking
fellow in his mid-thirties, with curly red hair cut short at the back
and sides, wearing a white shirt with the sleeves rolled up and a
black tie, got out of the Rover and opened the back door.

"Give us a few minutes, Bill, will you?" said Henderson.

"Good as gold, Mr Henderson," said the chauffeur, jutting his
chin at Walsh, his eyes flat.

"Did those chooks settle down after I left?" said Walsh, easing
into the back seat.

"They're not used to direct action."

"Best way," said Walsh. "We'd still be there."

"Agreed," said Henderson. "But don't worry. They may look like the Drones, but they're tough, successful, largely self-made fellas, fully aware of which way's up. We'll have no problems with them, don't you worry."

Walsh patted his pockets. A box of matches made a rattling sound. He took out a cigarette packet. It was empty.

"Have one of mine," said Henderson, opening his cigarette case.

Walsh took one of Henderson's smokes. He savoured the taste. "Not bad. I don't like filter tips as a rule."

"I'd have thought you would have been more of a loose tobacco type," said Henderson. "Out of solidarity with the working man."

Walsh tapped ash onto the floor. "You'd have thought that, would you?" He pointed to a leather satchel at Henderson's feet. "Is that for me?"

Henderson nodded. He lifted the satchel and passed it to Walsh.

"Quick work," said Walsh, opening the clips.

"Hall arranged it," said Henderson. "Bank of New South Wales."

The satchel was filled with bank notes rolled up and tied with rubber bands. Walsh reached in and took out a bundle. He thumbed the money.

"Hard to believe there's a thousand guineas in here," he said. "It's always disappointing. You think you'll need a wheelbarrow."

"Count it, if you like."

"No need. Crikey. If you can't take a Grand Sword Bearer's word, whose word can you take?"

Henderson looked at him for a moment. "How did you know my title?"

Walsh blew smoke towards the roof. "Oh, I imagine there's a few things you know about me too."

Henderson tapped a cigarette on the case and thumbed his lighter. "There is, as a matter of fact," he said, taking his time, drawing on the flame.

"Well?" said Walsh.

"Well, I know you shot a man in America in 1917," said Henderson, his lighter closing with a click. "An operative from the Pinkerton Detective Agency."

Walsh laughed. "Christ, I hope you didn't pay too much for that hoary chestnut."

"And I know you had to get out of Ireland in a hurry in 1920," said Henderson, as if Walsh hadn't spoken. "And with a different name. Landed as Pat Tuohy, left as Pat Walsh. Not sure why yet, but I'm led to believe it was connected to the murder of a British secret agent in the toilet of a Dublin boarding house. Member of the Cairo Gang."

"The *Cairo Gang*!" said Walsh. "My God, sounds like J.C. Williamson's latest, whatchamacall, West End sensation." He blew a smoke ring. It hung in the air between them. "You shouldn't poke around in areas that don't concern you, my friend. Violence is a last recourse for me, but I'm no angel. This talk of a Pinkerton man, now. I did kill a fella in America, but I didn't shoot him and he wasn't a detective. He was an enforcer for Anaconda Mining. Him and his cobbers seized a mate of mine, Frank Little — Wobbly organiser, Red Indian of some kind, as a matter of fact, good bloke — seized him from his room in a boarding house in this godforsaken copper town in Montana first thing, Frank wearing only his drawers, allowed the poor man no dignity, tied him to the bumper of a motorcar, dragged him down the main street, shot him in the back of the head and hung him dead from a railway trestle in broad daylight, a placard strung around his neck." Walsh drew a sign in the air. "'Others Take Notice! First and Last Warning! 3—7—77.' Know what those numbers mean?"

"Wouldn't have a clue."

"Size of a grave," said Walsh. "Three feet wide, seven feet long, seventy-seven inches deep. It's a vigilante warning from the Wild West. I found the stooge in a saloon that very night, laughing with his blackleg cronies, followed him into the dunny, garrotted him with my tie till his face turned blue and he voided himself."

Walsh pulled his fists apart in a sharp, demonstrative jerk, his eyes black.

"Now you know something that no one else alive knows. No one else *alive*, you foller?" He pointed at Henderson, his fingers forming the shape of a pistol. "What's that warning you blokes give to blabbermouths there at the lodge? 'Your left breast torn open, your heart plucked out and given to the wild beasts of the field and the fowls of the air'?"

"Are you threatening me, Walsh?" said Henderson. He turned and pointed out the window. "See him?" He indicated his driver, who was leaning into the Plymouth's now-open gullwing bonnet and explaining to Sunny how they'd got round the Chrysler's vapour lock problem in Libya by flipping the fuel pump and moving the bowl away from the heat of the exhaust manifold. "Long Range Desert Group. Chestful of gongs. Killed more Germans with his bare hands than Charlie Upham."

"Woo woo!" said Walsh, wiggling his fingers in the style of the Three Stooges. He pointed to Sunny. "See him? Unofficial heavyweight champion, Mount Crawford Prison, 1944 to 1946. Bare-knuckle scrappers those fellas, of course. Twenty-two bouts, twenty-one knockouts — knockouts, mind — one death. Burst some poor devil's kidney with a low blow. Apparently the blood just" — Walsh made a slow, unfolding gesture with his hand — "*pooof.*"

Henderson turned and made a point of staring. "Really?" he said. "That little bloke?"

Walsh snorted, not long, not loud, but with the hint of a smile, a concession to Henderson's concession. Henderson wound down his window, letting fresh air in and tension out.

"Look, it's nothing to me what you may or may not have done, Walsh," said Henderson. "Hell's bells, I've cut a few corners myself. I just want you to be clear with whom you're dealing."

"'With whom you're dealing'," said Walsh. He closed the satchel with a solid click and put it on the floor between his feet. "Right-o, my pellucid friend, I need some gelly. Two crates."

Henderson rested his cigarette on the edge of the ashtray.

"Gelly?" he said. "Do you mean dynamite?"

"No, I mean gelignite," said Walsh. "Dynamite is unstable. It sweats. Gelly doesn't. Gelly needs a detonator. It can be stored safely. It—"

"I won't allow killing."

"Don't worry," said Walsh, reaching over and squeezing Henderson's knee hard. "This isn't Chicago. I want to wake people up, not kill them."

CHAPTER ELEVEN

Molloy went into the Public Bar of the Occidental Hotel in Vulcan Lane and made his way through the heaving crowd, the clock inching towards six, men drinking, smoking, talking at the tops of their voices. He bought a jug and looked through the fog for Tom O'Driscoll.

"Johnny!" O'Driscoll shouted. "Over here."

O'Driscoll was standing at a crowded leaner, its surface covered in jugs and glasses and spilled beer, the metal ashtray in the centre overflowing. He was a short man with stiff curly hair shooting up at an angle. He wore a sports coat and a striped tie that stopped halfway down his shirtfront. He was the *Auckland Star*'s police roundsman. "You know these blokes?"

"How are you, boys?" said Molloy. The men at the leaner said "g'day" and went back to yelling at each other about the difference the Northland centre J.B. Smith would have made in South Africa in 1949.

O'Driscoll eased himself out of the pack. "How are you, cob?" he said.

"I'm good," said Molloy. "You all right?"

"I'm all right," said O'Driscoll. "Just got back from Matamata. Family funeral yesterday. Eileen? My sister-in-law? Bruce's missus?"

"Eileen died?" said Molloy.

"Polio," said O'Driscoll.

"Jeez, that's no good," said Molloy.

"It bloody isn't. Out of the blue, pretty much. Haymaking. Felt crook that night. Thought it was sunburn. Took the next day off. Out of character right there. Worked like a Trojan as a rule that woman, dawn to dusk. First she lost the feeling in her legs. Then her whole body seized up, apparently. Contractor called the doctor. Bruce was shearing in Waipuk. Doctor got hold of him. Bruce raced back quick as he could, but" — he shook his head — "kaputski."

This was more detail than Molloy needed, but even so.

"And four kids. Poor old Bruce. Mum's gone down to give him a hand. Tough on her, though. She's no spring chicken." He threw back the last of his beer. "So, yeah, bastard of a thing. Anyway, how can I help?"

"Oh, hell. Look, give my best to Bruce next time you see him."

"I'll do that."

"Knocks you for six, that sort of news." Molloy looked at O'Driscoll's beer. "You right there?"

"Could go another."

Molloy topped up O'Driscoll's glass. "Here's to Eileen," he said.

"Too right," said O'Driscoll. "May she rest in peace."

Molloy looked round. "I was just wondering if you'd ever come across a wharfie called Frank O'Flynn in your travels?"

"Irishman? On the WWU exec?"

"That's the one. You know him? Under your hat?"

"I don't *know* him. Know *of* him, sort of thing."

"What sort of things?"

"Ah, let me see," said O'Driscoll, taking a packet of cigarettes from his pocket and offering one to Molloy. "He had to get out of Ireland in a hurry before the war, not sure why. He was in Spain, those battles round Madrid in '36, early '37." He pointed with his cigarette. "Your old stamping ground, wasn't it?"

"Not Madrid," said Molloy. "How long's he been here?"

"Year or two? He was good mates with Barnes and them but they've had a parting of the ways, I heard." He drank the top inch, and lowered his voice. "There's a rumour he was caught with his hand in the till, but—"

He saw something over Molloy's shoulder. "Hey!" He waved. "Cait! Miss O'Carolan! Over here!"

Molloy turned. A young woman was standing in the entrance to the bar. There weren't many girls in the Occidental, and none of them looked like this one.

"Christ, would you look at her," said O'Driscoll, out of the side of his mouth.

"Who is she?"

"New cadet on the Women's Page. Came here from nursing. Imagine her giving you a sponge bath." He turned to Molloy. "She wants to be Martha Gellhorn, filing dispatches in the heat of battle sorta thing." He stubbed out his cigarette. "I encourage this ambition in the hope that she'll let me unfasten her stays."

"How's married life?" said Molloy. "Marge well?"

"The woman's a saint," said O'Driscoll, straightening his tie. "But still."

The crowd seemed to part as the young woman weaved her way towards them. "Hello, O'Driscoll," she said. She undid her scarf and shook her hair loose.

The other men around the leaner squeezed together.

"Evening, gents," she said.

"Evening," they mumbled back, blushing in unison.

"I finished the piece on the Rowley nuptials," she said to O'Driscoll.

"That was quick," he said. "I could go over it with you later if you like?"

"Later?"

O'Driscoll stammered. "Later tomorrow, I mean," he said. "Anyway. What would you like? Pimm's?"

"G & T, please."

"Coming right up," said O'Driscoll. "What about you, Johnny? Another?"

"Good as gold, thanks," said Molloy, pointing to his jug.

The young woman turned to Molloy. "Hello," she said. "I'm Caitlin O'Carolan." She put out her hand.

"Johnny Molloy," he said, shaking it.

"Oh, I've heard about you. You're O'Driscoll's friend, the private detective?"

Molloy watched as she pushed back her hair and fixed it with a pin. She was slender, about five feet four, with pale skin and black hair, and eyes the colour of the Irish Sea.

"It's not polite to stare at a girl, Mr Molloy," she said, opening her purse and taking out a cigarette case. "Didn't your mother tell you that?"

"My mother didn't tell me much about girls, Miss O'Carolan," said Molloy, coming to. "She left that sort of thing to Dad."

"Oh?" she said, tapping a tailor-made on the lid. "And what did he tell you?"

Molloy took a box of matches from his pocket. "I'm still waiting for him to get started."

"I bet you've managed to pick up a thing or two on your own, though," she said, touching his hands with hers as she drew on the flame.

"I was always careful," said Molloy, dropping the dead match onto the floor. "That's one thing Dad did tell me."

She tilted her head back, blew out a thin stream of smoke. "I don't think I've seen you in here before, have I?"

"I do most of my boozing in Grey Lynn."

"So what brings you here?"

"Oh, nothing much. I'm working on a case. Needed to check something with O'Driscoll."

"Gosh," she said, with the hint of a smile. "Working on a case."

For an instant Molloy felt as if there was no one else in the room. "*È stato un colpo di fulmine,*" as that rat Fabrizio said about Michael when the latter saw Apollonia for the first time. Struck by a lightning bolt.

"He was saying you used to be a nurse," he said, trying to return to earth.

"Well, I *went* nursing," she said, waving it off. "I never sat my States. A cadetship came up at the *Star*. That's all I've ever wanted to do. Be a reporter."

"Enjoying it?"

She rolled her eyes. "Oh, *enormously.*" She picked a tiny piece of tobacco off the tip of her tongue and managed to make it look elegant. "I cover the social round for the Women's Page. Deb balls, twenty-first birthdays, weddings, 'The bride's mother wore silk organza,' that sort of thing. It's the only position open to girls. Apart from copy holding or pool typing or waiting until, I don't know, you turn thirty and become a lesbian."

Conversation around the leaner stopped for an instant but Caitlin didn't notice.

"The minute I've completed my cadetship, woosh!" she said, her hand taking off like an aeroplane. "Home, never to return."

"What will you do over there?"

"Chain myself to the railing in front of the *Manchester Guardian* and not move until they give me a job."

"But wouldn't that mean living in Manchester?" said Molloy. "I've been there. It's like Wellington."

"Well, I wouldn't be in Manchester for long."

"Oh, that's right," said Molloy. "Tom said you wanted to be a war correspondent."

She frowned. "O'Driscoll's big mouth," she said. "But yes, I do. I want to be on the front line, wherever it is. I suppose you think that's too silly."

"There's nothing silly about the front line," said Molloy.

"No place for a girl, eh?" she said, blowing smoke straight at him. "Don't patronise me, please, Mr Molloy. I get enough of that at work."

O'Driscoll threaded through the crowd, shoulders hunched, carefully shielding a gin and tonic. "Sorry to take so long," he said. He was excited. "I saw Ross Jones from the *Herald*. He's been down in Wellington. He reckons they're going to ram through the Public Safety Conservation Act unless the wharfies back down. The Regulations have been set, just waiting for the Government to give the nod."

"There were soldiers in civvies prowling around Princes Wharf a few nights ago," said Molloy. "She's about to blow."

"You're so matter-of-fact," said Caitlin. "The Public Safety Conservation Act is draconian. It's something Hitler might have dreamed up."

"Oh, steady on, Cait," said O'Driscoll. "The wharfies are digging their own graves, don't you think?"

"No I don't, actually. I don't think that at all." She dropped her cigarette on the floor and stubbed it out with the delicate toe of an English shoe. "What do you think, Mr Molloy?"

Molloy shrugged. "I think the wharfies will come a terrible cropper," he said. "Pity, because I know quite a few of them."

"That's it?" said Caitlin, looking at the two men in disgust. "Honestly!" She put her glass down on the leaner. "Enjoy the swill, gentlemen." She turned and strode from the bar, moving without effort through the crowd. Molloy and O'Driscoll watched her go.

"Jesus wept," said O'Driscoll, shaking his head. "Those ankles."

CHAPTER TWELVE

Molloy left the pub and drove to Grey Lynn. It was just before seven. He parked in Chamberlain Street along from number 3. There was no sign of the Baby Austin. On the passenger seat was a camera, a Voigtländer Bessa. In 1945, in the run-up to Trieste, Molloy had found a German hiding in a bombed-out farm building, a bloke in his forties, Oberst i.G. Egon Turtz according to his paybook, a base wallah, hands up and shaking, keen to kamerad like so many of the master race at that end of the show. Turtz held out a photograph and whimpered, "*Meine Frau, meine Sohn*," a family portrait, himself in uniform, a woman and a child, everyone smiling, much happier in those confident days when *alles* was *über*.

Molloy knew the partisans would get him sooner or later, so when the German offered a suitcase full of money in return for his life Molloy had let him go. But not before souveniring his pistol — a Luger — and his camera. The banknotes were Fascist currency as it turned out, not worth two bob. Molloy had used them to buy a Jeep from an American quartermaster in Vienna a few weeks later, and he and two army cobbers, Rex Lawrence from Carterton and Gordon Slatter from Christchurch, had swanned up to Berchtesgaden to see where Hitler used to live. He had held onto the camera. And the Luger. One never knows, do one?

Molloy took the camera out of its leather case, unfolded the lens and framed the front door through the viewfinder, the bellows moving in and out as he turned the focus dial. He cocked the shutter and set the f-top for the darkening light. He put the camera on the passenger seat. Then he took a cheese sandwich from a paper bag and ate it, keeping an eye on the boarding house.

A car drove slowly up the street. Molloy checked his side mirror. A 1939 Chrysler Plymouth four-door sedan, the deluxe P8. He could hear the low rumbling of the big six-cylinder engine, tyres quietly crunching on loose gravel. What strings would you have to pull to get a motorcar like that into the country, he wondered. What sort of baksheesh would be involved? The driver kept leaning over and looking to his left, checking letterbox numbers. He stopped in front of number 3 and got out. He was a Maori, not a common sight in Grey Lynn. He walked up the front steps of the boarding house and knocked on the door.

Molloy reached for his camera and reframed the doorway. A man came out onto the verandah and then forward into the light. In his mid to late thirties, a tough, handsome face, dark wavy hair parted off-centre and pushed back, a cowlick sprung loose. He was wearing a brown sports coat and carrying a canvas ammunition bag under his arm, a hat in his hand. O'Phelan. Or O'Flynn, or whatever he was calling himself today.

Molloy hooked the kickstand over the edge of the half-open window, took a photograph, wound the film, took another and then another. He reframed to the left and got what felt like a good snap of the driver. It would be grainy but there was still enough light. The two men walked quickly to the Plymouth. Molloy slumped in his seat as the sedan turned and drove off down Chamberlain Street. He put the camera on the seat and started the ignition. He did a fast U-turn and almost crashed into the butcher's red panel van, which was backing out of a driveway. The driver got out and glared at Molloy.

"Got a licence to drive that thing?" he said.

"Sorry, cobber," said Molloy.

"Yeah, well."

Molloy put his car into reverse and backed up a couple of yards, changed into first and drove round the van. There was no sign of the Plymouth. When he got to the junction at the bottom of Chamberlain Street the road was empty in both directions.

CHAPTER THIRTEEN

Molloy parked in front of the Premier Building on the corner of Wyndham Street and Queen Street where he had an office on the fourth floor. It wasn't much of a place — one room with a desk and a filing cabinet, and a framed photograph of Phar Lap winning the Melbourne Stakes, left by a previous tenant — but it was somewhere to go during the day. He had the key to a tiny shared kitchen with an electric kettle and a compact Frigidaire, which had somehow made its way there from the US Navy Hospital in Victoria Park after the war. The plastic door on the freezer cabinet was shot and there was rust appearing around the rim, but it kept the milk cold.

He had set up a darkroom in an unused cupboard in the hallway. He closed the door, pulled a curtain across and turned off the safelight, took the roll of film from the Voigtländer and got to work. A few minutes later a strip of negative was clipped to a line with a wooden peg. He set the timer and went into the kitchen and made a pot of tea. He returned to his office and found the number of the Grey Lynn RSC in his notebook. He had applied for a phone line in May the previous year and Post & Telegraph had installed one four months later. It didn't ring very often but Molloy knew it was the future. He picked up the receiver and dialled, turning the pot twice as the phone rang.

"Are you there?" said Bones Harrington.

"G'day, Bones," said Molloy. "Johnny here."

"Who's that?" said Bones. "You'll have to speak up."

"Johnny Molloy."

"Oh, g'day, Johnny," said Bones. "It's chocker tonight. Cops raided the Dublin Club on Sunday. Closed it down, the bastards. Roughed up Basil and them. All their members seem to have come over."

"That's no good," said Molloy. "Is Billy Burgess there?"

"He is," said Bones. "Want me to get him?"

"If you wouldn't mind."

"Hang on a tick."

The receiver clattered onto the bar.

"Billy! You're wanted on the telephone!" Molloy heard Bones shouting. "Hey, Steve! Get Billy for me, willya?"

Molloy poured a cup of tea.

"Are you there?"

"Hello, Billy," said Molloy. "It's Johnny Molloy."

"How can I help you, son?" said Burgess.

"Wondered if there were any overseas sailings tonight. Auckland or Mangere?"

"There's nothing scheduled for the next two days," said Burgess. "The *Moana*'s going to Sydney on Thursday from Napier but she's just stopping for crew. Otherwise everything's stuck in the channel."

"Thanks, cobber," said Molloy.

"That's all right, son."

"Sounds like quite a show in there tonight," said Molloy.

"Aye," said Burgess. "All those bastards from the Dublin Club. You heard what happened?"

"I did," said Molloy. "See you later, Billy."

"'Night, Johnny."

Molloy checked his watch, stirred his tea, put his feet on the desk, and opened the previous day's *Auckland Star*. American, French and Dutch troops were fighting around the Han River near Seoul. The timer rang. He went back into the broom cupboard and unpegged the negative from the line. He got a sheet of glass and a piece of marine ply the same size from under the sink — a do-it-yourself printing frame, something he'd learned from an article in *Popular Mechanics*. Soon he was wiping a proof sheet with a sponge. The telephone rang. Molloy took the sheet into his office.

"Are you there?"

"Hello, Johnny," said Toomey, the police sergeant. "Pat here."

"Hello, Pat."

"I have some information on your friend O'Flynn," said Toomey. "Also known as O'Phelan."

"Fire away," said Molloy, opening his notebook.

"He was arrested for gross public intoxication and common assault on St Patrick's Day last year, and found to be in the country without permission," said Toomey. "I'm surprised he wasn't deported. He wasn't even charged in the finish."

"Any clue why he wasn't?"

"No," said Toomey. "The file was sealed."

"Is that unusual?"

"It's not *usual*, put it that way," said Toomey. "Particularly since the person he assaulted was a policeman. We look down on that sort of behaviour."

"I bet," said Molloy, taking a magnifying glass from his drawer. He looked closely at the images on the proof sheet. There were some good ones of both the Irishman and the Maori.

"On the matter of the licence plate, J328," said Toomey. "The motorcar is registered to a Miss C. Cotterill of Marine Parade,

Herne Bay. She's owned it since new. 1947. And before that she had a Whippet, which she had owned since 1927. I'm picturing a mature woman of a conservative bent."

"Thanks, Sherlock," said Molloy, hanging up. He wrapped the proof sheet in newspaper, locked his office and walked to Furst's hotel.

"That's him," said Furst. "As a cop you get a feeling. Little hairs on the back of the neck?" O'Phelan's Merchant Marine ID, the *Bulletin* story and the proof sheet were lined up on the writing desk in Furst's room. "You're sure he didn't see you?"

"Pretty sure," said Molloy.

"Any chance he's skipped the country?" said Furst.

"Only if he walked," said Molloy. "There are no sailings till Thursday."

"What about Pan American?"

"Nothing till Thursday."

"Maybe he swam."

"Yeah," said Molloy. "He's known to the police. Public intoxication. They tried to get him for assault on a policeman too, but the charges were dropped."

"Know why?"

"Not yet."

Furst picked up the proof sheet and ran the magnifying glass over it again.

"What do you want me to do?" said Molloy.

"Keep looking."

"It's your money."

"Spend it," said Furst. "I want this feller found."

CHAPTER FOURTEEN

Molloy tried the front door of the RSC but it was locked. He stepped back and looked up. The building was in darkness. He lifted the letter slot and could hear the low rumble of conversation. A red wire from an electric buzzer ran up the side of the door frame and through a hole drilled in the wall. Molloy pushed the button. He lit a smoke.

The letter slot opened. "Bugger off," a voice said. "We're closed."

"Bones, it's me, Johnny."

Locks turned and the door cracked open. Bones squeezed out and looked up and down Francis Street. "All right, Johnny," he said, stepping back. "In you come."

A heavy blackout curtain was hanging across the alcove.

"Bloody hell," said Molloy. "Expecting the *Luftwaffe*?"

"It's no joke," said Bones. "The police are threatening to come down hard. Committee's even talking about restricting this place to legal hours till things blow over. Plus the jokers from the Dublin Club. We might have to clear out the chairs and tables for a bit. Just one step away from the vertical swill. Bloody hell." He bolted the door.

The room was full of men talking in low tones. Smoke hung above them like cumulus. Tim was back on deck. Molloy ordered an eight.

"Really sorry to hear about Paddy, Tim," said Molloy, reaching across the bar to shake Tim's hand. "Bones told me."

"Oh, thanks, Johnny," said Tim. "Yeah, it's a bit of a bugger."

"Are you going to have a service of any sort?"

"Well, he'll be buried over there in Korea somewhere, of course," said Tim. "In one of them military cemeteries, I'd think." He took a deep breath. "We're having a do at St Joseph's on Friday morning. It'll just be small, Johnny, don't feel you have to."

"Wouldn't miss it, Tim," said Molloy. "Paddy was a good bloke."

"He wasn't a bad little bugger, was he?" said Tim, concentrating hard on the pour, some movement in his chin. "Good halfback."

"Bones and I were saying the same thing. Would've played for Auckland if it hadn't been for the war."

"The Kiwis even," said Tim. "That's what Scotty McClymont reckoned."

"He'd know," said Molloy. "I'm going to drop in and say hello to your mum tomorrow."

"She'd like that, Johnny."

Tim slid the beer across.

"Cheers," said Molloy, putting a shilling on the bar.

Tim leaned forward. "Strange thing, the same day she heard he'd copped it, she got a postcard from him. Sent a couple of weeks before Christmas." Tim drew words in the air. "Ended with something like, 'Please don't worry, Mum, and lots of love. Paddy.'" His eyes filled with tears. "And in her other hand she's holding the 'Regret to inform' telegram from Fred fuckin' Jones, pardon my French."

"Hell," said Molloy, at a loss.

"Hell's right," said Tim, blowing his nose into a tartan handkerchief. "Ah, well. Offer it up, as the nuns used to say. Anyway." He got change from the cash register. "Friday at ten. But don't feel obliged."

"Very good," said Molloy. "I'll be there."

Bones put a tray of dirty glasses and ashtrays on the counter next to where Molloy was standing.

"Billy still here?" said Molloy.

"Got the last tram," said Bones. He lowered his voice. "Maori boy in the corner's looking for you, though."

"Where?"

"Behind me," said Bones. "By the radio."

Molloy looked at the reflection in the mirror above the bar. "How did he get in?" he asked. "All those locks and buzzers?"

"Size of the bastard, who was going to stop him?"

The Maori had one hand on a leaner and was sipping beer from a five-ounce glass.

"G'day," said Molloy. "Johnny Molloy."

The big man put down his glass. It was an eight, Molloy realised, but in his big fist it looked like a five.

"Sunny Day," he said.

Day had a thick neck and broad shoulders. His skin was dark and his eyes were pale green. His nose was smeared across his face, brows held together by scar tissue. There were faded blue swallows tattooed on the webbing of both hands. His fists looked like hammers, knuckles large and misshapen and several shades of red.

"You're looking for a cobber of mine," he said. "Frank O'Flynn?"

"Am I now? What makes you say that?"

"Auckland's a small place," said Sunny, hooking a thumb. "He wants to talk to you, too. Car's out the back."

CHAPTER FIFTEEN

Sunny's Plymouth was parked across the other side of the yard. The passenger door faced away from the RSC and was shadowed by a dark line of macrocarpas. There was a figure in the passenger seat.

Sunny opened the back door. "In you hop," he said with a mock salute. As Molloy lifted his arm to take off his hat Sunny punched him hard in the side below the ribcage. Molloy's world turned red. Sunny spun him round and punched him with his other fist, this time in the solar plexus.

Molloy's legs gave way and he slid down the side of the car, toppled to his knees, and pitched slowly forward onto the bitumen, trying to suck in air through a pinhole.

The passenger door opened. "Need a hand, Sunny?" said a high-pitched voice.

"No. I think it's under control, thanks, Lofty."

Sunny squatted down and waited for Molloy's diaphragm to stop cramping.

"What do you want with Frank O'Flynn?" he said, eventually.

"Who?" said Molloy, somehow.

Sunny grabbed Molloy's hair, wrenched his head back and slammed his face into the ground. He rolled him over, picked him up by the lapels and sat him down against the left front wheel. Molloy slumped forward with his chin on his chest, his ribcage feeling cracked and on fire. Sunny's actions seemed effortless, as though Molloy weighed nothing at all. And Molloy was not a small man.

"One more time," said Sunny. "What do you want with Frank O'Flynn?"

"He's been cited as secondary party in a divorce suit," said Molloy, the words bubbling out around the blood that was filling his mouth and dribbling down his chin. "This solicitor wants me to get a photograph, that's all."

"Go on. What solicitor?"

"Furst," said Molloy, grasping at straws. "Something Furst."

"Who's he with?"

"He's got a practice down the line," said Molloy, hooking his thumb in a southerly direction.

"Down the line?" said Sunny. "Can you be more specific?"

"Napier," said Molloy, the first place he thought of.

"Napier. That's good. I know people in Napier."

A dog barked.

"Hey, you fellas! What's going on?" said a beery voice.

The passenger door opened.

"Bugger off, Grandad," said Lofty.

"What did I say, Lofty?" said Sunny.

"No, Sunny, I was just …" Lofty's voice trailed off. The door closed.

"Is that young Molloy?" said Davey Coulson. The old boy had both hands on his walking stick and was swaying on the spot in a slow, circular direction as though he was churning butter. His fox terrier stood stiff-legged beside him, furious.

"Is that you, Davey?" said Molloy.

"It is," said Coulson. He nodded towards the macrocarpas. "I was just going for a, you know, a piddle in the trees there," he said. "The latrine gets pretty busy this time of night and I don't like to be rushed and that annoys people, banging away on the door and that, so." He took a deep breath. "Anyway, I seen you fellas here and I thought, jeez, that doesn't sound too good. Can't see who in the dark, but I could hear someone gasping away like billy-o. And then I seen it was you, Johnny. You know, once me eyes adjusted?" He paused. "Everything all right, son?"

"Good as gold, thanks, Davey," said Molloy. "Got a bit carried away on the booze and had a big spew all over this poor bloke's white sidewalls. But we're all right now, aren't we, Mr Day?" He leaned to one side and spat a mouthful of blood onto the ground.

"I think we're putting two and two together, yep," said Sunny.

Coulson's dog growled.

"Geddown, Skip!" said Coulson. "Take no notice of him. He's a foxy." Coulson squinted at Sunny. "You're a Maori, aren't you? Foxies don't seem to care for you fellas too much. Funny thing." He pointed. "I grew up on the Hokianga. Knew a fair few Maoris. Good people, most of them. *Ka pai* this and that and so forth. But foxies seem to have this animus towards them." He gestured vaguely. "Any of your people from up that way?"

Sunny paused. "Not from up that way, no," he said. "More down that way and across."

"I see," said Coulson, after a moment. "Ah, well. Better go and, you know." He pointed towards the tree line. "I'll see you later, Johnny."

"See you later, Davey," said Molloy.

They watched Coulson and Skip walk away.

Sunny shook his head. "Jesus Christ almighty," he said. He turned back to Molloy, his voice low. "I'll check up on this Furst fella," he said. "Secondary party in a divorce, eh? O'Flynn's a lady's man, that's for sure. He's called Errol O'Flynn sometimes, so could be." He put his hand under Molloy's chin and jerked his head up. "But if you're making it up, by crikey you'll be sorry." He dropped Molloy's head and wiped blood and snot from his hand onto the detective's jacket. "Meanwhile, stay away from Frank. I find you sniffing around him again, you're dog tucker."

CHAPTER SIXTEEN

Molloy woke up feeling like he had spun out of control at seventy miles an hour and crashed into a wall. He was lying on his bed, on top of the blanket, in his shirt and underpants. He couldn't remember how he got there. He couldn't remember getting undressed. There was blood on his shirt and the buttons were missing. He brought his hand up to his face. There was dry blood caked on his chin, and the tip of his nose felt as if it had been scraped off.

He tried to sit up but the effort made him squeak with pain. He lay back, counted to ten, rolled to his left, ended up on the floor on his knees.

"Oh, Jesus Christ," he said out loud, not praying.

He put his hands on the edge of the bed and heaved himself up. His jacket and strides were in a pile on the floor, ripped and bloodied. He couldn't see his hat.

He stood. On his wall there was a small square mirror with bevelled edges hanging by a thin chain. He looked at his face. What a mess. His nose and chin were bloody and lines of dry blood connected the two. He scraped gently at the scab. Parts of it came away in large black flakes and fresh blood appeared immediately. He took a handkerchief from his drawer, dipped it in an enamel bowl and cleaned himself up as much as he could.

He took his other pair of strides from a hanger and put them on, wincing over each inch. He put on his socks and shoes, took off his shirt and singlet and got clean ones from his drawer. It took ten minutes. There was a knock on the door.

"Mr Molloy?" said Mrs Philpott. "Are you decent? Someone on the telephone for you."

"Thank you, Mrs Philpott. There in a tick."

He opened the door.

Mrs Philpott's hand shot up to her mouth. "Goodness!" she said. "Have you been in an accident?"

"Oh," said Molloy. "Bit of a dust-up at the RSC last night. I got between a couple of fellas."

"Well, don't look to me for sympathy," she said. "You know how I feel about drink."

"Drink wasn't the problem, Mrs Philpott," he said. "It was politics."

"Even worse," she said. "There's aspirin in the cupboard under the sink in the bathroom. I suggest you take two with a glass of water."

The telephone was on an occasional table in the hallway of the boarding house.

Molloy picked up the receiver. "Are you there?"

"Is that you, Johnny?" said Toomey.

"Hello, Pat."

"Regarding your cobber, O'Flynn," said the policeman. "There's been a development."

CHAPTER SEVENTEEN

Molloy rang the Hotel Auckland and spoke to Furst. His car was in the garage, his hat on the floor in front of the passenger seat. He must have driven home. He stopped in front of the hotel. Furst was standing on the footpath. The American flicked away his cigarette and got into the front seat.

"Holy Moly," he said when he saw Molloy's face. "The hell happened to you?"

"Fella suggested I stay away from O'Flynn," said Molloy. "Conversation went from there."

"I'd say it did!" said Furst.

"His name's Sunny Day," said Molloy. "He picked the Irishman up from the boarding house last night."

"You don't say," said Furst, taking a cigarette pack from his shirt pocket. "Smoke?"

Molloy shook his head. He put his arm out to indicate and pulled away from the footpath.

"Okay," said Furst, lighting up. "Tell me again what the cop said."

"His exact words were, 'Frank O'Flynn has taken his life, God rest his soul'."

"God rest his soul, my ass," said Furst, throwing his match out the window.

It took an hour and a half to drive the mostly gravel road to Piha. As they rumbled down the steep hill towards Lion Rock, Molloy wondered if the car would make it back up.

He parked beside a police car. There was a small crowd of people on the beach. A uniformed sergeant and a young constable were standing with half a dozen locals, all of them pointing in various directions but generally out to sea. The sergeant saw Molloy and Furst and came over to join them.

"Jeez, Johnny!" he said. "What happened to you?"

"Someone had a go at the RSC last night," said Molloy.

"Did they ever," said the cop. "You got a couple in I hope?"

"One or two," said Molloy. "Steven, this is Al Furst, from San Francisco. Al, Sergeant Murphy, who's in charge out here."

"Mr Furst," said Murphy, shaking Furst's hand. "Johnny taking you sightseeing?"

"I'm working with Furst on a fraud case," said Molloy. "This could be connected. Can you tell us anything?"

"Missing person at this stage," said Murphy. "But between you and me and the lamppost it feels like suicide. We get a bit of that out here." He pointed to an elderly man talking to the constable. "That gent was taking his dog for a walk along the beach earlier and saw a fella sitting on the sand staring out to sea. He said hello and that but the bloke didn't respond, and when he came back the other way there was no sign of him except for a pile of clothing and a letter stuck down with a piece of driftwood. There's a sort of rock shelf that goes out about fifty yards off the beach. It's visible at low tide. At the end's a sheer drop."

"No body?" said Molloy.

"Not yet."

"You got a name?" said Molloy.

"We have," said Murphy.

"Was it Frank O'Flynn?" said Furst.

Murphy looked at him.

"Oh. Pardon me," said Furst. He reached into his jacket and took a card from his wallet.

Murphy looked at it and turned it over. "Insurance investigator," he said, unimpressed. "I see."

"I had twenty years in the San Francisco Police Department," said Furst. "Retired two years ago as District Chief of Detectives."

Murphy nodded. "The letter was signed Frank O'Flynn."

"Any chance we could take a look?" asked Furst.

"That's how you'd do it in the San Francisco Police Department, is it?" said Murphy.

Furst put his hands up. "Fair enough," he said. "Worth a shot, though."

The policeman glanced around and stepped forward. He lowered his voice. "It's a goodbye-cruel-world sorta thing. He stole some money the Australian unions had raised for the wharfies, and couldn't live with himself."

"Yeah, that'd be tough," said Molloy. "You going to send someone out to look for the body?"

"In this rip?" said the policeman. "He'll wash up in a couple of days."

"If the sharks don't get him first."

CHAPTER EIGHTEEN

"What do you think?" said Molloy, closing his door with a wince and putting the key in the ignition.

"Not a lot," said Furst, lighting a cigarette. "For a seaman he doesn't have a lot of luck around water."

"No," said Molloy.

The office at the Piha camping ground had a few grocery items for sale, bread and milk, butter, lollies, soft drinks, yesterday's *Star*. Molloy bought four bottles of lemonade.

Molloy drove in silence up the Piha Hill, keeping an eye on the heat gauge. Just before the top he began to smell steam.

"Uh oh," said Furst.

Molloy pulled over and left the engine running. The two men got out. Molloy undid the bonnet. The motor was hissing and growling.

"Head gasket?" said Furst.

"Hope not," said Molloy. "The radiator hose is frayed. I have to replace it, but I've been putting it off." He got a rag from the boot and wrapped it round his hand, and slowly eased off the cap. Brown boiling water bubbled over the lip. He opened the lemonade and trickled it into the radiator. Both men stared into the core. There were no tell-tale bubbles.

They made it to Oratia and stopped at a bowser. There were pies in a warmer and they bought one each, and two bottles of Coca-

Cola, and sat on a bench in the sun while the mechanic replaced the hose and flushed out the radiator.

"You know, I've been thinking," said Furst, indicating Molloy's battered face. "How did this Sunny feller know you were looking for O'Flynn?"

"I was wondering that myself," said Molloy. "I only told two people. They know how to keep their traps shut."

Molloy dropped Furst back at the hotel and went home. It was a bit early for tea, but he wasn't hungry anyway. He closed the curtains and got undressed. The aspirin had worn off and he felt stiff and sore and tired. He sat on the edge of his bed, had a couple of belts from his flask, lay down and closed his eyes. He drifted off, and slept like a baby.

CHAPTER NINETEEN

Sergeant Pat Toomey liked his bacon crisp.

"What do you call this?" he said, waving a rasher above his plate.

Brigid was ironing. She took a deep breath. "I'm sorry," she said. "I'll put it back in the pan."

"Undercooked bacon and an overcooked egg," said Toomey. "Good thing I didn't ask for something difficult like toast. Or God forbid a cup of tea." He dropped the rasher onto the plate and wiped his fingers on a napkin. "No wonder your miserable family couldn't wait to shovel you off on me."

Brigid's reply was lost in the hissing of the iron.

Toomey put down his fork. "Beg your pardon?" he said.

"Nothing," she said.

"Don't tell me fibs, Brigid," he said. "What did you say?"

"Ma didn't want me to go with you at all," Brigid said, the words coming out in a rush. "She saw you from the first for the sleeveen you are."

In 1948, Toomey, a nephew of Monsignor Toomey from St Patrick's Cathedral in Wyndham Street, had received a special dispensation from the Church to have his late mother cremated, and making liberal use of a State Advances loan had taken her ashes back to Ireland to be buried next to her parents in the graveyard of St Theresa's in Clonakilty, on the coast in County

Cork. He had met Brigid through the parish priest of St Theresa's, Father Donovan. She was the sixth of eleven children of a clerk with the Rural Electrification Scheme. Her father suffered from the drink and the family's circumstances were modest. At twenty-three and unmarried, her prospects were not unlimited. Toomey looked like a catch.

"A *sleeveen?*" he said, standing and loosening his belt. It was thick leather, smooth and polished, and came out in an easy sweep. He doubled it over and smacked it into his hand, coming round the table, a black look on his face. She tried to run but the kitchen was tiny and he caught her easily, backhanding her with the belt, the leather drawing blood above the eye.

"I will not, *stand*, for that sort of, bog, Irish, traveller *filth*, in my *own house*, you hear me?" he said, hitting her from every angle until she collapsed in a corner.

It was over in seconds. He picked up a folded handkerchief from the ironing board and wiped his face, breathing heavily.

"I wish I was dead," she said through tears.

"I'll be home at six," he said, putting his belt back on, squaring the buckle. "For tea, God help me." He removed his uniform jacket from its hanger on the back of the kitchen door.

She touched her fingers to her mouth and looked at the blood. "I'll go to the station and report you to the superintendent, that's what I'll do," she said. "Your own pals will arrest you."

"Try that and they'll certify you, Brigid. You'll be locked up on Pakatoa Island with the nutcases and the inebriates and never heard of again."

"I won't be here when you get back. I can't stay with you no longer."

"You will be," he said, combing his hair in the hall mirror. "You've nowhere else to go. For my sins I'm stuck with you."

He picked up his helmet from the telephone stand. "Good day, Brigid," he said, closing the door quietly on his way out.

CHAPTER TWENTY

Molloy went to Leo O'Malley Menswear in Karangahape Road to replace his suit, ruined in the run-in with Sunny Day. Leo talked him into a new white shirt to go with the Cambridge two-piece.

He had scraped more of the scabbed blood off his nose and chin, leaving the skin in both places red and a bit raw but starting to settle, and his body no longer felt like it had been run over. He had had a good long shower at the Municipal Baths and that helped, and he had gone to Julian Maloney's barbershop in Victoria Street for a shave and a haircut.

He decided to treat himself to bacon and eggs and a pot of tea at the Piccolo. He read about the fighting round the 38th parallel, and the imminent arrival of the England cricket team, and in the Personals column, the source of a surprising amount of work, he saw a notice, inserted by the WWU, respectfully inviting friends of the late Francis Xavier O'Flynn to a memorial service later that morning. How Jock Barnes must have hated handing money over to the *Herald*, Molloy thought.

There was a crowd in front of the Trades Hall in Hobson Street, talking and smoking and gradually shuffling inside. Molloy parked his car round the corner and joined them. The hall was full, with people crammed in at the back and along the sides. Molloy stood just inside the main doors. There was a line of wooden chairs across the stage, with a lectern in the middle and an upright piano off to one side. A canvas backdrop hanging behind the seating depicted brightly coloured scenes from the eternal struggle of the working man woven round the stirring IWW declaration, *If Blood Be the Cost of Your Cursed Wealth, Good God! We Have Paid in Full!*

The Waterside Workers' Union executive — Mark Thomas, Malcolm Walker, Dennys Watkins, Peter Winter and John Green, with Toby Hill and Jock Barnes in the lead — clumped onto the stage and took their seats. The audience gradually stopped talking. Barnes stood in front of the lectern. He turned back and leaned down to whisper something in Hill's ear. He hitched his trousers and adjusted his tie. He took some sheets of paper from his pocket, shuffled them and put them down. He looked towards the ceiling at the back of the hall, turned to check that his officials were in place, and began.

"Brothers. And, ah, sisters, of course," he said. "Welcome. Sad day. As you'll have no doubt heard, our comrade-in-arms, Frank O'Flynn, has, ah, passed away, God rest his soul. O'Flynn was a true son of Ireland and, of course, a watersider. I spoke to Father Delaney earlier and the good Father felt that under the circumstances he's most likely to be in Limbo presently, given the whatchamacall, the current difficult circumstances, rather than, ah, you know?" He glanced down at the floor. "I think those of you who are RC in particular will appreciate that reassurance. Thank you, Father." Delaney nodded graciously from his seat in the front row. The parish priest of St Joseph's was one of those clerics who had, in the words of Pat Booth from the *Auckland Star*, enlarged the definition of papal infallibility to include himself.

Barnes looked at the lectern for an awkward few seconds. "Now, you're going to hear all sorts of stories about Frank putting his hand in the till and that, and I want to tell you it's pure bunkum from end to end. That's what the ruling class wants you to believe, see, because divide and conquer's how they play the game."

He patted his pockets until he found a handkerchief, unfolded it, and blew his nose loudly. It seemed to go on and on. Two little boys in the second row began giggling. A woman leaned over and clipped one of them hard on the ear. The boy turned and looked at her, shocked and wounded, his little face saying, "What was that for?" And then he caught his pal's eye and they were off again, hunched over, their little shoulders going up and down like pistons in a tiny, speeding car. Barnes folded his handkerchief and put it back in his pocket.

"When a man," he said, "takes his own life, who can understand it? Certainly, he was under pressure. It looks like, ah, he buckled. Well, that's no good. It's what the employers and the Government and Holland and the Yanks and them want, see. Capitulation. Well, it's not going to happen. So, ah, that's that."

Barnes took his notes off the lectern and left the stage. The executive turned in sync to watch him go and then turned back and looked at one another uneasily. The room was quiet.

"How do you spell *perfunctory*, Mr Molloy?" a voice whispered from behind him. Molloy turned. It was Caitlin O'Carolan, her hair tied under a black scarf.

"The only big word I know is *retainer*, Miss O'Carolan," he whispered back, after a moment.

Caitlin caught his arm. "Gosh," she said. "What happened to you?"

"Tripped on a rug," he said.

"Mr Barnes doesn't appear to be terribly upset by Mr O'Flynn's passing," said Caitlin.

Molloy looked at her. "Jock's probably the sort of bloke who does his bawling in private," he said.

Caitlin snorted.

Toby Hill stood up and walked to the lectern.

"Um, thanks, Jock, for those moving words," he said. "Yeah, no, good. Now, some of the boys would like to perform a song in Frank's memory. Frank was over there in Spain, a premature anti-fascist as our good friends the Yanks like to say, wounded and that, brave thing to do, so, ah, gents?"

The Watersiders' Chorale — Dave Galler, Eddie Mee, Peter Rogers, G.R.C. Howie and the Gillies brothers — lined up on stage. Paul Jeffrey, a seagull and part-time music teacher at Seddon Tech, who occasionally sat in for Crombie Murdoch with Ted Croad's big band at the Orange Ballroom on a Saturday night if Crom was out on the ran-tan with Ross Burge, and who dreamed of one day going to New York and playing those joints on 52nd Street — or Sydney, Sydney would be good, there was a scene in Sydney — carried a chair over to the piano. He began with an arpeggio in the hand-over-hand style of the Kansas City boogie-woogie master Pete Johnson, but funereally paced, as if the latter was suffering from a particularly bad case of the blues and didn't feel like stretching out. Jeffrey's versatility was dazzling. He stopped and cracked his knuckles. There was some coughing and shuffling from the crowd, and then silence. He squared his shoulders, nodded to Dave Galler, and gently played the opening chords of "Red River Valley".

"There's a valley in Spain called Jarama," Galler began in a high, sweet voice, with the others joining in on the second line, Eddie Mee's earthy *basso profundo* providing a pleasing counterpoint at the bottom end.

It's a place that we all know so well
It was there that we fought against the fascists
And so many of our brave comrades fell.

CHAPTER TWENTY-ONE

Molloy found Barnes in the corridor rolling a smoke, his hands shaking, threads of tobacco dropping to the floor.

"G'day, Jock," he said. "Nice eulogy."

"Bullshit," said Barnes. He looked up. "Cripes! Happened to you?"

"Walked into a door."

"Walked under a ladder looks like to me," said Barnes. He hooked a thumb in the direction of the singing. "Listen to them. The Red Army Choir. Desecrates the memory of decent men."

"How come?" said Molloy.

"You know Tom Spiller?" said Barnes. "Good bloke. Calls a spade a spade. He was in the French Battalion over there. Badly shot up. I got him to have a natter with Frank. Had me doubts, see. Tom reckons the waster was never in Spain. Hell, you were there. Did you ever see him?"

"No. But that doesn't mean much. I was further north."

"All right, well," said Barnes, unconvinced. He moistened the paper. Molloy lit a match.

"If you felt like that why'd you let him stick around?"

Barnes blew out a stream of smoke. His tone was flat. "It's a democratic organisation. The boys liked him. All that Irish malarkey. It was better to present a united front," he said.

Molloy looked around. "In the note the police found at the beach he said something about stealing money from the Welfare Fund."

Barnes dismissed the suggestion. "Toby wouldn't let him within coo-ee of our money. Or anything else, for that matter." He looked straight at Molloy. "He was a flippin' rat."

"A rat?"

Barnes' hands were shaking. "A rat," he repeated. "A stooge. A sell-out merchant."

"Come on—" Molloy began.

"Come on, hell," said Barnes, his face turning red. "Nobody yelled louder than Frank about the need to face down the employers and the Government and them, not even me. And now that we're out on a limb, facing the chop, what does he do?" Barnes dropped his half-smoked rollie on the floor and stamped it out with a large boot. "Goes to Piha for the waters."

"Who was he working for, do you reckon?"

Barnes shrugged. "Who stands to gain the most from the present situation?" he asked. "The ship owners? Sid Holland? The Yanks?" He put his big hand on Molloy's shoulder. "You're the detective, Johnny. You work it out."

He walked off down the corridor as the last notes of "Jarama Valley" died away.

From this valley they say we are going
Do not hasten to bid us adieu
Even though we lost the battle of Jarama
We'll set this valley free afore we're through.

CHAPTER TWENTY-TWO

Outside the Trades Hall people were talking and smoking. Molloy made his way through the crowd, nodding at familiar faces. A voice called out to him. "Mr Molloy! Wait." It was Caitlin O'Carolan.

"What did Mr Barnes say?" she asked.

"About what?"

"About Frank O'Flynn," she said. "I know that's why you went to see him."

"What makes you so sure about that?"

"I'm a reporter," she said. "I'm resourceful."

"You squeezed it out of O'Driscoll, you mean," said Molloy, shaking his head. "You're right. He does have a big mouth."

"Oh, don't be too hard on him," she said. "He lusts after me, poor man." She slipped her arm under his. "May I shout you lunch? I'd like to talk to you about something."

They crossed Hobson Street, dodging traffic, walked down to Smith & Caughey's and took the lift up to the third-floor cafeteria. After queuing to order lunch, they sat at a table by a window overlooking Queen Street.

"Did that song make you sad?" said Caitlin, removing her gloves finger by finger.

Molloy shrugged. "No. I'm over that business."

"The Spanish Civil War," she said, slowly enunciating. "*Brigadas Internacionales. Partido Comunista de España. ¡No pasarán!* It's so romantic."

"There wasn't anything romantic about it," said Molloy.

"What did you do there? Were you a soldier?"

"I drove an ambulance."

"An ambulance! My God," she said. "You were an idealist. And now you're a hard-bitten cynic. It's like something you'd see in the pictures."

"I don't go to the pictures much."

"Were you in the front lines?"

"Most of the time," he said. "It's where the casualties were."

"Oh, touché!" said Caitlin. "And after Spain, what then?"

"Joined up," said Molloy. "Like a mug."

"Where were you?"

"Greece, Crete, North Africa, Italy, all up through there." He caught himself. What was going on? He couldn't stand jokers who talked about the war, yet here he was, prattling away like a rear echelon skite at a battalion reunion.

"My father was in the 28th Battalion," said Caitlin.

Molloy looked at her.

"That took you by surprise, didn't it?" she said. "He was a medical officer. He lost a leg in Tunisia. A landmine."

"That's no good," said Molloy.

"No," said Caitlin. "Did you know Colonel Awatere, the CO?"

"I saw him once," said Molloy. "After Cassino. They lost a lot of men there."

"Father knows him well. He calls in occasionally. They go into the study and drink whisky and talk for hours. Father thinks the colonel is a broken man."

Molloy said nothing.

"'For God, for King, and for country — *au-e!*'" said Caitlin, an edge to her tone. "Did you feel that way?"

"Not particularly."

"Who's the toasted sandwich?" said a waitress. She had their lunch on a trolley.

Molloy nodded. "That's me, thanks."

"So you're the asparagus roll," the waitress said to Caitlin.

"I'm sorry for getting all maudlin out of the blue," said Caitlin, once the waitress had gone.

"Funerals can do that to people," said Molloy. There was a moment of silence. "Anyway, what was it you wanted to talk to me about?"

Caitlin leaned forward. "O'Driscoll said you were interested in Frank O'Flynn and that it was probably a divorce matter, since that's the sort of thing you do. Do you take milk?"

"Please."

"But I don't think that's why you're interested in him."

"Don't you?" said Molloy. "What do you think?"

She passed his cup. "I think Mr Barnes asked you to investigate O'Flynn. Because of the theft of money from the Welfare Fund. And you were giving him your report."

Molloy put a spoonful of sugar into his tea and stirred it slowly before answering. "Miss O'Carolan, may I ask you something?" he said.

"On one condition. That you please stop calling me Miss O'Carolan. It makes me sound like a Latin teacher. Call me Caitlin."

"Fair enough," he said. "Caitlin, why were you waiting outside Frank O'Flynn's boarding house in Grey Lynn the other night?"

He bit into his ham and cheese toasted sandwich. It made a crunching sound. He looked at her. "In a Baby Austin."

"I don't know what ..." she said.

"You don't know what … what?"

"What makes you …?" She picked up her napkin and put it down on the other side of her plate.

Molloy put down his toasted sandwich and reached into a pocket for his notebook. He thumbed its pages. "Who's Miss C. Cotterill of Marine Parade, Herne Bay?" He looked up. "Your mother?"

Caitlin glared at him. Then she smiled and shrugged. "My mother's sister, actually," she said. "My Aunt Caroline. She's in Melbourne and I'm looking after her home for a little bit."

"And her motorcar?"

"Yes. Not to mention feeding her blasted cats and a few other things. Dead-heading her roses when required."

"So why were you outside O'Flynn's boarding house?" he asked. "That's a fair way from Marine Parade."

Caitlin opened her purse, took out a compact and began dabbing powder on her cheeks. "O'Driscoll told me the Welfare Fund rumour last week and I thought it would make a good article. Not that the *Star* would be interested, of course, but it's the sort of thing that *Truth* might—"

"Cut it out," said Molloy. He pointed to the scab on his chin. "This happened because I was asking questions about O'Flynn. There are people out there who don't want him bothered, I don't know why." He looked at his watch. "I admire your pluck," he said. "And I can imagine you making quite a name for yourself at Home. But it's not a good time to be doing what you're doing here, for whatever reason you're doing it. I don't mean to patronise you, but you will get hurt. People think because nothing much happens in New Zealand nothing much happens. They're wrong."

He finished his tea and stood. "Now, I'm sorry, but I've got an appointment. Excuse me." He raised his hat.

CHAPTER TWENTY-THREE

Molloy crossed Queen Street and walked up through Albert Park to Princes Street. The university wasn't in session and there weren't many people about. The sound of a violin came from the open window of a merchant's house recently colonised by the Music Department, the last privately owned mansion in the street. Molloy went into the Clock Tower and asked the receptionist where he might find Archie Green. She looked at the watch pinned to her bosom. "Any weekday between half-past eleven and half-past two I would try the Staff Common Room," she said.

The Common Room had begun life as the officers' quarters for the 58th Infantry during the Maori Wars, and appeared to have had few improvements of any significance since. There was a closed-in fireplace at one end with a portrait of a college notable above it. The room had a high ceiling, and worn carpet faded by the sun which came in through a line of dormer windows. A Roll of Honour — *In Loving and Grateful Memory of the Men of This College Who Gave Their Lives for the Honour of the British Empire During the Great European War 1914–1918* — had been moved further along the wall to make room for a new roll honouring the men who'd given their lives between 1939 and 1945. A wooden ladder stood on a canvas drop cloth and there were tins and jars and brushes and paint-splattered rulers on the floor. The signwriter was working on names beginning with D. There were couches and armchairs, and a few people scattered about, all male, one of whom was Archie Green.

Green was Molloy's age, bony, with thinning red hair and freckled skin. He was sitting alone on a couch, legs crossed, reading an airmail edition of the *Observer*. A cup of tea and the remains of a thin white sandwich sat on greaseproof paper on a low table in front of him.

"Mind if I join you, Archie?" said Molloy.

Green looked up at him and froze. "I'm sorry, I think you've got the wrong chap," he said.

"No I don't, Comrade," said Molloy. "Johnny Molloy, remember? Young Communist League. Committee For—"

Green crunched his copy of the *Observer*. It was surprisingly loud for tissue paper.

"For God's sake!" he said, leaning forward. "Keep your blasted voice down."

He took off his specs and put them in the breast pocket of his shirt, struggling to find the opening, his eyes sweeping the room like a rat on a recce. "What do you want?"

"Your help," said Molloy.

Green spluttered. "Out of the question."

"Come on, Archie," said Molloy. "That's not very fraternal. Remember those singalongs round the bonfire out at Karekare? 'Arise, ye prisoners of starvation! Arise, ye wretched of—'"

Green shuddered. "Oh, God. I knew this would happen. The Party reaching out from the past to tap me on the shoulder."

"Steady on, Archie. I got out of the Party in 1939, the day Hitler joined."

"You never get out of the Party."

"That so?" said Molloy. "Well, it's not a Party matter, put it that way. I'm a private detective these days."

Green groaned. "For the College?" he said.

"Nothing to do with the College," said Molloy. "Army matter."

Archie paused. "What do you mean?"

"You were on Freyberg's staff during the war, weren't you?"

Green's little chest swelled. "Yes I bloody was," he said. "Intelligence officer. Mentioned in despatches *twice.*"

"How many of you were there?"

"What? IOs?" said Green. "Gosh. Me, Whitey, Dan Davin, Cox, Paddy Costello — now *there* was a Red, by God! — I don't know. Quite a few over the duration. Why?"

"Still keep in touch with any of them?"

"Not really. Possibly. When I'm in Wellington. Hard not to bump into chaps you know down there."

"Anyone who's remained in that area?"

"In that area?" said Green. "You mean …? Oh, dear. I think you're confusing the work of an intelligence officer in wartime with …" He lowered his voice. "We weren't *spies* by any stretch of—"

"Yes or no, Archie?" said Molloy, cutting him off.

"We can't talk here." Green was breathing heavily.

"Where?"

"Albert Park in fifteen minutes," said Green, just above a whisper. "By the floral clock." He let out an enormous sigh, and stood.

CHAPTER TWENTY-FOUR

Twenty minutes later Molloy was sitting on a wooden bench in Albert Park watching a young couple stretched out on the grass holding hands. Or rather she was holding his hand. Holding it back. The boy was trying to make a game of it, walking his fingers up her bare arm, his obvious intention to walk right up to her breasts and settle in. When his hand reached her sleeve she would take it in hers and place it on the grass and wriggle her fingers at him. Lots of giggling and whispering going on, but Molloy was impressed by the boy's relentless determination. It was like watching an ant at work, or the building of a pyramid.

Archie Green sat down next to him. He had put on a sports coat and a felt hat tilted forward so that his face was half in shadow. He had been dux of Auckland Grammar and a guild scholar at Cambridge before the war, and was making a name for himself as an academic, an economist in the area of price controls. There had been talk of a posting to the United Nations. And now here he was having a meeting with a private detective in a public park, like some grubby character, he thought, from *The Maltese Falcon*.

"Early political enthusiasms proving a bit of an embarrassment, are they, Arch?" said Molloy, offering him a smoke.

"There's a witch hunt here too, you know," said Green, leaning in to the match. His voice was a little steadier. Molloy smelt gin. "The

Americans are supplying lists. Names of known Communists and fellow travellers. Full of mistakes, apparently. Not that that would bother them." He drew on the cigarette. "It's not fair. Three years in the thick of it. Alamein, Cassino." He hooked a bitter thumb in the direction of the Clock Tower. "Means nothing." He rubbed his forehead, pushing his hat back on his head with the tips of his fingers. "If the College hears I was a Party member, I'm finished."

"Well, they won't hear it from me."

"On one condition, no doubt."

"Not a condition. A favour."

"Ah yes, a favour," said Green, feeling immensely sorry for himself. "And so it begins."

Molloy took an envelope from his pocket and put it on the bench. "There's an Irishman who was arrested last year for drunk and disorderly and one or two other things, and found to be in the country without papers. He should have been given the boot but he wasn't. I want to find out if someone pulled strings for him, and if so, who." He nodded at the envelope. "The details are in there. Not that there's much."

"And if I refuse?"

Molloy looked at him and said nothing. Actually, bugger all, he thought, but Archie didn't need to know that.

"I do some work with Industries and Commerce," said Green, putting the envelope in the pocket of his sports coat. "There's a chap there who ..." He shrugged. "I could talk to him."

"That'd be good."

Green's shoulders slumped. "My God, I was hardly a *Communist*. I joined the YCL as a way to meet fast girls, if the truth be known." He looked at Molloy. "Remember? 'The redder the bedder'? Fat lot of good that did me either."

He stood without a word and walked off, hands in pockets, head down.

Molloy gave him a minute. On the grass by the floral clock the boy's walking fingers had made it to the girl's shoulder, and they were kissing. He had subtly altered his angle of attack so that it was awkward for her to find his hand with her eyes closed. Molloy got up and watched as Green crossed Princes Street, and saw, beyond him, Miss Cotterill's brown Baby Austin parked on the other side of the road.

CHAPTER TWENTY-FIVE

Molloy drove to the Newton Police Station in Ponsonby Road and asked for Pat Toomey. He took a seat in the waiting room and read the race results from Saturday's *8 O'Clock*. It was shortly after two. The station was busy. Telephones rang, doors opened and closed, policemen came and went.

A boy about twelve with a black eye and grass stains on his knees sat sniffling on a bench next to his furious mother.

"I just don't know what I'm going to do with you," she said, her worn hands strangling the strap on her shopping bag. "God knows I've tried."

"They started it," said the boy, bottom lip poking out like a plate.

"Oh yes," said his mother. "It's always *they* with you. Just like your useless father."

Toomey leaned out of an interview room and hooked a finger at Molloy. "Johnny," he said.

There was a cardboard box on a table in the middle of the room with a typed label which read O'Flynn, F. X. personal effects of, and the address — Room 4, 3 Chamberlain Street, Grey Lynn — and a reference number. Toomey closed the door.

"Make it snappy," he said.

Molloy emptied the contents of the box onto the table. A worn toothbrush, a shaving strop, a cutthroat razor, two combs, some coins,

III

rosary beads, a Western — A.B. Guthrie Jr's *The Way West* — which Molloy had heard somewhere was pretty good.

"Is this the lot?" Molloy asked.

"What were you expecting, Johnny?" said Toomey. "A trousseau?"

"I dunno," said Molloy, flicking through the novel. "More than this though. Didn't he have any clothes? What about his work gear? He was a wharfie. He'd have had boots and a raincoat surely?"

"Perhaps he kept his work duds on the back porch?"

"Could be, I suppose," said Molloy. "What about personal stuff? Letters, that sort of thing?"

"Landlady probably threw them out," said Toomey. "Said she didn't but you know what they're like."

"I do," said Molloy, returning the items to the box and closing it. "Thanks, Pat."

Molloy drove to Grey Lynn and parked in Chamberlain Street. He climbed the steps at number 3 and knocked on the door. He heard someone shuffling up the hallway. The door opened. The landlady, a woman in her fifties with flaming red hair, glared at him.

"Yes?"

"I'd like to look at a room."

"Nothing available at the present moment. Which explains the 'No Vacancy' notice in the window," said the landlady, pointing. "Sorry."

She began to close the door.

Molloy put his foot on the step to stop her. "I'm not after lodgings," he said. "I'd like to have a look at Frank O'Flynn's old room."

"Are you a policeman?" she asked.

"I'm a private detective," said Molloy handing her his card.

She didn't look at it. "Then the answer's no," she said. "I've had policemen and whatnot through here all day, traipsing their dirt. I've only just finished cleaning up after them. The room has been let. New boarder is moving in on Saturday. Now move your foot or I'll ring a real detective."

Molloy turned and walked back down the steps. Over the road, on the corner of Brown Street, he saw the Baby Austin. He crossed the street.

Caitlin wound down her window and smiled at him. "Why, if it isn't Mr Molloy," she said. "Fancy seeing you here."

"You're asking for trouble, Miss O'Carolan."

"It's a free world, isn't it?" she asked. "Still?"

CHAPTER TWENTY-SIX

It was ten o'clock. Molloy was parked at the top of Chamberlain Street. The porch light at number 3 had gone out half an hour earlier and the boarding house was in darkness. He took a torch from the glovebox and walked delicately down the side of the villa. The grass was uncut and at one point he stumbled over an old tyre. He went slowly up the rickety rear steps and tried the door. It was unlocked. He let himself in.

Somewhere in the house a radio was playing. A toilet flushed and he heard footsteps along the hall and a door opening and closing. His eyes adjusted to the darkness. There were four doors on each side of the hall. Room 1 was closest to the kitchen. He crept up the hallway. Room 4 was locked. He ran his hand along the top of the frame but there was nothing. Where would the landlady keep the key? he wondered. It could be anywhere.

He went outside and around the side of the villa. The windows were at least six feet off the ground. He took one of the painting ladders from in front of the house and leaned it gently against the wall beneath the window of O'Flynn's old room. It was open a few inches, enough to air the room. He put his hands under the frame and pushed. It moved easily at first and then caught, making a shrieking sound loud enough to wake all of Grey Lynn. He waited. Silence. He lowered the window slightly so that it was square and then pushed it up, and let himself in.

The room had a single iron bedstead with a rolled-up mattress, a small table and chair, a tallboy and a chest of drawers on top of which was a flowered jug and a bowl on a freshly ironed doily. There was a mat on the wooden floorboards in the middle of the room. On the wall above the chest of drawers was a small mirror on a chain, and on the opposite wall a framed picture of Windsor Castle cut from the lid of a chocolate box.

Molloy lifted the chair and leaned it against the door, its back under the knob, locking it in place. He took the drawers from the chest and turned them over to see if there was anything taped to the bottoms. Nothing. He searched the tallboy and ran his hand around the top. Nothing. He took down the mirror and the picture and turned them over. Nothing. He unrolled the mattress and checked where it might have been cut and resewn. He ran his hand around the bed frame. He lifted the mat. He checked the floorboards for signs they had been moved. He took the chair from under the doorknob and stood on it to look at the light shade. *Nada*. The whole place was as clean as a whistle.

He returned the chair to its position against the door and sat on the bedstead. The springs groaned. He looked at the picture on the wall. He took it down again. Its backing was held in place by metal clips, recently folded. He straightened them and removed the cardboard. There was a folded slip of card in the corner between the illustration and the frame. He put the picture on the bed and opened the slip. It was a left-luggage ticket from the Auckland Railway Station. It was new.

There was a banging on the door. "Hey," a voice shouted. "Who's in there?"

"I've telephoned the police," a second voice, the landlady, threatened. "They're on their way."

"I've got a cricket bat," someone else called.

"Yes," said the landlady. "Bring it."

Doors opened. "What's going on?" yet another voice said.

"Someone's broken in," said the first voice. "Bastard's not going anywhere though."

"Language!" said the landlady.

"Round the back! He'll get out the window!"

But Molloy was already there, dropping to the ground and running along the side of the house towards the street. Lights were coming on. He could hear yelling from inside. The front door burst open. Two figures ran out onto the front porch and then stopped.

"Quick," said the first.

"What?" said the second.

The landlady pushed her way between them. "Police," she yelled. "There he is."

Molloy ran across Richmond Road. He could hear footsteps behind him.

Headlights picked him out. He saw nothing but brilliant white. A car cut in front of him. Its passenger door swung open and he heard Caitlin call out, "Quick, get in."

The car accelerated down Richmond Road.

"Well, Miss O'Carolan," said Molloy, looking over his shoulder for signs of pursuit and seeing nothing. "You're wasted on the Women's Page, I'll give you that."

"That's big of you, Molloy," she said, checking the rear-vision mirror and charging along Ponsonby Road.

"Where are we going?"

"There's someone who wants to talk to you," she said. "Actually, he's an old friend of yours."

She drove down College Hill and up Victoria Street, bent over the wheel like Juan Fangio. She turned into a side street and then into another. It was lined with two-storey wooden buildings. There were shops at ground level and flats above.

"Here we are," she said, turning off the ignition and pulling the handbrake. The motor ticked into silence.

Molloy looked around. "Where?"

There were pubs on opposite corners, the Criterion and the Shamrock. Other than the blue glow of the Criterion's neon sign, and faint lighting from one or two of the flats, the area was in darkness. There would have been commercial travellers in the house bar of the Criterion, and after-hours customers boozing in the Shamrock, but for all the people around, they might as well have been in Wellington.

Caitlin leaned across him and pointed to a light coming from behind the curtains in a room above Progressive Books.

"There," she said.

An unlocked door next to the bookshop opened onto a narrow stairway lit by a single bulb. Caitlin led the way. At the top of the stairs was a small landing and a plain door halfway down a corridor. Molloy could hear the rolling of a Gestetner.

Caitlin knocked.

"Who is it?" said a voice that Molloy hadn't heard since before the war.

"Me," said Caitlin.

"Just a tick."

Molloy looked at Caitlin. "Well, whaddya know?" he said.

The door opened. An older man, lean and muscular, his nose

bent and his ears rumpled, a big grin on his ugly mug, stood there wiping his hands with a rag. He was wearing a black beret, an ink-stained white shirt with the sleeves rolled up, and high-waisted trousers tied with a worn leather belt. The metal frames of his round Health Department glasses caught the light from the bulb and his green eyes glinted from behind thick lenses.

"Fraternal greetings, Comrade Molloy!" said V.G. Parker, General Secretary of the Communist Party of New Zealand.

CHAPTER TWENTY-SEVEN

Molloy was driving a tip-truck on the Mangakino deviation, a Public Works Department scheme for the Main Trunk Railway, when he first met Vince. It was 1934. Parker was an organiser for the Drivers' Union and recruiting for the Party on the side. Molloy was union to the core and the latter was an easy next step, especially in the middle of the Depression when it seemed the only factories in the world with their lights on were in the Soviet Union.

In 1937, on Parker's instructions, Molloy went to Spain as a driver with the Spanish Medical Aid Committee ambulance unit. There were three nurses: René Shadbolt, Isobel Dodds and Millicent Sharples; Trevor Haysom, a school teacher and Party member from Palmerston North, there to maintain ideological discipline; and Molloy, the unit's driver-mechanic. After a briefing from Comintern representatives in Marseilles on what to expect once they crossed the Pyrenees, Haysom had had second thoughts. He went out for tobacco and never returned. The nurses were seconded to the International Brigade hospital in Huete. Molloy was sent to the front.

During the Huesca Offensive his ambulance was hit by a bomb dropped from a Nationalist aeroplane — a Junkers trimotor which he got to know better in Crete four years later. Dorthe Scheffman, a nurse and staunch Trotskyite from Denmark, who died of TB in the

French internment camp at Gurs in 1940, was riding in the back with two German casualties from the Thälmann Battalion. Dorthe was all right, just shaken. One of the Teds was killed. Molloy had a broken leg and concussion.

He was invalided to Barcelona, just as the Spanish revolution began to turn upon itself. On the 3rd of May three motor lorries of assault guards from the Karl Marx Barracks attempted to occupy the anarchist-run telephone exchange in the Plaça de Catalunya. Barricades made from sandbags and paving stones, and manned by workers armed with rifles and petrol bombs, appeared on every corner. Five days of street fighting followed. Molloy was lucky to escape with his life. A goon squad from the XV International Brigade, sent to the hospital to liquidate the patients, most of them wounded from the barricades and POUM militiamen from Huesca — George Orwell's old mob — was commanded by an Australian, a good bloke named Richard Warren. Molloy knew him. They had knocked about a bit together in Paris while in transit to Spain. The *Internacionales* came into the ward with their machine pistols on automatic and worked their way down the narrow aisles, shooting methodically and without concern, their tunics soon shiny with blood and viscera, the air thick with mattress feathers and gun smoke.

Warren recognised Molloy. He put the barrel of his weapon next to Molloy's cheek and fired into the pillow. Molloy jerked and slumped and managed to pull the canvas blanket up over his face. The shot careened round his skull for months afterwards, and he still didn't hear as well as he should out of his left ear, but he was alive. He didn't like to think what became of the Australian. The International Brigades were no place for sentimental blokes.

Molloy landed back in New Zealand at the end of July 1939. Parker wanted him to do a public speaking tour around the country to raise funds for Spanish refugees in France. The announcement of the Nazi-Soviet Non-Aggression Pact upset that plan — Stalin and Hitler on the same side. For a few days there was silence from Vince. Then he showed up at Molloy's to fill him in on the revised Party line. The impending European conflict was an imperialist one, Vince said, of no significance to the working class.

Molloy exploded. What about anti-fascism? What about the Popular Front? What about ¡No pasarán!?

They'd had a go, in the kitchen, out on the front lawn, along Arthur Street, neighbours egging them on. The plods had come and broken it up and both men had spent the night in the cells behind Newton Police Station, cooling off. Next day Molloy resigned from the Party and a few months later he was in Egypt with the First Echelon. He hadn't seen Parker since.

"Well I never," said Molloy. He turned to Caitlin. "A cadet reporter who takes her orders from a red-hot Commo." He turned back to his host. "I've got to hand it to you, Vince," he said. "This really is revolution from within."

"Takes orders?" said Parker. "Not Cait. She bows only to the will of the proletariat, isn't that right, Comrade?" He put out his hand. "Good to see you, you backslider. Come in."

CHAPTER TWENTY-EIGHT

One wall of Parker's room was lined with bookshelves. There was a single bed in the corner. A small postcard of Lenin unveiling a memorial to Karl Marx in Voskresenskaya Square in 1918 was pinned to the wall above the mantelpiece. An open window looked across rooftops, curtains deliberately arranged to obscure the view of Smith & Caughey's, bourgeois emporium that it was. On the table stood a Gestetner machine and ink and wipers. Washed dishes dried on a bench next to a gas ring and there was an open bottle of milk and a half a pound of butter under a net cover on the windowsill in the breeze.

"Have a seat," said Parker, pulling the stools out from under the table. He put the duplicating equipment on the floor and pushed aside a floral curtain under the sink.

"Let's have some plonk," he said, taking out a flagon. "Pass us those cups will you, dear." He poured three nips of sherry. "This stuff's not bad," he said. "Old Dally out West called Farac makes it. His uncle was a *Potemkin* man, he reckons, although he could be pulling me leg."

He raised his cup in salute. "*Za vas*! Here's to the Great Patriotic War, eh? I heard a bit about your army exploits, Johnny. Big hero and that."

"What do you want, Vince?" said Molloy.

"Never any beating about the bush with Comrade Molloy," said Parker, putting the flagon on the floor. He pointed at the dried scab on Molloy's nose. "That wasn't from the thumping I gave you that time, was it?" He shook his head. "Those were the days, eh? When you could get an argument going? Now all they're interested in talking about is footy and the ponies." He straightened up. "Anyway, you want to know why we brought you here?"

Molloy shrugged. "My line of work, you end up in some odd places."

"Work? Is that what you call it?" Parker shook his head. "One of my proudest moments," he said to Caitlin. "When I brought this fella into the Party." He reached for the flagon. "Now look at him. A *Pinkerton* man."

"Right-o," said Molloy, reaching for his hat.

"Comrade!" said Caitlin, looking sharply at Parker.

"Yeah, no, that was out of order," said Parker quickly, holding up one hand. He put his cup on the table. "Sorry, Johnny. I'm not meself. Have a seat, please. It's this waterfront business. I can't sleep worrying about it. Will you hear me out?"

"Go ahead," said Molloy. "But don't take all night."

"Good. That's good. I appreciate it." He pointed at the postcard of Lenin on the wall. "First of all, let me read you something that little fella wrote. For context." He leaned over and opened a drawer in a cupboard next to the bed. He took out a booklet. It was bulging with little strips of torn newsprint denoting key passages. He opened to a bookmarked page. "This is from his *On the Foreign Policy of the Soviet State*."

He began reading. "'The struggle of the workers becomes a class struggle only when all the foremost representatives of the entire working class of the whole country are conscious of themselves as a single working class.'" He looked up. "You see that? 'Conscious of themselves as a *single working class.*'" He gazed at the hectoring Lenin and shook his head in admiration. "The *acuity* of the bloke." He put the booklet back in the drawer. "Three Musketeers sorta thing. All for one and one for all. United we stand, divided we fall. The *collective will.* Yet there's Barnes and them, off down the adventurist road, *on their own.*"

He ticked his fingers one by one. "Oh there'll be talk of solidarity, but when it comes to the crunch? The Meat Workers won't stick with them. Disciplined, see, they know how to take advice. The Seamen? Not a show. Drivers? Likewise. Postal Workers? Never. Magnificent, those bastards. That parasite Walsh has the Clerical Workers and the craft unions wound round his little finger, so forget them. Of course there'll be the usual renegade elements. Carpenters spring to mind, the ungrateful swine. Miners? Possibly — who can predict which wild path those West Coast Doolans will follow? But no one of *significance*, you get it? None of the *foremost representatives.*" He leaned forward. "The wharfies are walking into a trap pretty much on their own. The wharfies! The Brigade of Guards of the industrial movement! Hard bastards. Street fighters. Control the waterfront, you've got the country by the throat. But not these clowns. Not Barnes and them. Jock's strutting round with his chest puffed up like flamin' Mussolini, but he's no Ulyanov, I think you'd agree, you know, in terms of strategic foresight. Instead of controlling the waterfront they're giving control away! Handing it to Holland and his Yankee cobbers. So why are they doing it? Who's pulling the levers? Who's the *controlling element?*" He slammed the table. "*What the fuck is going on?*" He looked at Caitlin. "Pardon me French, Comrade."

She brushed it off. Molloy sipped his sherry. He wasn't a sherry man as a rule but Parker was right. It wasn't bad.

"There's an agent provocateur in the WWU," said Parker. "We think it's — or *was* — Frank O'Flynn. We know you're poking around, asking questions about him. Can you tell us why? For old times' sake?"

"Jock wants to know the same thing," said Molloy.

Parker threw up his hands in disgust. "*Now* he does, when it's too flippin' late! I tried to warn that ditchdigger about O'Flynn but he didn't want to know."

"Can you help us?" asked Caitlin.

Molloy put his cup down on the table. "What's in it for me?"

Parker made a growling sound. Caitlin ignored him. "We know something you might find useful," she said.

"Try me," said Molloy.

Parker reached for the flagon. "Ah, go ahead, tell him," he said to Caitlin, pulling the cork.

"O'Flynn isn't his real name," said Caitlin. "Which you probably know. But did you know he spent time in prison in Ireland for Republican activities?"

"What sort of activities?"

"He was part of an IRA bomb squad," she said.

"What the Fenians call the Chemical Wing," said Parker, putting the flagon back on the floor. "He tried to assassinate the Earl of Galway at the opening of the Cork Town Hall in 1938, amongst other things."

"He was caught but he escaped," said Caitlin.

"From *Mountjoy Gaol*." Parker shook his head. "In the heart of Dublin! More people have escaped from blimmin' Alcatraz than the Joy."

"What are you saying?"

"That he ratted on his cobbers," said Parker. "So the authorities let him go. See, this is a bloke with a history of informing."

"How do you know all this?" said Molloy.

"It's the Party's business to know. He was given a new name and passage to America. Perfect place for a rat."

"How did he end up here?"

"Bugger off," said Parker. "It's your turn."

Molloy paused for a moment. "Well, Miss O'Carolan saved my bacon tonight. So I'll tell you what I know."

"Jolly good," said Parker. He tapped the flagon. "Touch more?"

Molloy shook his head. "There's a Frank O'Phelan wanted in California for insurance fraud," he said. "Swept off a boat and drowned, supposedly. The insurance company thinks that O'Phelan might be this O'Flynn."

"The same one as supposedly drowned at Piha?"

Molloy nodded.

"Bloody right!" said Parker, holding up his sherry. "More likely to have drowned in this. Johnny, look," he said, getting serious again. "We can work together. Let Caitlin help you. She's as smart as a whip. Time is running out."

"What do you want to know?"

"Someone's paying this stooge. We find out *who* we find out *why*."

Molloy finished his drink and put the cup on the table. "I think your offsider's going to stick to me whether I want her to or not. And I owe her one for tonight." He stood. "I'll be in front of the Auckland Railway Station tomorrow morning at nine. There's something I want to check. Caitlin, if I see you there, I see you there."

"I'll be there," said Caitlin.

Molloy put on his hat.

"Would you like a lift back to your car?"

"No thanks," said Molloy. "I need some fresh air. See ya, Vic."

"*Das vedanya*, Comrade," said Parker. "When this blows over we'll have a beer and a proper natter, eh, what do you reckon?"

CHAPTER TWENTY-NINE

Sunny Day stopped the Plymouth on a gravel road and switched off the motor. A hand-painted sign — PRIVATE PROPERTY! NO ADMITTANCE! — was nailed to a padlocked wooden gate. A dirt track led down to a hydro site. The track was steep and rutted. At the bottom, a narrow river widened out in front of a small concrete dam with a race on either side.

In a cleared area next to the dam was a green corrugated iron Ministry of Works shed with a flat roof. The site was deserted. One side of the valley was gorse. From the river up the bank on the other side was steep, dense bush.

Sunny had two keys, one for the padlock on the gate and the other for the shed. He thought he would probably rip the sump out of the Plymouth going down the track, and even if he didn't, he doubted he'd be able to get her back up.

He took off his jacket and left it in the front seat of the car. He took a hammer and a torch from the boot. He unlocked the gate and made his way delicately down the track, dancing over ruts and cowpats, his leather-soled shoes sliding on the wet grass. He walked around the shed. No windows, strictly for storage. The padlock was sound. There was a sign on the door warning KEEP OUT! and one below it saying DANGEROUS GOODS. NO SMOKING! He put down his tools and walked over to the dam, shaded his eyes and checked for trout, but the morning sun was on the water and he could only see himself looking back.

He unlocked the padlock and opened the door, switching on his torch. There were some tools in the corner, a metal drum with a lid, a pile of empty sugar bags. There was a shape against the wall covered with a tarpaulin. Sunny removed the tarp. There were five wooden boxes, one smaller than the others. He took the smaller box and one of the larger ones outside and opened the lid of the larger with the claw of his hammer. He peeled back the waterproof paper.

Beautiful. Red Diamond tunnel gelatin, made by the Austin Powder Company of Cleveland, Ohio. Gelignite. Sunny loved gelly. Stable, dependable, deadly. Rhymed with jelly, smelt like marzipan, safe-crackers called it soup. When he was a kid he'd worked as a second-storey man for a safe-cracker named John Newman, blowing strongboxes in provincial picture theatres in the Lower North Island. Newman began by tying the office typewriter to the bolt work handle. He then wrapped a tiny amount of gelly around a detonator and poked it into a French letter, pushed the Frenchie, through the keyhole with the detonator hanging out, stuck the shebang in place with chewing gum, and lit the fuse. The resulting explosion, no louder than an empty cake tin dropping on a kitchen floor, shifted the levers holding the bolt for an instant, just long enough for the falling weight of the typewriter to turn the handle, opening the safe. The first time Sunny had seen the operation he had laughed out loud at its simplicity. You'd be a mug *not* to be a crook. All right, you ended up back in the jug eventually. But then you learned a new skill.

Sunny opened the other box. Hunkin T Series detonators. He kept one stick of gelly aside, closed the lid and tapped the nails gently back into place. One never knows, do one? He untwisted the bottom of the stick and poked a detonator a couple of inches or so into the base. He walked over to the bank, lit the fuse, threw the stick into the dam, dropped to the ground and covered his ears. The explosion rocked up the valley and water rained down all around him. At least twenty fat brown trout and as many eels floated to the surface.

He took off his shoes and socks and trousers, waded into the river, and made a considered selection — three hens, each at least four pounds. He gutted the fish on the bank, using his pocketknife. He washed the blood and slime off the knife and off his hands and wiped them on the grass. There was watercress growing in the shallows. He cut an armful.

He got dressed, put the trout and watercress in a sugar bag from the shed, lifted the box of gelly and the detonators under his arm, and walked back up the hill to the Plymouth. It was nine o'clock in the morning and just starting to get hot.

CHAPTER THIRTY

Sunny Day was known as Sunny for the same reason the Governor-General, the tall and rotund Lord Freyberg, was known as Tiny. There was nothing sunny about him. He was trouble from the word go. He was darker than his Ngati Porou cousins and self-conscious about it. His maternal line was Ngapuhi, a legacy of the war parties that raided up and down the East Coast during the Musket Wars. There may have been some African in there too. The crews of the American whaling ships that called into Kororareka in the 1820s often included Cape Verde Islanders, expert harpoonists and boatmen from the west coast of Africa. His green eyes were anyone's guess.

He was sentenced to a year in a Delinquents' Home when he was twelve for breaking and entering, and then two years in a Borstal for assault. By seventeen he was bare-knuckle boxing at carnivals and A&P shows throughout Taranaki and the Waikato, and a ringie for a two-up promoter. If a game was going against the house he had the presence to call a foul toss and the size to silence any objections. At eighteen he was back-up man for the Ohakune sly-grogger, J.R. Rowley, making regular trips into the dry King Country, the back seat and boot of Rowley's Austin Twelve loaded with whisky, a sawn-off .22 under his seat. He had a reputation for reliability and lack of compunction. He was a master of the left hook and the king hit. In 1939 he was sentenced to nine months for burglary following an attempt on the strongbox of the Hastings Laundry Company after a day spent drinking in the Public Bar of the Albert Hotel with three steam-iron operators, one of whom, a girl named Wilhelmina, knew where the office key was hidden.

He was released from Napier Prison in January 1940. His father, a fine-looking man with a thick black moustache and a long Maori name, but known in the Pakeha world as Tom, was waiting for him outside, leaning against his truck, smoking a pipe. The old man took the pipe from his mouth and checked the bowl, patted his shirt pocket for a box of matches, struck one, held it over the tobacco, and took several gentle draws — his lips making a lop-sided popping sound that Sunny remembered — while he kept his eyes on his son, expression neutral. Eventually the pipe took.

"You all right?" he said.

"Oh, y'know," said Sunny. "What do you want?"

"A fulla from Gisborne was around asking about you," said Tom. "Neville? Some name like that? Pakeha fulla? And a few of those bad Gisborne Maoris. Didn't say why."

Sunny knew why.

"You need to pull your head in for a bit," said Tom.

"I was thinking of the South Island," said Sunny. "Got a cobber in Christchurch."

"No," said Tom. "Further than that. Hop in."

They made the two-hour drive over pot-holed gravel roads up the coast and inland towards Ruatahuna, where Sunny had grown up, stopping at Tikitiki, outside the Post Office.

There was a poster on the wall. A column of soldiers, rifles shouldered, marching in formation towards the words,

YOUR PAL
IS IN THE
FIRST ECHELON
DO YOUR SHARE!
ENLIST TODAY

"Wants to join up," said Tom to the postmaster. "For King and country."

"He's not twenty-one though is he, Tom?" said the postmaster. "Has to be twenty-one, see."

"He's twenty-one enough," said Tom. "Just get the form."

"Right you are," said the postmaster, after a pause. He was small and Tom was big. And Tom had *mana*. "No skin off my nose." He pointed to the poster. "Second Echelon now. Made the quota for the first before Christmas." He took a form from a drawer and squared it on the counter.

"Use Eru's name," said Tom. "Twenty-eighth of the seventh 1917 where it says 'date of birth'."

"What will Eru say?"

"You let me worry about what Eru says," said Tom. "You get writing."

Sunny filled in the details. Say one thing for the penal system, it gave a young man a chance at the things that count in life — how to give and take a hiding, how to stare down a challenge, how to read and write at a rudimentary level.

"Sign there," said the postmaster, pointing.

Sunny signed.

"And if you'd witness the signature," the postmaster said to Tom.

Tom wrote his full name and underlined it, as florid as John Hancock's on the Declaration of Independence.

"Very good," said the postmaster. He stamped the bottom of the form, tapped the impression with blotting paper, and added his initials. Two weeks later Sunny was in camp at the Palmerston North Showgrounds, part of the Main Body, allocated to C Company, (28) Maori Battalion.

He took to the training, less so to the discipline. If nothing else, it was better than prison and fighting was in his blood. Firing a rifle. Stripping a Bren. Twisting a 14-inch bayonet into a sugar sack filled with sand.

He was punished for minor infractions on a number of occasions and charged with assault following a mêlée in the Soldiers Club in Russell Street, just off the Square. Someone from C Company threw a penny into a group of recruits from B Company. B Company was drawn largely from the area around Rotorua and the Bay of Plenty, and was nick-named "the Penny Divers" after the children who dived off bridges for tourists' coins at Wharewakawaka. The coin spun high into the air, not feathering in any way, thrown by someone who knew how to throw. The B Company boys took exception to this slight. The brawl wrecked the Public Bar of the Soldiers Club and spilled outside before being broken up by provosts and police.

Sunny, who had been in the thick of it, was brought before a magistrate. Inconsistencies in his recruitment details were discovered — his prison record, for example. Sunny thought the game was up. But the beak said that society was better off with him "over there" rather than "back here". He was fined seven days' pay and Confined to Barracks for ten days, the latter timed to coincide with the battalion's embarkation from Wellington on the troopship *Aquitania*, in convoy with the *Empress of Britain* and the *Empress of Japan*, and the destroyer HMS *Leander*, part of the 2nd New Zealand

Expeditionary Force. They were joined in Cook Strait by the *Andes*, carrying soldiers from Burnham Camp, and its escort HMAS *Canberra* — and, briefly, a humpback whale, which C Company in particular saw as a providential *kaitiaki*, Paikea's mythological saviour from Hawaiki-nui. The convoy was heading for Egypt to join the 2nd Division but diverted to Britain en route, crossing the Irish Sea a few weeks later past wreckage from a sunken liner and another vessel burning fiercely, the water slick with oil, arriving in time to learn of the death of Cobber Kain and the evacuation from Dunkirk and the capitulation of France, in time to hear Winston Churchill say on a radio broadcast, "The whole fury and might of the enemy must very soon be turned on us. Hitler knows that he will have to break us in this island or lose the war."

He was in the army now.

The Maori Battalion spent six months in England waiting for the Germans to invade. It was based at Doddington — or, as the censors insisted, "somewhere in England" — fifteen miles from the Kent coast, directly below the flight path that German bombers followed to London. The Battalion suffered its first casualty of the war, Private Tokena Pokai, a despatch rider from the East Coast, struck and killed while leading a blacked-out convoy on the Folkestone Road at night. There were artillery exchanges between Calais and Dover, the distance from Te Kaha to White Island. There were dogfights overhead on summer afternoons. King George VI made an inspection, as did his brother, the Duke of Gloucester. Winston Churchill took the salute. A Battalion rugby team, wearing white jerseys and black socks, played Wales and lost, 12-3. The men impressed with their manners. No domestic chicken was safe.

But the expected invasion didn't happen. The New Zealanders transferred to Egypt to join the first echelon at the beginning of

January 1941. Three months later Sunny was in Greece, separated from his platoon during the withdrawal from Mt Olympus, making his way to the evacuation point at Porto Rafti in an endless column of New Zealand and Australian and Greek soldiers, Palestinians and Cypriots from labour battalions, Albanian and Bulgarian and Yugoslav refugees, civilian and military vehicles.

An empty 6th Australian Division ammunition truck gave him a lift. The driver and the passenger were sappers from 2/3 Field Regiment. The ragged convoy stopped near Thermopylae while a tank was brought up to push the wreck of a petrol tanker off the road. The three men got out of the truck and under the cover of a tree.

"You're a Maori, I suppose," said the driver.

"He thought you was a blackfella at first," said the passenger. "No offence."

"I did! I said jeez, they're getting desperate!" said the driver. "Y'know?"

"But I seen your shoulder flashes. I said, nah — he's a New Zealander, mate. He's a Maori!"

Sunny wasn't offended. Besides, the Australian had a submachine pistol strung across his chest. Plus Sunny needed a ride. Being offended could wait.

"Never met a Maori before."

"What about that little fella played for Wests?" said the passenger. "Whatsaname, Albert Herewini? He was a Maori."

"Yeah, but I didn't *know* him. Knew he was a Kiwi, that's all. That's different." The driver turned to Sunny. "You heard of him?"

"Doesn't ring a bell," said Sunny.

"Nuggety little bugger. Tough? Jeez he was tough. Ran like a rabbit too."

They shook hands. Mick. Red. Sunny.

"What happened to your outfit?" said Mick.

"Got separated coming off the line."

"Yeah? Us too. Jerries just smashed through. CO gave us forty-eight hours to get to Kalamata, every bastard for himself. He said, 'We've got to hook it tonight, men. Whether we get through or not is just chance.'" Mick shook his head. "Just chance! What a bloody shambles. We're going to lose this flamin' war."

"What'll happen then, you reckon?" said Red.

"To us? Not much. Follow orders. Same as usual."

"You haven't got any grub I suppose, Sunny? Anything tucked away?" said Mick.

"I've got some booze and a tin of gyppo pickles, I think they are," said Sunny. "If you've got something to open it."

Sunny's canteen was filled with Greek brandy, which he'd found in an abandoned hut, along with a tin, rusted around the seal, Greek script and a faded illustration of what appeared to be a member of the cucumber family on the label, his first food in two days if he could work out how to get into it. He had no weapons, having abandoned them during the pitch-black night climb over Mt Brusti following the German break-through along the Aliakmon Line. He'd attacked the tin with a rock but just succeeded in changing its shape. He'd thrown the tin away in anger and then gone looking for it.

"I'll open it with me teeth if I have to," said Red. "Let's see." There was a pack at his feet. "Look at me swag." He opened the flap and took out a pistol in a leather holster. "I've got a Luger. Nine millimetre Parabellum. Put a bullet through a tank this bastard they reckon. I've got two bayonets. This is a motorcycle pennant. Sort of a bush hat. Belt with a swastika on it. Smokes. Pills for staying awake." He held up a small canister and rattled it. "The Italians had these in Libya. Supposed to make them want to fight." He looked at Mick. "Remember that, Mick? Italians fighting?" The Australians laughed. "How long have we been awake? About four days? You want to try one?" he said to Sunny.

"I'll give it a go," said Sunny. "Where'd you get this stuff?"

"Some Greek blokes we met a few days ago," said Mick. "Come down from Albania. I swapped all this for a five-gallon drum of benzene. Could've got a machine gun on a tripod, you believe that? Could've got a tank probably. Me nephew wanted a flag, the little bugger, and me dad'll be tickled with the pistol."

"Pass me one of them bayonets," said Sunny.

He put the tin on the ground and stabbed the lid with the bayonet. He worked the blade round the rim and bent the lid open. He took out a pale green vegetable of some kind, sniffed it, and dropped it into his mouth like a sardine. He wiped his mouth and passed the tin to Mick, who took one and then handed the tin to Red.

"Jeez," said Mick, after swallowing. "Gyppo's right. Hard to believe what the people over here call food. Most of their stuff you wouldn't give to the dogs. Funny, because they sorta look like us." Mick had a small blue swallow tattooed on the webbing of his hand.

Sunny unscrewed his canteen. Red took a packet of German cigarettes from his breast pocket, *Eckstein No. 5*s. Holding out a lighted match Mick noticed the same blue swallows on Sunny's hands.

"Where'd you pick up the birds?" he said.

"State ward back home," said Sunny, hooking a thumb.

"Me too!" said Mick. "Put it here, mate!"

Mick had spent five years in the Magill Reformatory for Boys in South Australia. Sunny was impressed. Magill was the Sing Sing of antipodean juvenile reform, a gladiator school. They discussed their shared history of delinquency and the efficacy of moral training. They sipped the Metaxa.

"Bloody hell," said Mick, shaking his head fondly at the memory. He looked at Red. "What do you reckon? Shall I?"

Red shrugged. "Ask him," he said.

"You up for something?" said Mick to Sunny.

"You bet," said Sunny. "What?"

The paymaster unit of 6th Div's Headquarters Company had requisitioned the Athens branch of the Thomas Cook travel company on arrival in Greece two weeks earlier because it had a secure vault.

"Not *that* secure," said Mick.

"Only two weeks ago?" said Red. "Seems a lot longer."

Red had been sent to beef up the alarm. There was a branch manager — a Pom about fifty, soft — and two girls, Greek locals he thought. A couple of provosts had arrived with document satchels while Red was stringing wire, and the Pom had unlocked the grille in front of the vault and opened the vault itself, which had a combination lock. A table in the middle of the secure room was chocker with cash, just sitting there, notes in bundles, stacks of them, wrapped in clear paper. Even the Red Caps had whistled.

"We're going to make a little detour when we get to Athens and grab that money," said Red. "It'll be chaos."

"We could use another bloke if you're interested," said Mick.

"Sure I'm interested," said Sunny. "I haven't got a weapon though."

"We can get you a weapon," said Mick. He tapped the submachine pistol hanging across his chest. "You can use this little beauty."

"What will you do with the money?"

"Get rid of it in Egypt," said Mick. "No problem."

"Will it be guarded?"

"Greeks?" said Mick, looking at Red. "We can handle Greeks."

"Yeah, but what if they're Australians?" said Sunny. "Or Tommies?"

Mick turned to Sunny.

"Like the CO said, it's every bastard for himself."

"I'm in," said Sunny, tipping back the last of the brandy.

Central Athens was crowded. Civilians filled the streets and cheered and cried as military vehicles and civilian motorcars eased through. The Greeks' mixture of grief and farewell and foreboding seemed genuine. The three soldiers had little trouble getting past Military Police traffic control posts. So long as they were heading in a direction that was generally south no one asked any questions.

The Thomas Cook office was closed, its double-doors locked. There were no guards. Sunny racked the machine pistol and the Australians checked their pistols. They had removed any identifying badges or kit and carried empty packs. A woman in black came up and threw her arms around Mick and said, "*Niké.*" When Mick said, "Don't speaka da lingo, sorry," the woman said, in English, "Victory" and held up her fingers in the V-sign. Mick laughed. "Victory?" he said. "Is that what this is? Good on you, Mum." They crossed the street, banged on the grille, and identified themselves as Australian Military Police.

After some back and forth the door cracked open. The manager was holding a pistol, a big Webley Mk VI, in a trembling hand. He stepped back and brought up the weapon. "What do you want?" he said. "You're not MPs."

"You're right there," said Mick. "Careful with that thing, you old coot. You might shoot yourself in the foot."

"I was in the last show," the manager said. "I know how to use this."

"Bully for you," said Sunny, grabbing the barrel and wrenching the pistol away. The three men pushed through the door and fanned out.

"Open the vault."

"Out of the question," said the manager. "It's more than my job's worth."

"Your job! There's a war on, ya knucklehead," said Mick. "I wouldn't be worrying about your job for a while."

"The vault's empty," said the Englishman. "Your lot came two days ago and took everything."

Sunny cocked the Webley and held it to the manager's chest.

"Open it anyway. I'm counting to three," he said. "One, two—"

"All right!" said the manager. "The grille keys are in the top drawer of my desk."

"Which?" said Mick a moment later, holding a bunch.

"The one with the red tag," said the manager.

Mick unlocked the grille and swung it open. "Hop to it, mate," he said, pointing to the combination lock in the middle of the vault door.

The manager's hands were shaking so badly he couldn't hold the dial.

Sunny passed the pistol to Red and moved the manager to one side. "Call them out," he said.

The manager swallowed. "Ah, ah, left 24. Right 16. Left, um, 9."

Sunny twisted the dial. The door swung open.

Bundles of notes sat on a table in the middle of the room and others spilled out on the floor. Strongboxes had been opened.

The notes were mostly military scrip, colourful but soon to be worthless.

"Bloody hell," said Red. "This is no good."

"Where's the safe?" said Sunny.

"The safe?"

"You deaf?" said Sunny, raising the Webley again.

"Behind the clock," said the manager, pointing to a clock hinged to the wall.

Sunny swung the clock open. There was a Birmingham Automatic Machine Company safe embedded in the wall.

"It's unlocked," said the manager.

Inside was nearly £100 in sterling and US dollars, gold coins, passports — French, British, Bulgarian, Greek — and a fistful of jewellery and watches. Mick put it all in his pack.

They drove south. At Tripolis they pulled over and divided the spoils into three. Sunny took a watch, the first he'd owned, and some money and jewellery. They separated, making a loose arrangement to meet up at the Fifty-Fifty Club in Sydney for a beer after the war.

Sunny took the blast of an exploding shell on the beach at Porto Rafti and was evacuated to Maadi with concussion. The surgeon recognised Sunny's new watch as a 1935 Patek Phillipe rectangular and reported it to his colonel, who in turn summoned the provosts. When Sunny's kit was searched they found his share of the money and jewellery from the Thomas Cook robbery. He was court-martialled, served nine months in the 1st Australian Detention Barracks in Palestine, and was then sent home. A year later he was in Mt Crawford Prison in Wellington, serving two years for an unrelated matter.

But he'd missed out on Crete, so it could have been worse.

CHAPTER THIRTY-ONE

With its vast symmetrical facade, terrazzo floor, imported marble, fine bronze detailing, embossed metal ceiling three storeys overhead, palm-lined concourse sweeping around in front, and the swarms of men in uniform — drivers, guards, conductors — the Auckland Railway Station felt to Molloy like the sort of place in which Mussolini might have lived had *Il Duce* chosen Auckland over Rome.

He was sitting on a step, finishing a smoke, watching Caitlin hurry across the road between vehicles and run up the steps.

"Sorry," she said. "I wasn't sure where to leave the car."

"That's all right." He dropped his smoke on the ground, grinding it out.

"I hope you're not annoyed about last night," said Caitlin, taking a cigarette case from her purse and opening the lid.

"You saved my neck," said Molloy, striking a match. "Who taught you to drive?"

"My Uncle Pat," she said. "He held the Wanganui to New Plymouth land speed record before the war."

"He did a good job," said Molloy, lighting his own cigarette.

"Vince was pleased to see you." She tilted her head back, blowing a thin stream of smoke skywards.

Molloy laughed. "I bet he was."

"No, he was. He has a real soft spot for you, I can tell."

"Yeah," said Molloy. "He's a big sook all right." He checked his watch. "Let's go."

The left-luggage department was a long narrow room at the end of a corridor off the Main Trunk platform, lined with metal shelving filled with suitcases and boxes and parcels and other items, each tagged with a cardboard label. There was an electric clock on the wall and posters advertising rail excursions to Chateau Tongariro, the Winter Wonderland, and Rotorua, the Thermal Wonderland.

Molloy gave the ticket to an NZR clerk.

"Won't be a tick," said the clerk.

He walked down an aisle towards the far end of the room, moved a ladder on wheels into position, climbed up and shook a case loose.

"What are you looking for, can you say?" said Caitlin.

"I found a left-luggage ticket in O'Flynn's room last night."

"Not one of those bodies in a trunk that keep turning up in London, I hope," said Caitlin.

"You never know," said Molloy.

The clerk humped the suitcase onto the counter. It was made of cardboard with cheap leather facings. There were embarkation stickers pasted on the sides and it was tied with twine like a parcel. He twisted the tag on the handle so that Molloy could check the number against the number on the receipt. "AF612," he said. "That the one?"

"That's her," said Molloy.

"Get you to sign your life away," said the clerk, spinning a ledger and handing Molloy a fountain pen. "And she's all yours."

Molloy rang Furst from a phone booth at the railway station and arranged to meet him at the Premier Building. Caitlin drove and they parked in Queen Street and took the lift to the fourth floor. Furst was waiting for them, leaning against a wall in the corridor, reading the *Herald*. Molloy introduced Caitlin as his assistant. Furst raised his hat and said what a pleasure it was, and judging by the way he looked at her, it was.

Molloy unlocked his office door and showed them in. If they were impressed with his set-up they managed to contain themselves. He cleared the top of the desk and lifted the suitcase onto it. He took out his pocketknife and cut the rope and tried the catches. They were rusty and locked. He put the point of the knife in behind the stems and wiggled the blade. The locks snapped. He closed his knife and put it back in his pocket. "Let's have a look," he said, opening the lid.

There was old clothing packed along the top of the suitcase. A jersey, a raincoat, a pair of galoshes wrapped in newspaper, woollen socks.

"Winter stuff," said Molloy, handing the items to Caitlin, who held them at a distance. There was the smell of camphor. At the bottom of the suitcase were four Western novels and a cardboard shoebox. The shoebox was full of a traveller's bric-a-brac — a cheap writing pad with five blank pages; two par avion envelopes; a pencil; a key with a long stem; a bundle of US banknotes tied up with a rubber band, two hundred dollars or more. And a photograph, a strip of three taken in a photomat. A couple, laughing in the first, taken by surprise in the second, kissing in the third. A blonde woman with a large lipsticked mouth and sleepy eyes, her arm thrown casually around the neck of a man in his thirties with a tough, handsome face, black wavy hair parted off-centre and pushed straight back, a cowlick sprung loose.

"The happy couple," said Furst. "O'Phelan and his hop-head girlfriend, Valma."

He picked up the bills and peeled back the top few. He put the money down and took a notebook from his pocket, flicked to a page, ran a stubby finger along a line, squinted at a note, and then another, and closed the book with a slap.

"Bingo. This is part of the money US Life paid out to Valma after O'Phelan drowned in the Bay of Alaska in 1949," said Furst. "How's it end up two years later in his suitcase on the other side of the world?"

"He didn't drown in 1949," said Molloy.

Furst beamed. "Nossir, he did not."

"What now?"

"I'll cable head office, let them know where we've got." He put on his hat. "I'm going back to my hotel to send a telegram. Maybe the two of you would care to join me tonight for a meal in the dining room? This is good work, son. We've got something to celebrate."

"Sounds good," said Molloy.

"Swell," said Furst. "The house bar around six? I'll leave your names at the front desk." He tipped his hat. "Miss O'Carolan."

They listened as his jaunty tread disappeared along the corridor.

"'Good work, son,'" said Caitlin. "Honestly. Patronising Yank."

"He's not a bad bloke."

"If you say so," she said. "What now?"

"He'll get instructions from his head office. It'll be a police matter from now on. But if he wants me to keep looking for him then that's what I'll do. If not?" He shrugged.

Caitlin looked at him. "But you said you'd help us."

"I said you could tag along while I looked for him. As of now I'm not looking for him."

"So, what exactly? On to your next divorce, I suppose," said Caitlin. "Blow you, Molloy. I'll find O'Flynn myself." She picked up her purse and flung it over her shoulder. "Vince was dead right about you. You really are living on your knees now, aren't you, *Comrade*?"

She went out the door and slammed it hard but the glass was mesh and held. Molloy heard her high heels clacking furiously along the corridor.

He returned the items to the shoebox. The phone rang. Molloy picked up the receiver.

"Are you there?"

There was a mechanical sound as someone pushed button A. An echoing voice said, "Don't say my name. You know who this is?"

"Yeah, I know who this is," said Molloy.

"Same place. Five o'clock this evening."

"Right-o," said Molloy.

The phone rang off.

CHAPTER THIRTY-TWO

Archie Green was sitting in Albert Park, his hat pulled low, hiding behind a copy of the *Auckland Star*.

"Is that you, Archie?" said Molloy.

Green lowered the newspaper a couple of inches. "Of course it is."

"Well?"

"I spoke to a friend of a friend. A policeman. Special Branch."

"And?"

Green paused and took a deep breath. "O'Flynn has powerful friends. One in particular."

"Who?"

Green scanned the park, checking they were alone. He looked at Molloy and slowly mouthed three words, enunciating with great drama.

Molloy shook his head. "You'll have to speak English."

Green leaned in, his voice full of portent. "Fintan. Patrick. Walsh."

"Walsh," said Molloy, after a moment. "Did your cobber say why?"

"He didn't," said Green, some of his old confidence coming back. "And I didn't ask him. Walsh helping out a fellow potato-eater, I'd imagine."

CHAPTER THIRTY-THREE

In Dublin in January 1939, the seven men who made up the Army Council of the IRA, an outlawed organisation in Ireland, declared themselves the legitimate government of the Irish Republic, with the attendant right to use force and wage war against an occupying power. Drawing on this lofty mandate the council put the United Kingdom on four days' notice to remove its troops from Irish soil, reserving the prerogative of "appropriate action without further notice in the name of the unconquered dead and the faithful living" if, upon the expiration of that period of grace, the demand remained unmet.

It did, so on Sunday, the 15th of January 1939, in a communiqué to Lord Halifax, the British Foreign Secretary, the IRA declared war on Great Britain.

The Army Council immediately set off a campaign in England, known as the S-Plan or the Sabotage Plan, which called for the destruction of power stations, transmitters, military installations and aerodromes on the British mainland.

The next day explosions went off in London and Liverpool. Bombs exploded under electricity pylons stretching across the Manchester Ship Canal. In London, gas mains were damaged. A fish porter cycling to work was killed by a flying manhole cover. Special Branch began rounding up the usual suspects. In the weeks following the initial explosions there were dozens of arrests. In

Manchester, two women were caught in possession of a barrel of potassium chlorate, two Mills bombs, forty-nine sticks of gelignite, and ten electric detonators — "the whole Sinn Fein conjurer's kit", in the words of the Irish writer and IRA Volunteer Brendan Behan, who was himself arrested, aged sixteen — and, most significant, a copy of the S-Plan. The IRA was unbowed. Two bombs exploded in the London Underground, one at Tottenham Court Road station and one at Leicester Square station. Police patrols around Whitehall were strongly reinforced and all ships arriving from Ireland were searched.

The campaign continued well into the summer. Two bombs exploded in the left-luggage department of Kings Cross railway station, resulting in the death of a bystander. In Liverpool, tear gas bombs went off in picture theatres, causing fifteen injuries. Incendiary bombs started fires in eight British hotels. Eleven bombs exploded in public lavatories throughout the Midlands. The advertising department of the *News Chronicle* in Fleet Street was the target of a bomb. London branches of the Midland Bank, Lloyds Bank and Westminster Bank suffered a series of explosions. Letter bombs exploded in twenty postboxes. One went off in a London sorting office and another in a Birmingham mail lorry. Every postbox in London was searched for further IRA devices. In short, there were bombings galore. The above list barely scrapes the surface. But in late August the campaign took a darker turn. A bomb exploded in the carrier basket of a bicycle leaning against a wall in the busy shopping district of Broadgate in Coventry. Five people were killed and more than fifty wounded. There was widespread revulsion at this outrage, and fury in Dublin. Death was not on the S-Plan. The fish porter hit by the manhole cover and the bystander at Kings Cross Station were accidents. The Coventry killings felt deliberate. The bomb maker who leaned his armed bicycle against the wall and walked away whistling was Francis Xavier O'Phelan, aka Frank O'Flynn, and the Army Council wanted his head.

He was picked up a week later at the dogs in Limerick where he had gone to watch the grand final of the Irish Greyhound Derby, arm in arm with two harlots from Wicklow, the White sisters, oblivious to the danger he was in. As the boxes rose it was a streak of greased lightning called Marching Through Georgia who took the lead and held it to the finish by a distance of two lengths on good going, setting a track record of 30.05 with odds of 13–8.

Lining up at the tote to collect his winnings, O'Phelan felt the barrel of a revolver in the small of his back and was surprised to see that two IRA gunmen, Ginger Shaw and Roibaird Orland, had joined him in the queue. Shaw had spotted him earlier and sent Orland to fetch his lorry and some rope. The White sisters melted away.

The IRA men drove O'Phelan to a safe house in Bunratty owned by a Mrs Coogan, where his legs were tied and he was locked in a ground-floor room. A telephone in the hallway rang constantly and muffled voices came and went. The two gunmen guarded him in four-hour shifts. Shaw told him that an IRA hard man named John Fay, "a first-rate knee surgeon" in the brutal vernacular of Republican discipline, was driving down from Belfast for a session of rigorous interrogation.

Orland was of a gentler disposition. When he took over guard duty he and O'Phelan discussed Marching Through Georgia's pedigree and then the broad strokes of the S-Plan. It became apparent to O'Phelan that the IRA planned to execute him for his role in the Coventry bombing. Orland offered O'Phelan a nip from his flask, had two or three himself, and soon dozed off.

O'Phelan undid the rope, gently lifted the revolver from the pocket of the sleeping gunman's coat, climbed out the window and made his way to the Bunratty Garda station where he gave himself up.

The term "to grass", meaning "to betray", evolved from the rhyming slang for policeman: a "grasshopper" is a copper. Over the years the term has taken on a particularly Irish resonance. O'Phelan, feeling abandoned, threatened to grass like the grass in Phoenix Park, rolling green acres of names and details, the S-Plan stripped bare. In the backstabbery of Republican politics, such spillage suited no one, but O'Phelan was not without his champions in the upper reaches. They remembered how close he had got to the Earl of Galway the previous year, and at considerable personal risk.

An arrangement was made for him to be sprung from Mountjoy Gaol and shipped to Boston with a new name and one hundred pounds, part of the proceeds of a raid on the Amiens Road Post Office in Dublin, in return for a firm promise to keep his gob shut and never come back to Ireland. The deal was worked out by the former Officer Commanding, 2nd Tyrone Brigade, a shadowy figure named Peter O'Regan, who, in 1920, as a member of the Twelve Apostles, a squad set up by Michael Collins during the Irish War of Independence to assassinate the British agents known as the Cairo Gang, had known Fintan Patrick Walsh.

Ireland is a small place too.

CHAPTER THIRTY-FOUR

"Walsh, that Freemanite, I knew it!" said Parker. He turned to Caitlin. "You see, Comrade? You misjudged Johnny. A principled beggar when you get right down to it, just like, whatchamacall, Sam Spade and them." He picked up the sherry. "Wash those cups will you, sweetie?" he said to her. "This cries out for plonk."

Molloy put his hand up. "Not for me," he said. "I'm not staying. I came here to warn you, Caitlin. Walsh is a nasty piece of work. Ask Parker about him. You and Fintan are old cobbers, aren't you, Vince?"

Parker waved away the suggestion. "I haven't said boo to that splittist in twenty years," he said. "But you're right. He's a hyena." He pulled the cork from the flagon. "You won't have a drop?"

Molloy shook his head, tipped his hat to Caitlin and left the flat. He was lighting a smoke when he heard someone running down the stairs.

"Molloy, wait!"

He turned. Caitlin crossed the footpath, putting on a cardigan at the same time, her purse getting tangled in one sleeve. "I'm sorry," she said. "I owe you an apology."

"You don't owe me anything." He took his keys from his pocket. "Be careful, that's all." He looked up to the first-storey light. "And

159

don't rely on Vince to look after you." He shook his head. "How did you get tied up with that no-hoper?"

"Buy me a drink and I'll tell you."

He looked at her for a second. "Okay," he said. "Hop in."

CHAPTER THIRTY-FIVE

Molloy pressed the RSC buzzer and waited. Locks turned and the door cracked open. Bones squeezed out and looked up and down Francis Street. "All right, Johnny," he said. He stopped when he saw Caitlin. For a moment he was speechless. This was a gross breach of protocol.

He leaned towards Molloy. "Hell's bells, cobber. I'm not sure about this. We don't have a sort of separate area for" — he jerked his head — "you know?"

"Miss O'Carolan's a newspaperman, Bones," said Molloy. "Unshockable. Caitlin, this is Bones Harrington, old friend of mine. Bones, Caitlin O'Carolan."

"Mr Harrington," said Caitlin, putting out her hand.

"Oh. Yeah. How d'you do?" said Bones, at a loss. Women weren't his strong suit. He dropped his head and spoke out of the side of his mouth. "The boys aren't going to be too happy, Johnny. Wouldn't be surprised if this goes to the committee." He stepped back, without enthusiasm.

Molloy held the blackout curtain to one side and Caitlin entered the bar. The conversation dropped and then stopped, and then slowly resumed. Molloy took her elbow and showed her to a table in the corner.

"I feel like one of the Scottsboro Boys," she whispered, sitting down.

"What do those boys drink?" said Molloy.

"If I asked for a gin and tonic would it start a fight?"

"We'll soon find out."

"Don't be long."

"Yell out if there's trouble."

Tim was behind the bar. He gave Molloy a black look, his specialty. "Johnny," he said, his voice accusing.

"Evening, Tim," said Molloy. "Gin and tonic, and a whisky and water, thanks."

"That'll be singles? This late?"

"Doubles," said Molloy. "But we'll be quick."

"Yes. Right-o." Tim poured the drinks in silence.

"I called in to see your mum this arvo," said Molloy.

"She said."

"She seemed pretty good. You know. Considering."

"She make you look through his old footie photos?" said Tim, still frosty, but warming slightly. "You would've been in half of them."

"She did, yeah. She had pikelets. Still a good cook, your mum."

"She's a tough old boot, but hell's bells," said Tim. "Korea? What was he thinking?" He put a chunk of lemon in the gin. "Five bob, thanks, Johnny."

Molloy paid and carried the drinks over to the table.

"*Nostrovia*," said Caitlin, taking a sip. She screwed up her face. She put her finger in the glass and stirred it a couple of times and took another sip. "I'm sorry for getting huffy this afternoon." She reached into her purse for her cigarette case and offered him one.

"Didn't bother me," he said, taking a cigarette and lighting a match.

Caitlin leaned into the flame. She was spectacular in the smoky light.

"All right," he said, putting the match in the ashtray. "How did you get tied up with Parker? Through the Party?"

She laughed. "You're not a provocateur, are you?"

"I'm just curious," he said. "Red girls tend to be, I dunno, more homely."

"You chauvinist!" she said. "But thank you." She spoke in a low voice. "I joined a Marxist-Leninist study group that met once a week in the Parnell Library. We passed a unanimous resolution to get together at eight o'clock every Monday night until the day of the Revolution. Our group had a cover name. The Succulent Propagation Society." She smiled, tilted her head slightly, and blew a thin stream of smoke into the air. "The library didn't know that what we were propagating was the extinction of the bourgeoisie. Vince gave us a talk once." She shrugged. "He thought I showed promise."

"I bet he did," said Molloy. "Are you a Party member?"

"I believe in what the Party stands for," she said. "I'm not a slave to it."

"Things must have changed a bit. They didn't allow the distinction in my day."

"Why did you leave?"

Molloy tapped the ash off his smoke before answering. "Same reason you stop going to church, I suppose. You know? Contradictions?"

There was a pause. Caitlin sipped her gin and tonic. "What do you mean?" she said. "Contradictions?"

"Oh, hell," said Molloy. "Was this the sort of thing that got batted around at the Succulent Propagation Society?"

She frowned. "It's a serious question."

Molloy knew he was sunk. "All right." He spun his glass on the table a couple of times. "Everything I thought I knew about left and right and right and wrong got turned upside down in Spain. Everything."

"But that's because you fell in with Trotskyites. Vince told me."

"Come off it. They weren't Trotskyites. They were those salt of the earth workers and peasants the Party talks about so much. *Compañeros.* They wouldn't have known a Trotskyite from a Mickey Mouse-ite half of them. Or cared." He made a small gesture, raising his left arm, fist angled towards his cheek, thumb facing out, the salute of the Left Opposition. "They knew the difference between *Don* and *Camarada* though." He picked up his whisky and knocked it back. "And they were betrayed."

"Betrayed?" said Caitlin.

"Yes, betrayed," said Molloy. "By the Comintern. By the *Partido Comunista de España.* By Stalin. In the way the Non-Aggression Pact was a betrayal. I saw it happen."

"No, *you* come off it," said Caitlin. "The Non-Aggression Pact wasn't a betrayal, as well you know. It was a temporary and pragmatic reaction to the impending abandonment of the Soviet Union by the West. If—"

"Finished with that, miss?" said Bones, pointing to Caitlin's glass.

"No!" she said. "You'll know I'm finished with it when it's empty!"

"Right you are," said Bones. He replaced the ashtray with a clean one and mumbled to Molloy, "Ask you to sorta knock back the arguing a bit, Johnny, all right, if you wouldn't mind? We're trying to keep politics to a minimum at the moment, what with one thing and another."

"Good as gold, Bones."

"We're closing pretty soon, anyway," said Bones. He wiped the table and walked away.

Molloy looked at Caitlin. "Look, it's like Rachel Barrowman said. 'When the fight against fascism finally came, the Soviet Union wasn't part of it.'"

"Wasn't part of it? Other than the God-knows-how-many Soviet citizens who died, you mean?"

She finished her drink, bringing the glass back down to the table with a loud bang. "Would you mind taking me to my car, please?" she said, standing. "This was a mistake."

CHAPTER THIRTY-SIX

Molloy's car was parked in Francis Street. He went around to open the passenger door for Caitlin.

"I'm perfectly capable of opening my own door, thank you," she said.

He drove out of Francis Street into Richmond Road and headed up Great North Road. Caitlin lit a cigarette and stared straight ahead. Smoke seemed to be coming out of her ears.

"So what is it exactly that you're saying?" she said suddenly, glaring at him. "Are you saying that the Non-Aggression Pact was motivated—"

"Hang on a tick," said Molloy, cutting her off. "Vince isn't having us followed, is he?"

"Oh, don't be so dramatic. How would he have us followed? I'm probably the only person he knows with a motorcar."

"Then hang on to your hat," said Molloy, stepping on the accelerator.

The car shot forward. Caitlin jerked back against the seat. "You all right?" he said, keeping one eye on the rear-vision mirror.

Caitlin looked at him and then back over her shoulder. There was a set of headlights gaining on them.

"Who is it?"

"No idea," he said, suddenly pulling the hand brake and spinning the wheel. The car glided round forty-five degrees. Molloy tapped the foot brake and the vehicle straightened and shuddered across the tram tracks towards the intersection with Ngatea Street.

"See them?" he said, as the pursuing vehicle overshot and continued up Great North Road.

"Big American car. And it's turning, I think."

Molloy changed gear and sped up the narrow street and round a corner.

"Do you know who it is?" Caitlin asked.

"I do," said Molloy, turning another corner and suddenly jumping on his brakes. "Watch out!" he yelled, as they spun around and ended flush with a high wooden fence. The street was a dead end.

He pushed open his door and got out. "Come on."

"I can't!" Her door was jammed against the fence. Molloy reached back in and she somehow folded into him and slid from the car just as the Plymouth came around the corner and slewed to a halt, full beams blinding them both. Molloy put Caitlin down. Doors slammed. Sunny and Lofty stepped into the light. Sunny was holding an axe handle, smacking it into the palm of his hand.

"I told you," he said. "I bloody told you."

"She's got nothing to do with this," said Molloy, moving in front of Caitlin. "I just met her."

"Lucky you." Sunny skipped forward, his leather soles scraping on the ground, bringing the handle up over his head like a club. Molloy raised his arms to protect himself but Sunny changed his swing to a crosscut motion, like Bert Sutcliffe taking care of a short-pitched delivery wide of off-stump.

The handle smashed into Molloy's ribcage, but his jacket was hanging away from his body where he'd lifted his arms, and his wallet was in his inside pocket. Both absorbed some of the blow, so it could have been worse. It was certainly bad enough. He slammed against the car.

Caitlin cried out, covering her mouth with her hands, eyes bugging. Lofty grabbed her. "Not like the pictures, is it?" he said. He pushed her towards the Plymouth and into the back seat.

Sunny jabbed the handle into Molloy's chest and lifted it so the point was under his chin. "Get in the back with your girlfriend, buster," he said. "We're going for a ride."

CHAPTER THIRTY-SEVEN

The Black Death came to Sydney in January 1900, when a flea hopped off an infected rat and bit a deliveryman named Gavin Mbali. The following month Sydney was declared a plague-infested port. A Plague Department was established. All drains, gullies, sinks and outside toilets in an area around Darlinghurst were flushed with hot water, then carbolic water, then lime chloride. All household rubbish, food scraps, ash, stable straw and horse manure was removed and burnt. Rat catchers were paid tuppence per rodent. Photographs show groups of nonchalant, moustachioed men in bowler hats, some wearing bow ties, hands on hips or holding metal buckets and mesh traps, standing by piles of dead rats three and four foot high. By October, 108,308 rats had been caught, 1759 people had been quarantined and 103 people had died.

The conditions that brought bubonic plague to Sydney — ships, rats, overcrowding, the haphazard collection of rubbish — were equally present in Auckland. A decision was made in 1903 to build a destructor, sited in Freemans Bay, a giant furnace complex with a brick chimney ten storeys high. This was in the days before Cameron Brewer. By 1951, 120 tons of refuse a day was being burnt in the furnaces, which had an operating temperature of 2000°F, several hundred degrees hotter than a crematorium.

From the outside at night the building seemed to glow. Sunny spun the Plymouth into the entranceway at speed, the car fishtailing up the heavy wooden ramp to the tipping platform, whitewalls thudding on the traction rails. Molloy and Caitlin were thrown across the back seat.

Spilled light from dull electric lamps set high on concrete walls picked out the edges of machinery and the heaving outline of thirty-foot piles of God-knows-what. Burning rubbish fuelled two huge, howling Babcock & Wilcox boilers. The place shimmered with rats, countless pinpricks of red light, and there, hat on, coat off, was the biggest rat of all. Fintan Patrick Walsh.

Sunny and Lofty opened the rear doors and pulled Molloy and Caitlin from the car.

"Who's the girl?" said Walsh, yelling above the noise.

"She was with him," Sunny yelled back.

"She's not tied up in this," said Molloy, before Caitlin could answer.

Walsh turned to Molloy. "Is this the fella who was told to stay away from Frank and didn't and now poor Frank's dead, God rest his soul?" said Walsh. "Is this him?"

"That's him."

"You know who I am?"

"I know who you are," said Molloy.

"Then you'll know what I'm capable of. The stories you've heard aren't even the half of it, you foller?" Walsh grabbed Molloy's shirtfront. "What's your game, you nosey bastard? And none of that bulldust about solicitors in Napier."

"What solicitors?" said Molloy.

"Oh, Jesus," said Walsh, waving a hand. "Sunny."

Sunny slung Caitlin over his shoulder and swung open the furnace door. The roar was like an aeroplane engine, ten times louder than before. It was an evil sound and its heat and force knocked them backwards.

Caitlin screamed. Sunny swore. Walsh shaded his eyes, his face glistening. Caitlin kicked her legs frantically and Sunny almost dropped her. "Give me a hand here, Lofty, you useless bugger!" he yelled.

Lofty wrapped one arm over Caitlin's legs and then grabbed her ankles. Sunny took her wrists. They started to swing her, like children in a playground, getting closer and closer to the raging furnace.

"Johnny!" she screamed.

"It's an insurance job," Molloy shouted.

"Keep talking," said Walsh, flaming shadows leaping and dancing on the walls behind him. "And you two keep swinging."

"O'Flynn rorted an insurance company in California and faked his death. I was hired to find him."

"Who hired you?"

"A Yank called Furst. He's staying at the Auckland, that flash pub in Queen Street."

Walsh looked hard at Molloy. "What do you think, Sunny?" he said. "Is he telling the truth this time?"

"I think he could be."

"I agree," said Walsh. "Drop her."

They did.

"See, son," he said to Molloy, flicking open a white handkerchief and wiping sweat off his face. "You're not as tough as you think. Not by a long shot. But I am."

CHAPTER THIRTY-EIGHT

Lofty opened a storeroom and pushed Molloy and Caitlin inside. He slammed the door and crashed the bolt into place. Molloy felt round for a light switch. There was a bare bulb in a copper fitting above the door. The room was small with a concrete sink and a single tap. A shelf held paint tins and stiff brushes. A worn broom stood upside down in the sink. In one corner was a rust-speckled forty-four-gallon drum with a skull and crossbones label on the lid. The floor was wet and water dripped from a skylight which was set in a sloping roof.

"Come here," Molloy said, and Caitlin fell into his arms, sobbing. He put an arm around her.

"My God," she said, eventually. "Would he have done it?"

"He was bluffing," Molloy said, not believing a word.

He took a handkerchief from his pocket, and Caitlin wiped her eyes and put on what her aunt would call a brave face. "What now?"

"I've got to warn Furst before they get to him."

He looked around and up at the skylight. There was a rope on a pulley attached to the wall. He pulled it. The skylight opened.

"This isn't Colditz," he said. "Just a matter of getting up there somehow."

"I'll do it," said Caitlin, blowing her nose.

"Come off it."

She took a couple of deep breaths, formed her mouth in a circle, and blew away her doubt. "I won the Blessed Jo Rice Shield for gymnastics three years in a row at Baradene. This is a piece of cake."

She took off her shoes and threw them through the opened skylight. They clattered on the corrugated-iron roof. Molloy pushed the drum into position. He climbed onto the lid, the effort burning his bruised ribs, and pulled her up. They were very close.

"Squat down," she said. "Don't worry, I've got very good balance."

She climbed onto his shoulders, one hand lightly pressing the side of his head.

"Ready?" said Molloy.

"Chocks away," she said.

He stood slowly. The soles of her feet eased upwards as she straightened her legs.

"I feel like an heiress on a bi-plane," she said, her arms outstretched.

"Don't be a dope." Molloy could feel her balancing on her toes. "Are you there?"

"I can't quite get my fingers on the ledge."

"What about if you stand on my hands and I push you up?"

"Let's try."

She put one foot and then the other onto the heels of his hands. He lifted her up like a circus strongman, trying to ignore the pain in his ribs. He could feel her take her own weight as her elbows went through the gap and rested on the frame.

"*Et voilà!*" she said, and then she was on the roof.

"Try to walk on the nail lines if you can. It's probably rusty."

Molloy could hear corrugated iron groaning as Caitlin moved delicately along the roof. Silence. "I can drop down to the street."

"How far?"

"Not far."

"Find the night watchman," he said.

"What should I tell him?" she said.

"Oh, I don't know. What would Martha Gellhorn say?"

CHAPTER THIRTY-NINE

A concrete parapet about a foot thick ran along the edge of the building overlooking Drake Street. Caitlin sat on the ledge, her legs dangling over the side. The paving stones seemed a long way down. She took a deep breath. She put her hands across her body, gripped the inside edge of the parapet, and swung around so that now she was facing the building and hanging by her fingers. Hoping for some pommel horse magic, she lost out to gravity and dropped, vaguely aware of scraping down the wall, and then landing, crumpled, on the footpath.

She lay there for a while. Then she got up onto her hands and knees and somehow stood, leaning against the wall for support. She tried a few steps. Nothing felt broken. Amazing. I'm made for this, she thought.

She walked down Drake Street, keeping close to the wall. Hot air came out of an entranceway. She stopped. She could hear furnaces roaring. She took a few steps up the ramp. Across the vast hall she could see the boilers. There was no sign of the Plymouth.

She forced herself to think about what had happened earlier. Lofty had taken them across the floor to a metal stairwell. She walked over to it. There was light at the bottom. She eased down the stairs, her hands on the rail. A corridor led off to the right.

A burst of laughter sent her back against the wall, mouth dry, heart pounding. A door opened and a middle-aged man with a sweat-stained face and a dirty brown dust-coat came out of a doorway, hoicked onto the floor and swung up the stairs, his hobnail boots clanging on the metal treads just above her head. One of the night-shift men going to check the boiler?

Who else was laughing? Walsh and his cronies?

Now what? The only way forward was past the door. Caitlin could hear pieces of conversation. She leaned against the far wall, in shadow, and slowly moved her head to see inside. Two men in overalls were sitting on opposite sides of a long table, playing cards.

"Good game's a fast game," said one of the men. He was about eighteen, tall and skinny, bony chest visible where the top few buttons of his overalls were undone, the dirt stopping at his pale white skin.

"Bugger off," said the other man, reordering his hand. "I like to take me time." He was English, his accent northern and thick.

"You're telling me," said the boy. He reached for the tea pot in the middle of the table and began topping up his enamel mug.

Caitlin was weighing up the best approach when a voice said, "Hello-hello."

She jumped. Her head snapped around. It was the workman who had gone up the stairs a few moments earlier. He was not much taller than Caitlin, big bellied, and sweet faced under the dirt.

"Hey, you blokes. We've got a visitor."

The card players turned and looked at her. The younger one stood. Well brought up, she thought. Hopefully.

"Young lady like you doesn't want to be in a place like this. Especially at night," said the man in the dust-coat.

"You all right?" said the Pom. "You don't look too good."

"Oh. I fell, and …" said Caitlin, pointing vaguely.

"How did you end up in here?" he said.

"Well …" she began.

Something slithered across her shoe.

A rat.

She screamed.

"Caitlin!" Molloy's voice not too far away.

"Crikey," said the boy, with a laugh. "It's like blimmin' VE Day."

"Oi," said the Pom. "Lady present."

But Caitlin was already running down the corridor.

"Molloy?" she yelled.

"Here!" yelled Molloy.

She slid the bolt and opened the door.

"About time," he said.

CHAPTER FORTY

The barman put a DB coaster down in front of Furst, placed a glass on it and stood back.

Furst studied the cocktail. "Okay," he said. "Number one, that's not a martini glass. Martini glass is shallow, comes in at an angle." He demonstrated with his hands. "Puts you in mind of a voluptuous woman, see?"

The barman, round-shouldered with long teeth and liver spots on his hands, nodded. Furst took the slice of lemon floating on the top of the drink and held it up. "You don't want that," he said. "You want an olive. Or if you're from New York, maybe an onion."

"An onion? Yeah?"

"Got to have ice," said Furst. "Ice is critical."

"I put some ice in it," said the barman, pointing.

"Ton of ice. So that when you shake the ingredients together the ice bruises the gin. Gets the flavour out. That's why it's better to use a shaker than a pitcher, see."

"I see," said the barman. Yanks, he thought to himself. Jesus.

"O-kay," said Furst. "Time for the drum roll."

He picked up the glass, had a sip, rolled it round in his mouth, swallowed it, sucked in some air and thought about it for a second or two.

"You know what? It's not bad for a first-timer." He had another sip. "Get you shot in any self-respecting joint west of the Mississippi, but like I say, not bad."

"Well, you know, little country," said the barman, sourly. "That'll be two and six, thanks."

"But what a *great* little country," said Furst, toasting its greatness with a third sip. "First time, but I'm sold."

"Yeah?" said the barman. "You like it?"

"Very much so."

"Lot of you blokes here during the war."

"Oh, sure. They talk about it all the time."

"Do they?" said the barman. Maybe this Yank wasn't such a bad sort of a fella after all.

Furst looked around the bar. It was empty.

"What time you kick us all out?" he said.

"No hurry," said the barman. "I could make you another one, if you like."

"Hell, why not?" said Furst, putting the glass down on the bar. "Join me?"

"Oh, yeah. Might give it a go."

"Joint could use some music," said Furst.

There was a Regal Fleetwood on a ledge above the bar. The barman turned it on and twisted the dial to 1YA.

"Onions?" he said, waiting for the valves to warm up. "What? Like tripe and onions onions?"

"Cocktail onions. Little ones," said Furst, demonstrating the size. "I'm an olive man, myself." He tapped out a cigarette and lit it.

The barman put a second martini down in front of Furst. Les Paul and Mary Ford came on the radio. Furst hummed along.

"I'll have a whisky and milk," a voice said. "Not too heavy on the milk."

Furst glanced. Solid feller. Ruddy, raw-boned face. Good suit but lived-in.

"Are you a guest in the hotel, Mr Walsh?" the barman said.

"Get me the drink, son."

"Whisky and milk coming up," said the barman, in a small voice, reaching for a glass.

"Where's the dunny?" said Walsh.

The barman pointed. "Through that door, end of the hall, Mr Walsh."

Walsh put his hat and some coins on the bar. "Keep an eye on my hat."

The barman watched until Walsh had disappeared into the toilet. He leaned towards Furst and lowered his voice. "Big wheel in the unions," he said, putting an ice cube into a glass and the glass under a whisky jigger.

"That so?"

"Real hard man," said the barman. "I could tell you some stories about that joker."

"What sort of stories?"

The barman put the whisky on the bar and drew his finger across his throat. "Those sort of stories."

"You don't say?" said Furst.

"Too right. Reckon he threw a stoker overboard in the middle of the Tasman once. Bloke said something Walsh didn't like? Over the rail into the drink he goes."

"Well I never."

The barman poured a splash of milk into the whisky. The song finished. Walsh came back into the bar. He picked up his glass.

Furst put out his hand. "The name's Furst," he said. "I'm staying here at the hotel."

"Walsh," said Walsh, and sipped the whisky. "I'm picking you for a Yank," he said.

"You're right," said Furst. "San Francisco."

"Frisco?" said Walsh, with joy. "Know it well."

"No kidding?"

"Lived there for a bit, oh, this'd be a good thirty years ago, even more," said Walsh. "Still remember the address. 2011 Turk, Apartment 4H."

"I'll be darned. I worked the Tenderloin for twenty years. San Francisco Police Department."

"Go on?" said Walsh. "I thought you looked familiar."

They both laughed.

"What took you to the Golden State, Walsh?"

"Between ships," said Walsh. "Met a gal, as you blokes say, decided to stay put for a bit. Pat, by the way."

"I arrived there at the end of the war. Took my discharge and stayed. 1919," said Furst. "I'm from New York, originally, and call me Al."

Walsh tapped the bar with his knuckles and pointed at his glass. He turned to Furst. "Top you up there, Al?"

"Hell, why not?" said Furst, finishing his martini.

"What brings you down this way?" said Walsh, as the barman made the drinks. "Chasing a bank robber?"

Furst chuckled. "I'm retired. I work for an insurance company now."

"Insurance, eh? What sort? Life? General?"

"More the investigation side. Fraud."

"Really?" said Walsh. "Sounds interesting."

CHAPTER FORTY-ONE

Molloy and Caitlin walked quickly up College Hill. A truck passed them. One or two cars. A woman walked in the opposite direction with her head down, high heels clacking on the footpath. There was a phone box on the corner of Geraldine Street. They crammed in.

Molloy looked up the Hotel Auckland in the telephone book. He put two pennies in the slot and rang the number. The operator put him through to Furst's room. No reply. He asked her to try the house bar. She doubted it would still be open. Molloy insisted.

"House bar," said the barman.

"Is there a bloke called Furst there?" said Molloy. "Big Yank, about fifty. Staying in the pub."

"Yes there is."

"Can I speak to him?"

"Just a tick," said the barman, putting down the receiver.

The barman walked over to the unlit fireplace where Furst and Walsh were sitting in armchairs, smoking cigars and telling war stories.

"Excuse me, sir," he said. "You're wanted on the telephone."

Furst looked at his watch.

"Must be head office," he said. "You mind?"

"Go for your life," said Walsh.

Furst went to the bar and picked up the receiver. "Al Furst," he said.

"Al?" said Molloy. "It's me. Johnny Molloy."

"Hey," said Furst. "You stood me up tonight, you limey bastard, you and your Girl Friday." He was in a good mood.

"Got tied up," said Molloy. "I'll tell you about it. But listen, there are people who are on their way over to see you. Watch out."

"Oh, yeah? Who?"

"The Maori who did me over the other night. His name's Sunny Day. And a lanky kid called Lofty," said Molloy. "They work for a bastard named Walsh."

"Fintan Walsh? Union bigshot?"

"Yeah."

"Hell, I'm having a drink with him right now."

"Furst, listen to me," said Molloy. "The other two nearly threw Miss O'Carolan into a furnace an hour or so ago on Walsh's orders."

Furst laughed. "Oh my, Molloy, you're giving me the vapours. Telephone me in the morning and we'll tie up the loose ends, okay?" He hung up.

Molloy stared at the receiver for a moment before putting it in the cradle. "They're boozing together in the house bar," he said. "Best of pals."

The phone booth was suddenly flooded with light. Molloy grabbed Caitlin and drew her in. The light swept past. A car driving down College Hill.

Molloy relaxed his hold. They were an inch apart.

"Wow," said Caitlin, a little breathless.

"Don't get excited. I thought I recognised that car for a second."

"Whose did you think it was?"

"Does it matter?" said Molloy, his throat dry.

"Not to me," said Caitlin, softly, closing her eyes and tilting back her head.

Molloy tightened his arms around her and felt a stab of pain.

"What?" she said, alarmed.

"Nothing," he said, trying to brush it off. "Ribs are a bit sore, that's all."

"Oh dear. Are they broken, do you think?"

"Wouldn't think so."

"Good thing I'm almost a nurse," she said. "Come on. There's a taxi stand in Three Lamps. I'm taking you home."

CHAPTER FORTY-TWO

Home was an elegant two-storey bungalow in Herne Bay set back off the road behind an enormous tree. Creeper grew around the entrance and along the top of a large picture window, and in the moonlight Molloy could see a chimney made of river stones.

"Will you marry me?" he said.

"It belongs to my aunt, you dope," said Caitlin, squeezing his arm.

The kitchen was at the back of the house with a view down a lawn and over a wooden fence across the harbour to the Chelsea Sugar Refinery in Birkenhead.

Caitlin turned on the light. "Take your coat and shirt off."

Molloy stood in his singlet.

"Where does it hurt?"

"Sort of here," said Molloy, pointing.

She put an ear to his chest. "Take a deep breath."

He looked down at her hair. She splayed her hand on his ribs, applying pressure. "I doubt it's broken. If it was, you'd know about it. There's not much I can do. I'll bandage it. These sorts of injuries fix themselves. I'll find you some painkillers. Won't be a tick."

She left the room. Through the kitchen window Molloy could see a small boat moving up the harbour past Watchman Island, a lamp swinging on its bow.

Caitlin came back into the kitchen with a bottle of aspirin, a bandage and some Johnnie Walker. She poured neat whisky into two kitchen glasses and gave one to Molloy. She shook two pills into his hand.

"Good health," she said. They clinked glasses. He swallowed the pills. She unravelled the bandage.

"Take off your singlet."

"I'm really surprised you didn't continue with nursing," said Molloy, as Caitlin wrapped the fabric around his chest. "That bedside manner."

She looked at him. "Oh, I've got a bedside manner, all right," she said, securing the bandage with a safety pin. "Don't you worry."

The air between them crackled.

"Look," said Molloy, after a moment. "I better be off."

"Why?" said Caitlin, putting down her glass.

"Let's not get carried away," he said.

"Why not?" she said, slowly undoing the top button of her blouse.

"Because I've been around the block a couple of times," said Molloy, putting his hands gently on her shoulders. "And you're a girl with her whole life ahead of her."

"So?" She was wearing a sheer corselette with a deep plunge. "It won't be my first time, if that's what you're worried about."

CHAPTER FORTY-THREE

Furst was struggling to put on his pyjamas when he heard a knock at the door. Matching Walsh drink for drink had been a mistake. He had rung the front desk and asked for analgesics to be sent up. But rather than the night porter, his visitor was a peroxided nymph straight from the lurid cover of an Erle Stanley Gardner mystery, as *fatale* as *femmes* come.

"Hello," this vision said, her open and friendly tone belying her sultry appearance. "Are you Mr Furst?"

"That's me," said Furst. "Are you the night nurse?"

"If you like," said the girl. "I'm Brenda. A friend asked me to come up and keep you company."

"A friend, huh?" said Furst, pulling the folds of a dressing gown over his stomach. "And who would that be?"

"Mr Walsh. F.P. Walsh."

"Did he now, by God?" said Furst, looking quickly up and down the hallway. "Well, come right in, honey. Brenda, was it?"

"Brenda, yes. Although I'm thinking of changing it to something more modern. Gosh, this is a nice room." She kicked off her shoes and sat on the bed. "Oh!" she said. "Is this one of them inner-sprung mattresses?"

"You know, Brenda," said Furst, feeling better already. "I believe it is."

CHAPTER FORTY-FOUR

Lofty parked the Chrysler in front of a grocer's in New Lynn. Sunny was letting him drive. Lofty went inside and bought a loaf of bread, a pound of butter, milk, tea, chocolate biscuits, Weet-Bix, half a dozen eggs, six slices of bacon, rolling papers, tobacco and a box of matches. The shopkeeper put the items in a cardboard box. Lofty loaded it into the boot of the Plymouth, next to the box of gelly, a canvas carpenter's bag filled with tools, and a crate of Waitemata, and got back in the car. They drove to Laingholm and then down a gravel road to Huia. Lofty stopped outside a fibrolite bach set back off the road. O'Flynn was sitting on the back porch with a mug of tea, his nose peeling, one hand shading his pale green eyes from the morning sun.

"The cavalry has arrived," he said. "About time."

"Put the kettle on," said Sunny.

Lofty put the box of groceries and the beer on the porch. Sunny placed the gelignite and the detonators and the canvas toolbag next to it.

O'Flynn came out with a teapot and cups. "I've no sugar."

"Not for me," said Sunny.

"Me neither," said Lofty.

"You didn't bring a girl, did you?" said O'Flynn. "Jaysus, I could use one." He winked at Sunny. "Even your man's looking sweet."

"Hey!" said Lofty, stepping backwards.

"Do we have a day for the spectacular?" said O'Flynn, taking the lid off the box of gelignite. He took out a stick and threw it to Lofty. "Think fast!"

"Oh, jeez," said Lofty, fumbling the catch. "What did you do that for?"

"This Saturday," said Sunny. "There's a boat to Sydney at midday. All the girls you want in Sydney."

"So I've heard," said O'Flynn. "What's today?"

"Wednesday. I'll pick you up at seven o'clock in the morning. You'll be out of the country by lunchtime."

"And the fella who's sniffing round? The shamus?"

"He got the message, don't worry."

"There's another thing," said O'Flynn.

"What?" said Sunny.

"I've a suitcase in left-luggage at the railway station."

Sunny paused. "You should have thought of that," he said.

"We left in a hurry you'll recall."

"Even so. What's in it?"

"Oh, items of a sentimental nature. Letters and the like."

"Travelling money?"

"A hundred greenbacks give or take."

"Give me the ticket. I'll see what I can do."

"That's the problem. The ticket's still in me room at the boarding house. Hidden in the backing of a picture. I was in me cups when I put it there. Sober, I thought it was in me wallet."

"Well," said Sunny. "Do you remember the number on the ticket?"

"Funnily enough now, I don't."

"Then you're buggered. Mr Walsh wouldn't take the risk at this stage."

"I thought as much," said O'Flynn. "Ah well, I'll offer it up." He stretched. "Three more days in this dump. I'm going mental. I'm down to reading the dunny paper."

"There's a Western in the glovebox," said Sunny. "Not sure what it's called."

"Sounds grand," said O'Flynn.

CHAPTER FORTY-FIVE

Walsh had gone to San Francisco in 1948 as the Federation of Labour's representative at a Cold War boondoggle called the International Longshoreman's Congress. He booked in at the Army–Navy YMCA. He gave a boiler-plate address to the plenary session, something about the effects of the first Labour Government's amendment to the Industrial Conciliation and Arbitration Act as it applied to the implementation of the 40-hour week, and got back to his room early, intending to have a drink or two, go out for a meal in Chinatown, visit a cathouse. But there was a note pushed under his door. *Café du Nord,* the note said. *Tonight at 9.*

There was no name, just a salutation, *One of The Particular Ones.*

What the hell?

Nothing really frightened Walsh, but this gave him pause.

He made a telephone call from the lobby to the office of the maritime union, the ILWU, and asked for Harry Bridges, saying he was an old friend from down-under, that Harry would want to talk to him.

"Who is this?" said Bridges.

"Harry, it's a voice from the grave," said Walsh. "Pat Tuohy."

There was silence. "Well, fuck me," said Bridges. He still had an Australian accent after twenty-five years in America. "It is a voice from the grave. I thought you were dead."

"The report was an exaggeration," said Walsh.

"Obviously," said Bridges. "I just assumed that someone would have got to you by now."

Walsh and Bridges first met as crewmen on a Mexican oil tanker shipping crude from the Gulf Coast port of Tampico to New Orleans. They went back to California by way of Texas, bumming their way across the country, riding freight cars, dodging railroad bulls, living in jungles, mooching food. Boys really, though Walsh had killed people by then.

"Are you in Frisco?" said Bridges.

"I'm at the International Longshoremen's Congress," said Walsh. "I thought you'd be a guest speaker."

"Don't be stupid," said Bridges. "It's a front organisation. Look at the lickspittles on the executive — Willis, Rabe, Littlejohn, Paniora. Those canaries'll be spilling their guts to the Un-American Activities Committee next, the pack of bastards. What the hell are you doing there? You haven't jumped the fence too, have you?"

"Don't be a dope," said Walsh. "The State Department paid my fare. They think I was born yesterday? Hell, I'll take anyone's money if it means seeing the Paris of the West one more time. I'm getting on, Harry."

"Mate, we both are," said Bridges. "What are you up to? Let's have a drink."

"I'm at the Army–Navy Y," said Walsh.

"Perfect," said Bridges. "The Old Ship Saloon on Pacific Avenue's a short walk. Remember the Ship? It was a speak in our day. Say thirty minutes?"

"Good," said Walsh. "Oh, one other thing, Harry. I need to get my hands on a gun."

Harry Bridges had always been a handsome bloke in what might be called an Australian way — long face, long nose, hooded eyes, hair slicked straight back. He looked like a Sydney bookie. He had aged of course. His hair was now grey and rippled, his skin was marked with lentigines of various sizes and shades of brown, the legacy of a life spent on decks and wharves and picket lines, his once-smooth face could have done with an iron and press. He walked with a cane, the result of an altercation with a mounted policeman in 1933. But his eyes were as sharp as ever and he held himself well. He was wearing an ILWU button on the lapel of his check sports coat, and he carried a brown paper bag.

He was born in Melbourne in 1901. He had jumped ship in Los Angeles, been in the Wobblies with Walsh, at the violent centre of West Coast waterfront militancy from the word go, elected President of the ILWU in 1937. He made the cover of *Time* magazine that same year — Bridges in a singlet with a big grin and the caption, "Trotsky to Stalin's Lewis?", a reference to his nemesis, the black-browed boss of the Congress of Industrial Organizations, John L. Lewis, the most powerful union figure in America. The US Government spent twenty years trying, unsuccessfully, to have him deported back to Australia for sedition and his case went to the US Supreme Court twice. He shook Walsh's hand, ordered a pitcher of beer, and moved to a corner table.

They swapped war stories for half an hour — "Remember when?" "What the hell happened to?" "The problem today is" — before Bridges pointed to Walsh's glass, barely touched.

"You haven't given up the booze, I hope?" he said.

"I'm meeting someone later," said Walsh. "Need to keep my wits about me."

"Oh, that reminds me," said Bridges, sliding the paper bag across the table. "You're not planning to knock anyone off, I hope?"

Walsh moved the bag onto the bench next to him. "Just want it in case."

Bridges leaned in. "It's a Colt something, bit of a lady's gun, but I'm told it'll make a big hole. I got it through a third party in Tacoma when we were building up for the '34 strike. I thought I better get some protection. For the wife and kiddies as much as anything. Hell, you know the drill, goons throwing petrol bombs into people's living rooms, police looking the other way. It's untraceable. You'll see where the serial number's been ground out. I've never used the bloody thing, wife didn't want it in the house. When you're finished with it, smash it up if you can and drop the pieces down a drain, just to be on the safe side."

"You don't want it back?" said Walsh.

"I'm too old. So are you, by the way. What's this about?"

"Someone put a note under my door asking to meet at a place called Café du Nord at nine tonight. Note was signed, 'One of The Particular Ones'. That mean anything to you?"

"Should it?"

"It does to me. You know that old saying, 'your blood runs cold'? Mine did, I tell you, just for a second. Listen. I got involved in some grubby business in Dublin after the war — the first one that is. The IRA assassinated, I dunno, fifteen British secret agents right across the city one Sunday morning."

"How were you involved?"

Walsh's hand was on the table. He closed his fingers into the shape of a pistol, his thumb moving like a hammer.

"Good job," said Bridges softly, raising his glass in a toast. "Here's to the death of secret agents. So who are 'The Particular Ones'?"

"We had a list of about thirty of these jokers from memory, but we only got half. Faulty intelligence, jammed weapons, failure of nerve, the usual operational stuff-ups. Not that fifteen in a couple of hours wasn't pretty good! Some of the ones who got away were particularly important in terms of the wider struggle. It was a tag that stuck to those we missed. They were the ones the Intelligence Wing had targeted *in particular*, see? They took it as a badge of honour, being English."

"And one of them's seen you here and tracked you down, you think?"

"That's what I'm assuming."

"What's your plan?"

"Plan? What's this Café du Nord?"

"It's a basement bar in Market Street. Been around since the year dot. Used to be a speak too, as a matter of fact. Dark. Not very big."

"I'll go along. See what he wants. What they want."

"Is that smart?"

Walsh shrugged. "He could have been waiting in my room earlier, he could have shot me walking over here. Anyone can be killed, we both know that."

"I wish I could come with you. Watch your back sorta thing."

"And what? Whack him over the head with your stick?"

"Hey! I've still got plenty of pep!" said Bridges. "No seriously, mate, I wish I could but I mean I just can't. I have to be sensible. You know, my position? The flippin' Department of Justice has been on to me for twenty flippin' years, trying to boot me out of the country. I get tied up with something involving a gun and a card-carrying Commie?" He hooked a thumb. "Outski."

"Forget it," said Walsh. "One old man's bad enough. I'll be all right." He nodded towards the paper bag. "Especially with this."

"Tell you what, though," said Bridges. "I could send along a couple of boys from the local to keep an eye out. I could set that up in a heartbeat."

"Thanks, Harry, but I'll handle it. You're a mate," he said.

"A mate?" said Bridges. "Jeez, after what you did for me that time with those bastards in Coeur d'Alene?"

"You would've done the same for me," said Walsh.

"Well, I'd like to think so, but," said Bridges.

Café du Nord was in the basement of the Swedish American Hall. Walsh caught a tram, arrived early, watched the entrance from the shadows across the street for half an hour, went inside and down the stairs. He ordered a glass of beer, checked the rear exit that opened onto an alley, went into the Gents, closed the door, and took the pistol from the paper bag. Bridges was right. It was a lady's gun. He could barely fit two fingers around the grip. It was the sort of weapon Brigid O'Shaughnessy might have carried. But it was simple. There was a slide safety catch and a grip safety catch and the magazine popped out easily and what else did he need to know? It fitted into the pocket of his jacket. He could pull it out without snagging. He went back to the bar, sat over his beer, and waited.

The room was quiet. It was a Tuesday night. There was a couple in the corner talking. Two salesmen drinking cocktails. Three office girls laughing softly. A radio station played jazz with the volume turned down. The barman straightened bottles and wiped glasses with a tea towel, all the time keeping an eye out for the raised finger. Two bruisers came in, ordered a pitcher of beer and a checkers board, and sat by the door, Harry's boys from the union local, Walsh assumed. He didn't see the Particular until he was beside him. He must have come in through the rear exit by the Gents and been waiting in the darkness of the hallway. He leaned against the bar to Walsh's left and began talking softly.

"I've been watching you for ten minutes," he said. "You're drinking with your right hand, which means you're right-handed, which means your gun is in your right-hand pocket." His accent was Irish. "Which is why I'm on your left with me gun pointing straight at yiz."

Walsh picked up his glass with his right hand and drank it to the bottom, looking at the reflection in the mirror behind the bar. The Irishman had a tough, handsome face, black wavy hair parted off-centre and pushed straight back, a cowlick sprung loose.

Walsh put the glass down and wiped his mouth. He spoke in a whisper so that the Irishman had to lean in. "What if I'm drinking with my right hand because I'm left-handed and I wanted to keep my left hand free to go for my gun which is in my left-hand pocket?" He turned abruptly, jabbing the barrel of the Colt into the Irishman's thigh. "Eh?" he said. "How about that?"

"Jaysus," said the Irishman, his voice low and urgent. "Hold your horses! What if my mention of holding a gun on you was purely hypothetical? If there was no such gun in other words? What if I just wanted to talk?"

"Just wanted to *talk*? If that was all you wanted I'd take you out the back and put two in your knees right now for wasting my bloody time," said Walsh. "What's going on? You're not English. You would have been in short pants in 1920. Why should I want to talk to you?"

"Exactly! Me point entirely! If I'd approached you directly you'd have given me the brush-off! Go on, put the gun away, please. I meant you no harm. Me uncle's Fintan O'Phelan."

"Never heard of him."

"You must have forgotten. You two were in the Apostles together. Uncle Fintan was Michael Collins' bodyguard."

"Not much of one, apparently." Collins, the IRA Chief of Staff, was assassinated in 1922.

"That was hurtful. Uncle Fintan died in the ambush himself."

Walsh put the pistol on the bar, spinning the barrel to face the Irishman, masking it with his right hand. "What's your name?"

"O'Flynn," said O'Flynn. "Born O'Phelan. I had to change it. Francis X. But people call me Frank."

"All right," said Walsh, eventually. He nodded to the barman and indicated his glass. "Top me up and one for the Fenian here. And a pitcher for those two palookas by the door." Harry's gorillas were lost in their game of checkers.

The barman poured two glasses of beer.

"*Sláinte*," said O'Flynn.

"Start talking."

"Right you are," said O'Flynn. "Well, me father and his pals used to carry on about this hard man from the other side of the world, Pat Tuohy, and the Apostles, and why you chose Walsh for your name, and being on the run and all that. You were sort of a legend to me growing up, like the Scarlet Pimpernel or something."

"Was your father a Volunteer?"

"Of course! B Company, Cork Brigade."

"Where did he stand on the Treaty?"

"Oh, let's not get into that. He was a good man, shall we leave it there, do you mind?"

Walsh shrugged.

"All right now," said O'Flynn. "There was a poster for the Longshoremen's Congress on the noticeboard at the union hall the other day and I was looking at it idly, like, and I saw your name on the list of speakers. I thought to meself, I wonder if that's him? I mean, New Zealand? It's a small place, is it not? It's a possibility. Ireland's not big and those sort of coincidences happen there. And when they introduced all of you on stage on the first afternoon I said, by God, it's him indeed, the man himself."

"How did you know what I looked like?"

"Ah ha! Good question. And one that I anticipated." O'Flynn moved his glass out of the way and wiped the area with his sleeve. "I'm just going to take something from my pocket, all right? It's not a gun."

A sepia photograph, cracked and worn, folded in quarters. Frank straightened it carefully and put it on the bar. Walsh leaned in. Six young Irishmen in uniform, Sam Browne belts, boots and puttees, holding an assortment of weapons, Webley Top-Break and Smith & Wesson .38 revolvers, a Lee-Enfield Mark V11. "That there's me pa," said O'Flynn. "That's me Uncle Fintan, of course, God rest his soul. These three fellas you'll know. And that there" — he pointed — "is you."

Walsh picked up the photograph and held it to the light. "I should have gone to Hollywood," he said after a while.

"You'd have been bigger than Edmund O'Brien," said O'Flynn.

"I was thinking Tyrone Power."

"Bigger than both of them."

"I remember your father now. Bernard, wasn't it?" said Walsh.

"The same."

"Quiet fella from memory."

"He opened up with a Bushmills."

"Don't we all? So why did you change your name?"

"I got into a spot of bother with the authorities back in Ireland, you know how it is."

"I do. Where's this going, son?" said Walsh. "It's my first night on the town here in thirty years and I was looking forward to a decent chop suey and a brace of strumpets to mark the occasion."

O'Flynn looked at his watch. "You're a bit late for the chop suey joints probably, but I know a number of strumpets and I'd be honoured to make the introductions."

"Never needed help in that area," said Walsh.

"All right. I'll be brief." O'Flynn took a quick sip. "I'm planning a, what would you call it, a caper, a *shenanigan* soon — nothing violent, nothing political, but lucrative if it comes off — and I'm going to have to disappear for a bit, lay low, and I was thinking Tahiti, Fiji, one of them, and then I thought, when I saw you on the stage, why not New Zealand?"

"Some caper."

"If it works I'll be well set up. Obviously, I can't talk about the procedural details."

"Why are you talking to me at all?"

"I'd appreciate the assistance of someone of influence to get me across the border without having to face too many awkward questions. Someone such as yourself."

"What's in it for me? Hypothetically."

"There would be a fee. And I have certain abilities that you might find useful."

"Such as?"

O'Flynn leaned in. "I was in the Chemical Wing of the IRA for nine years. There's nothing too small or too big that I couldn't open or blow to smithereens. I've worked undercover. I've shot a man from a mile off and a few this close." He held a finger close to Walsh's temple. "There's no job I couldn't do."

"Hell's bells," said Walsh. "I think you've got the wrong idea about the South Pacific, sonny. You might be better off looking at Chicago."

O'Flynn stiffened. "Is that so now?" he said, reaching for the photograph and refolding it delicately.

"Hey, hey!" said Walsh. "Don't get all sulking Paddy on me." He took a notebook and a fountain pen from his breast pocket. Fats

Waller's "Ain't Misbehavin'" was playing on the radio. He ripped out the page and handed it to O'Flynn. "Get in touch if you go through with it. I'll see what I can do."

"You won't be sorry," said O'Flynn.

"I hope not," said Walsh. He pointed towards the music. "As that fella said, 'One never knows, do one?'"

CHAPTER FORTY-SIX

Walsh got out of the lift on the third floor of the Grand Hotel, nodded to the uniformed policeman standing opposite, and walked along the corridor to the Royal Suite, so named because the Prince of Wales had stayed there for two nights in 1929.

It was just after eight o'clock in the morning. A tall man in shirtsleeves wearing a shoulder holster was sitting in a chair by the door, reading the *Herald*. On a side table within easy reach was an ashtray with a lighted cigarette balanced on the edge, and a pistol, a Smith & Wesson .44 Special. Walsh liked the .44. It had a well-deserved reputation for accuracy, one which he had put to good use during a dust-up in Idaho in 1916. The man stood as Walsh approached.

"Good morning, Mr Walsh," he said.

"Get the door, son," said Walsh, with a flick of his hand.

Sid Holland, the Prime Minister of New Zealand, was standing in the middle of the room in his underpants and singlet, black socks clipped to garters. He had his hand in one shoe and was buffing the toe with a brush.

"Good morning, Sid," said Walsh.

"Morning, Walsh," said Holland.

"You know you can leave your shoes outside the door with a couple of bob, and some flunky will do that for you?"

Holland picked up the second shoe and held it alongside the first. "I'm the Prime Minister," he said, putting the brogues on the floor. "I can't ask any bastard to clean my shoes."

He took a breakfast tray from the sideboard to the table and sat down. Weet-Bix, a hot dish under cover, damp toast, orange cordial, a pot of tea.

"Don't mind if I eat in my undies, do you?" he said, removing the cloth and tucking it into his singlet at the throat. "Tea?"

"Not for me. You go for your life."

"I will, don't worry," said Holland. "Flew up on an aeroplane last night from Wellington. Got airsick over New Plymouth and had my head in one of those brown bags all the way to Whenuapai. Empty as billy-o now. How did those Bomber Command blokes do it, night after night?" He poured milk onto the Weet-Bix and sprinkled on a tablespoon of sugar.

"What's on your mind, Sid?"

"What's on my mind? Anarchy, that's what. Those blasted watersiders." He turned in his seat and pointed towards the door with his spoon. "See that bruiser outside? Assume he's still there? A *bodyguard*. With a *revolver*. In New Zealand, for goodness sake."

"So what's the story, do you reckon?"

"Depends," said Holland, wiping a trickle of milk from his chin. "Where does the Federation of Labour stand? Will we have your support if we crack down on the wharfies?"

Walsh sat on the edge of a chair, balancing his hat on his knee. "Depends, Sid," he said. "You take half measures, the Federation risks getting caught in the middle. No telling how the membership will react."

"The membership will react in the way you damn well tell them to react, won't they?" said Holland, sliding the Weet-Bix to one side and taking the cover off the dinner plate. "Isn't that how it works?" Bacon and eggs and a watery tomato.

Walsh ignored the comment. "If you come down hard on the wharfies, using the full force of the Emergency Regulations, you'll have no trouble from us."

Holland threw up his hands. "Not you too? Everyone thinks those blasted Regulations are the answer! They're not! They're incomprehensible! It would take a Philadelphia lawyer to understand them. I should have left the damn things in the drawer."

He sipped his tea and put the cup down on the saucer with a clatter. "Barnes and Hill are a couple of ding-dongs, no question," he said. "But there are good men in the rank and file from what I understand, blokes who'll see reason. I'm giving a speech at the Town Hall tomorrow. I'll send them a clear message."

Walsh stood and put on his hat. This was going nowhere. "You're the man of the hour, Sid," he said. "I've every confidence you'll do the right thing when the time comes."

He left the hotel. Sunny was leaning against the Plymouth, one foot up on the running board, a smoke dangling from his bottom lip, talking through the open window to Lofty. He straightened up, flicked the cigarette away and opened the rear door for Walsh. He went round the front and got into the driver's seat.

"Jesus Christ and the saints eternal," said Walsh, sinking into the leather. He let out a long sigh. "Give me a smoke, someone."

"Right here, Mr Walsh," said Lofty, passing a packet over his shoulder.

"You had a word with O'Flynn?" said Walsh, lighting a match.

"Yep," said Sunny. "He's getting fidgety about Molloy."

"So am I," said Walsh. "And his girlfriend. And Furst, for that matter. Is Brenda at the hotel?"

"I told her to stay put till we said otherwise."

"She coping all right?"

Sunny laughed. "Rita Hayworth's little sister," he said.

"You've got the uniform, Lofty?" said Walsh.

"Wearing the strides," said Lofty, pointing. "Tunic and helmet are in the boot."

"Good," said Walsh. He lit a cigarette. "Right-o. Time to get rid of the Yank and his pal the private eye."

"Get rid of?" said Lofty, after a moment.

Walsh laughed. "I keep telling people," he said, "this isn't Chicago."

CHAPTER FORTY-SEVEN

Furst opened his door an inch or two and squeezed his face between the gap, looking out into the corridor. He was wearing a vest and holding up his pants with one hand. He had pulled them on in the hallway, bouncing along on one leg. He was unable to find his boxers. They were probably curled up in the sheets or hanging over a lampshade. His hair was dishevelled and his face felt sticky with lipstick and sweat. There was sunlight in the corridor.

It was shortly after nine in the morning. There was no obvious reason why he should be receiving a visit from a purse-lipped hotel manager and a uniformed policeman at this time. His heart was thumping, and not just from his recent exertions.

"Can I help you, gentlemen?" he asked.

"Is your name Furst?" said Lofty, in the sort of flat, accusing tone he had heard so often directed at himself. He was holding a helmet under one arm. Next to him was the hotel manager in a morning suit, glaring. The Auckland was the city's deluxe hotel. It had never once been mentioned in *Truth* and he didn't need any American riff-raff soiling its good name.

"That's me. What appears to be the problem, officer?"

"You're under arrest," said Lofty, taking a set of handcuffs from his back pocket.

"Arrest? What for?"

Lofty rose slowly on the balls of his feet. "Unlawful carnal connection with a minor," he said, enjoying himself.

"A minor?" said Furst. "I wasn't aware that she—" No, *stop*, he said to himself. My God. What were the rules around self-incrimination in this South Pacific hellhole? Let alone the rules around carnality?

"What's going on?" said Brenda, appearing from behind Furst. She was wearing a hotel towel, loosely arranged.

"What age are you, young lady?" said Lofty.

"I'm sixteen," said Brenda. "Just about."

"You're *fifteen*?" said Furst. He turned to Lofty. "I had no idea."

Lofty shook his head in disgust. "No. No, I bet you didn't. Your type never does."

"Now, look here. I'm a retired San Francisco—"

"Can you hold your wrists out, please," said Lofty.

Brenda stepped forward and put her hand on Lofty's arm. "Now hang on, buster," she said. "Have you heard of Fintan Patrick Walsh? He asked me to come over and keep company with Mr Furst, who's visiting New Zealand for the first time. There was no funny business. You should keep your impure thoughts to yourself." She tossed her hair and adjusted the towel over her cleavage, giving the manager an advertent eyeful. "What do you take me for?"

"F.P. Walsh?" said Lofty. His confidence seemed to wane.

"What's he got to do with anything?" asked the hotel manager.

"You'll find out, Grandad," said Brenda. She turned to Furst. "I'll sort this out, sweetie," she said, giving him an incriminating kiss on the cheek. "Don't worry."

Furst rubbed the spot furiously, checking for lipstick. Brenda turned and walked down the hallway towards the telephone, giving the men a good view of her undulating behind. "Won't be a tick."

She dialled. There were cigarettes on the table. She tapped one on the glass top and lit it. "Yes, hello, operator," she said. "Can you connect me to 33176, please?"

"Good girl," said Walsh, talking into the House phone in Reception. "Say, 'yes, I'll wait'."

"Yes I'll wait," said Brenda. She turned to Furst. "Don't worry about a thing," she said, indicating Lofty.

She turned back to the telephone. "Mr Walsh? It's Brenda. Brenda. Yes. Good, thank you. There's a bit of a problem with Mr Furst. He's being arrested. Yes, arrested. Carnal knowledge with a minor. Beg pardon? Me. Yes. Almost. In August. That's right, fifteen. Didn't I? Gosh, sorry. There's a policeman here and a funeral director. Just a minute." She put her hand over the receiver and called out to Lofty. "Mr Walsh would like to talk to you, Constable."

She sat on the end of the bed and crossed her legs, the towel barely in place, then leaned back and blew a thin stream of smoke towards the ceiling. The hotel manager was spellbound.

Lofty took the phone. "Are you there?" he said.

"Just say your name," said Walsh.

"Constable Doolan," said Lofty.

"Now just say, 'yes' a few times, then 'certainly, Mr Walsh', then hand the phone to Furst."

Lofty said 'yes' a few times with a varying intonation, and 'certainly, Mr Walsh', then turned to Furst. "He wants to speak to you."

"What the hell, Pat?" said Furst.

"Al, I apologise. I thought you could use a bit of company. I had no idea she was little more than a child."

"A chi—?" said Furst. "Oh, my God." He sat on a chair and covered his face with his free hand.

"Best thing for you to do would be to get out of the country quick as a flash," said Walsh. "There's a flying boat going to Sydney tonight. I'll send one of my blokes around to pick you up in half an hour."

"What about the police?" said Furst, mumbling into the phone.

"Don't worry about them. Put the plod back on. In the meantime, pack your bags."

"Grateful to you, Pat, I mean it."

"After what you blokes did for us in the war, least I could do."

Furst handed the phone to Lofty, who listened, said "will do", and "I understand, Mr Walsh", and hung up.

Lofty glared at Furst and shook his head and then edged past him out into the hallway.

"What's going on?" said the hotel manager.

"Nothing to see here," said Lofty, with what sounded like disgust.

CHAPTER FORTY-EIGHT

V.G. Parker sat at his kitchen table, hands wrapped round a mug of tea, one foot jiggling, rollie buried in his nicotined fingers, eyes fixed on the postcard of Lenin pinned to the wall. There was something about the jut of the Chairman of People's Commissars' goateed chin that always reminded Vince of Frank Sargeson. A comparison he kept to himself, obviously.

He thought of the arch-revisionist Tyrkova's description of Lenin, which he knew by heart: "From his youth his revolutionary work was characterised by the spirit of cold intrigue and by the cruel arrogance of a man convinced that he was the bearer of absolute truth, and, therefore, absolved from all moral obligations." It was intended as a denunciation, but to Parker it was an ethos. "What is to be done, Vladimir?" he asked the postcard. "What is to be done?"

Parker was one of the eighteen men and women who attended the foundation meeting of the Communist Party of New Zealand at the Wellington Socialist Hall in April 1921. Pat Tuohy, recently returned from America with a new name, F.P. Walsh, and full of bluster about his role in the underground world, was another. Parker drew up the Party manifesto, based on the 1903 Bolshevik programme — the organising of a socialist revolution, the overthrow of capitalism, and the establishment of the dictatorship of the proletariat. Walsh seduced a delegate from the Christchurch

Tailoresses and Pressers Union on the first night of the gathering, and the wife of an English academic on the second. A miner, James Dyer, was elected first Party Secretary. Branches were established on the West Coast and in the four main centres. The Party was riddled with factionalism and undermined by Impossibilists from the beginning. Members were shadowed by policemen looking for evidence of seditious behaviour under the War Regulations Continuance Act, and subject to constant harassment and arrest.

In 1927, Parker was tapped by the powerful Australian Communist Party apparatchik L.L. Sharkey to attend a one-year course of study at the Lenin School, the Comintern training centre in Moscow, the so-called "Sorbonne of the Revolution", whose aim was to develop disciplined and reliable political cadres for assignment to Communism's front lines, and whose students were considered the *crème de la crème*. They studied Marxist theory, physical education and the clandestine arts. Travelling under the pseudonym "Fred Evans", after the Waihi martyr, Parker went to Japan and then to Vladivostock, and from there, in the company of two Party members from Montreal and one from Chicago, on the Trans-Siberian Railway to Moscow.

They arrived in time to hear of Trotsky's expulsion from the Central Committee and found themselves caught up in the turmoil that followed. When the United Opposition organised a demonstration in Red Square to be addressed by Lenin's widow, Krupskaya — ostensibly to celebrate the tenth anniversary of the events of October, 1917, but clearly a provocation, the beginning of an attempt to rewrite history to the detriment of the Party and the glorification of Trotsky — the two Canadians urged their fellow students to attend as a show of revolutionary solidarity. The Chicago comrade caught Parker's eye and gave him the slightest shake of the head. Not that Parker needed guidance. It was obvious to him that Trotsky and his hirelings were promoting the very left opportunism that had so undermined the CPNZ in its founding years. The following day the Canadians were missing from the classroom and were not seen again, nor was their absence noted, except that their seats were kept empty for three weeks, books in place. Then one day the books were gone too. It was a valuable lesson to Parker and the rest of the cadre. Keep your eyes on the road to socialism and ignore the seductive provocations of traitors, spies and saboteurs.

Vince looked at his watch. Five minutes past. Making me wait, eh? A tactical move. Two can play at that game, cobber. He undid the strap and put it in his pocket. Not wearing a watch would suggest an indifference to appointments of any kind. Late for our meeting? Don't apologise, Comrade. I'd forgotten we were even having one!

A car door slammed. Parker waited. Heavy footsteps coming up the stairs, in no particular hurry. All right, thought Parker. He stubbed out his rollie and stood. He got his tobacco pouch from the mantelpiece. There was a loud insolent knock on the door. He shaped a paper in one hand, loosened some leaf with the other, spread it evenly, rolled the smoke between thumb and fingers, ran his tongue along the edge, tidied the overhang, pinched the ends, struck a match, inhaled, exhaled, left it hanging off his bottom lip.

A louder knock. "Come on, Parker, you little prick," said Walsh. "Open up."

Parker opened the door.

Walsh's suit coat was slung over his shoulder, his hat set back on his head.

Parker bowed mockingly and doffed his black beret. "'The bloody assassin of the workers, I presume'," he said.

Walsh's lips peeled back in what might have been a smile. "'The scum of the earth, I believe'," he said.

"Come in, Comrade. It's been too long," said Parker.

"Not long enough, if you ask me," said Walsh. "But anyway."

"Too right," said Parker. He pointed to the table. "Pull up a chair," he said. "There's plonk, or I could put on another brew."

"Nothing," said Walsh, taking off his hat. "I won't be here long." He looked around. "Nice bivvie. You're a man of simple tastes, obviously."

"I don't need much," said Parker, topping up his tea from the pot. "Just enough to fit in a *veshmeshok* and be out the back door one step ahead of the *Okhrana*, that's what they taught us."

"The romantic life of the revolutionist," said Walsh.

"All right, Pat," said Parker, sitting down. "To what do I owe the pleasure?"

"First off, this is a matter of mutual interest," said Walsh. "There's something in it for you and something in it for me."

"Jeez, where's me money-clip?"

"I want to stop this nonsense on the wharves from going any further. I want you to tell the unions you control, I want you to say to them, *enough!*" said Walsh.

"The Party doesn't control anything. The Party reflects the will—"

Walsh raised his hand. "Yes yes, yackety-yack. Jesus. Listen. It's you and me talking turkey in your kitchen. Two old comrades sharing difficult truths, not some extraordinary session of the Central Committee."

"Talking turkey?"

"Gloves off. Cards on the table. Doesn't leave this room."

"So what are we talking about here exactly?" said Parker. "You know. This hypothetical turkey."

Walsh looked at him for a moment.

"I was thinking you might be interested in taking over Timber Workers and Related Trades for four years," he said.

"Chicken feed," said Parker, waving the suggestion away.

"Round figures, eight hundred members? Threepence a week per member? Some chicken."

"The word I heard was turkey."

Walsh twisted his neck as though jamming a cork into an explosion. "Hamilton and New Plymouth Clerical Workers. Brings it up to a thousand, give or take. Final offer."

"Keep your shirt on, Comrade, jeez. We're bargaining here. How?"

"I can make sure you're elected Secretary. You take responsibility for the bookkeeping. Allocation of subs would be your decision. You might feel some of it should go into a, I dunno, a *special fund*, for example."

"And after four years? Theoretically, I mean. In the unlikely event that the Party—"

"Up to the members. If they feel their interests are being handled in a constructive manner, well ..." He raised his hands. It was in the lap of the Gods. "I can certainly assist them in reaching that decision closer to the time."

Parker thought it over. "They need measured direction, that's for sure," he said. "We have to combat this Butlerite tendency wherever it rears its contemptible head. Timber workers could be particularly vulnerable."

"You'd be doing them a favour."

"Well, that's right." A pause. "And in return?"

"The Drivers."

Parker laughed. "You're joking."

"And the Storemen & Packers."

"Them, possibly. The rank and file won't like it but the delegates aren't mugs, so that's not out of the question. But the Drivers? Never. They think they're the Red Cavalry."

"Get them talking about it, that might be enough," said Walsh. "Get someone to propose a resolution."

"Undermine the appearance of solidarity?" said Parker. "I could give that a go."

"Good."

"Anything else?"

"It's a matter of extreme urgency."

"Of course it is." Parker shifted in his chair. "I'm not going to lie to you, Walsh, there's a distasteful element to this conversation." He took a thoughtful sip. "On the other hand, the Party's most unhappy about the adventurist direction the wharfies are taking. And funding is an ongoing headache, it hardly needs saying."

Walsh pointed to the postcard on the wall. "Remember Ulyanov's observation, 'There are periods in the life of the proletariat when conscience turns out to be obsolete and we have to put it to one side.'"

"Stalin's observation actually but it's a fair point," said Parker. "If it's good enough for Josif Vissarionovich then who am I to quibble?" He turned his cup slowly. He sighed. "It's a long way from 1921, eh, Pat?" He clenched a mocking fist. "You know? The dictatorship of the proletariat?"

"The revolutionary road is a long and winding one, Comrade," said Walsh. "This is not the time for introspection."

He picked up his hat and spun it round his index finger. "One other thing. There's been a private detective floating around poking his nose."

"A hooligan named Molloy," said Parker. "He was a Party member before the war. Lost his way so we booted him out."

"And the girl? Little flit of a thing?"

"Isn't she, though? A petty-bourgeois. Could have her uses. She's a cadet on the *Star*."

"I don't like that."

"Why not?"

"I just don't in these times. Get rid of her."

Parker hesitated. "Get rid of her? What——?"

"Jesus H. Christ!" said Walsh. "You too?"

CHAPTER FORTY-NINE

Molloy parked in front of the Hotel Auckland and went up to Furst's room to check he'd survived his evening with Walsh. The door was open and there was a linen trolley outside. A maid was making the bed. The windows were wide open and the curtains pulled. The room smelt of perfume and sweat. There was no sign of Furst's luggage or, for that matter, Furst.

"Excuse me? Where's this guest gone?" Molloy asked the maid.

"Left, I suppose," she said, shaking a pillow into a fresh slip. "They'll know downstairs."

In the foyer, a short middle-aged man in a navy blue reefer jacket with lawn bowling regalia on the lapels was double-checking his room service bill, denying he had ordered whisky to be sent to his room.

"What's your name, young lady?"

"Esme."

"Now listen to me, Esme, I don't drink whisky."

"I'll have to get the manager," said Esme.

"You can get the Pope if you like," said the guest. "I don't drink whisky. I didn't order whisky. I'm not paying for whisky. And that's that."

Esme tapped on the manager's door and went in.

The lawn bowler turned to Molloy and shook his head in wonder. Get away with murder if you let them, these beggars, his look said, one man of the world to another. The flush on his nose suggested to Molloy that he was no stranger to plonk of some sort.

Esme came out of the manager's office. "He'll be right there," she said. She pointed to Molloy. "Would you mind waiting while I attend to this gentleman?"

The man pushed back his sleeve and looked at his watch. "Go ahead," he said. "Haven't got all day though."

Esme moved along the counter to Molloy. "Gosh," she said, pointing at Molloy's nose. "What happened to your conk?"

"Walked into a door. Has Furst gone?"

"Paid his account and skedaddled this morning." She took an envelope from a pigeon-hole. "He left this for you."

Inside were ten fifty-pound notes and a message. *Molloy*, he had written, *Have gone to Sydney at short notice. Will explain by telegram soonest. Bonus as mentioned. Yours etc., Furst.*

"How did he get to the aerodrome?" asked Molloy.

"Big Maori boy picked him up. The size of a bus."

Molloy frowned. "May I use the telephone?"

He rang the *Auckland Star* and asked for Miss O'Carolan. He waited for some time and began to think he had been disconnected. The telephonist came back on the line.

"Who's there, please?" she said.

"My name's Molloy."

"Just a minute."

More silence.

"Are you there?" said a male voice, eventually.

"Yeah," said Molloy. "Who's this?"

"Tom O'Driscoll."

"Tom, it's Johnny Molloy."

O'Driscoll lowered his voice. "You're looking for Caitlin?"

"I am."

"She's been given the heave-ho," said O'Driscoll. "Plain-clothes blokes took her away. She's a Commo. Red-hot one, apparently. Someone turned her in. Bloody hell, Johnny, it's like Moscow round here all of a sudden."

CHAPTER FIFTY

Molloy drove fast to Herne Bay. Morning sun lit up the front of the bungalow, and the creeper, a bougainvillea, was a brilliant red against the white plaster. A uniformed policeman was sitting in the shade of the huge tree, a puriri, his white summer helmet on the bench next to him.

"Hold it," said the policeman, flicking a cigarette away and moving towards Molloy, one hand up, squinting into the sun. "You can't come in here."

"Who's going to stop me, Rat?" said Molloy. "You?"

"Who's that? Molloy! Bloody hell. Couldn't see your rotten mug. Sun was in me eyes."

"Isn't it against the law to imitate a policeman?" said Molloy. Russell Baillie had been in the same class at St Joe's.

"I am a policeman," said Baillie.

"Yeah? How did that happen?"

"They changed the height minimum during the war," said Baillie. "*Carpe diem*, as the nuns used to tell us."

"Did you get overseas?"

"Reserved occupation," said Baillie, with a smirk.

"Bad luck," said Molloy.

"Oh, broke me heart," said Baillie. "Anyway. This is a no-go area to members of the public."

"A friend of mine lives here," said Molloy. "A Miss O'Carolan."

"She's not home. She's at Newton helping with enquiries."

"Enquiries about what?"

"Wouldn't you like to know?"

"I would, yeah," said Molloy.

"Well, then."

Molloy opened his wallet and found a pound note.

"Oi, what's this?" said the policeman, glancing at the money and then at the street and then at Molloy. "'An attempt to unlawfully influence an authorised person in the conduct of his duties, being an offence under section 62 of the Crimes Act'? Surely not? Not Johnny Molloy, the war hero?"

"That's pretty clever, Rat. For a bloke who was in Third Technical for three years."

"The brothers had it in for me, the pervs." He folded the note and put it in the pocket of his tunic. "And by the way, no one calls me Rat anymore."

"What do they call you?"

"Russell, of course," said Baillie. "Which is my name, as you bloody know."

"Is it really?" said Molloy. "I always thought Rat was your name."

"Ah bullshit you did," said Baillie. "Hey, you're a cobber of Sergeant Toomey's, aren't you?"

"I know him," said Molloy.

"The blimmin' gaming squad," said Baillie, shaking his head. "That's the story." He rubbed the tips of his fingers together. "Bookies paying you to look the other way. All sorts of sheilas. Bugger this walking the beat for a joke. You couldn't put in a word, could you? Tell him we were cobbers at school sorta thing?"

"I'll see what I can do."

"Good on ya," said Baillie. He lowered his voice and hooked his thumb in the direction of the house. "It's a Special Branch matter. They sent us round to watch her place and I got the short end. Stuck here for the rest of me shift."

Molloy looked up at the cloudless sky. "She's going to be a scorcher."

"Good day to be outside in a serge uniform, you mean?" said Baillie. "Thanks."

CHAPTER FIFTY-ONE

In the billiard room of the Northern Club, David Henderson was doing the *Punch* cryptic crossword, a glass of sherry and some plain biscuits on a side table next to his armchair. Two men played snooker on table four, talking quietly now and then amongst the clacking of balls and the occasional rattle of the bridge. A steward was restocking the bar at the other end of the room. There was the faint sound of a radio coming from somewhere.

Walsh sat down opposite him, creating a slow burst of air from leather cushions.

"Walsh," said Henderson, looking up from the magazine. "Eight letters. 'A vessel at sea or stuck on the bar'. Starts with 's'."

"'Stuck on the bar'?" said Walsh. He tapped his chin. "Try 'schooner'."

"Very good," said Henderson, filling in the squares with his pen.

"I talked to our bold Prime Minister," said Walsh.

"And?"

"Useless. He thinks he can charm the wharfies."

Henderson made a dismissive noise. "Ah, yes," he said. "The famous Holland charm. And the Emergency Regulations?"

"He thinks they'll lead to anarchy."

"*Lead* to anarchy? Isn't that what we've already got?"

The steward arrived.

"Sherry?" said Henderson.

Walsh shook his head.

"No thank you, Locke," said Henderson. "And could you do something about that blasted radio?"

"Certainly, sir," said the steward, backing away.

"Have you talked to your friend Parker?" said Henderson.

"I did," said Walsh. "He poked round in his store of Party maxims until he found one that justified stabbing his cobbers in the back."

"No shortage there I should imagine."

Henderson glanced at the men playing snooker, made sure the steward was tied up.

"Well? What now?"

"Almost ready for kick-off."

"Can you be more specific?"

Walsh looked at him. "Eight letters, starts with 't'," he said. "'Root worm, ruined later.'"

"What's that? An anagram?" said Henderson, writing down the clue. He looked up. "Tomorrow?"

"A few minutes after midday. Will you be there for Sid's address?"

"Have to miss it, I'm afraid," said Henderson. "Sailing down to Waiheke first thing. Longstanding engagement. We're lunching at Connell's Bay."

"A better place to be," said Walsh, standing.

Henderson picked up his sherry. His hands were shaking slightly. He spilled a drop on his tie.

CHAPTER FIFTY-TWO

Molloy walked down the side of Pat Toomey's house. Brigid was hanging out the washing, covered in billowing sheets. He coughed. She cried out and turned suddenly and then looked away, but not before he saw the bruise on her cheek.

"Hell, Brigid," he said. "What happened to you?"

"It's nothing," she said, back towards him. "I'm clumsy, that's all."

"Has Pat seen it?"

Brigid said nothing.

"Is he home?" said Molloy.

"Johnny, please."

"I need to talk to him. About something else."

"He's at the station," said Brigid. "You could ring him on the telephone if you like. We've got one in the hallway."

Molloy telephoned the Newton Police Station and asked for Sergeant Toomey.

"Are you there?" said Toomey, after a minute.

"It's me, Pat," said Molloy. "Johnny Molloy."

"Hello, Johnny."

"There was a girl taken in for questioning this morning," said Molloy. "Her name is Caitlin O'Carolan."

"There was," said Toomey. "What's your interest in this unfortunate young woman? Is she a friend of yours?"

"Well, that. And a client. Sort of."

"Sort of," said Toomey. "Not the ideal person to have as either, just at the moment. She's a fellow traveller, Johnny, a Red. Very slippery customers. Not that I need to tell you."

"Is she still there?"

"She was released on her own recognisance about half an hour ago," said Toomey. "Her father's some big Epsom doctor. Arrived with Frank Haig, the lawyer. A real anarchist, this friend of yours."

"She's young, Pat."

"Not that young," said Toomey. "If you get my meaning."

"Why was she picked up?"

"We received a tip-off," said Toomey. "Anonymous, of course. Someone on the telephone. That's the way it's done nowadays. The muffled phone call has replaced the poisoned letter."

"Any idea who?"

"Middle-aged or older male, according to the sheet. That's all we've got."

"What did he say?" said Molloy, knowing who it was.

"That she was a Party member with connections to the Waterside Workers' Union. Red rag to a bull just at the moment. What's your interest? I thought you'd put all that Communist business behind you."

"Once a Catholic sort of thing, I suppose, Pat. You know how it is."

"You should keep your head down, Johnny," said Toomey. "With things the way they are."

"Thanks for the advice. Hey, Pat, that's quite a shiner Brigid's sporting."

"She enjoys a tipple," said Toomey, after a moment. "Between you and me."

CHAPTER FIFTY-THREE

Molloy took the stairs beside Progressive Books two at a time and stormed down the hallway.

"Parker, you gutless bastard," he shouted. "Get out here."

The door flew open. Parker dropped into a boxer's stance, shoulders hunched, fists around his face, weight on the left leg, right heel off the floor. He had been a pretty handy fighter in his day, losing on points to Jimmy Hegarty at the Theatre Royal in Taumaranui, Hegarty's last amateur fight. He'd never been any great shakes as a scientific performer, but he always went straight at his opponent, fearless.

"Yeah, come on, have a go, ya class traitor," said Parker, unhooking his glasses and flinging them onto the bed. "I'll give you the hiding I should have given you ten years ago."

Molloy moved towards Parker and feinted a jab. Parker slipped and threw a right. Molloy turned and caught the punch on his shoulder, and then came under Parker's arm with a hook that caught the wiry Commo in the ribs. Parker made a *hunnh* sound and moved backwards, catching his breath.

"Sting a bit?" said Molloy. "Shit hot."

They circled each other.

"You sold her out, didn't you?" said Molloy. "Following Walsh's orders, you rotten bastard. Who's next on the auction block? The wharfies?"

"*You're* lecturing *me*, you turncoat?" said Parker. He threw a sudden right that caught Molloy on the cheek and knocked him back against the kitchen table. He stepped in, shoulders coiled for the king hit, but Molloy weaved and wrapped him in a clinch.

"I'd sit down with the flamin' Devil himself if it was in the best interests of the proletariat," Parker hissed into Molloy's ear as they danced on the spot.

Molloy turned abruptly and shook Parker off, lowered his shoulder, jabbed with his left and threw an overhand right that hit Parker on the nose and sent him crashing backwards onto the bed.

Parker pulled himself up, shaking his head. Blood dripped onto the floor. He put out a hand. "Pax for a tick, all right?" he said, breathing heavily. He touched his nose delicately. "Think you broke the bastard."

"Why did you do it?" said Molloy, keeping his fists in a loose position.

"Why?" Parker dabbed at his nose with the back of his hand. "Caitlin's a useful idiot. A pretty one, certainly, and sexually progressive which, y'know, shit, good on her, but a dilettante. It suited Walsh to get rid of her and was no particular loss to me."

"That's it, is it? Walsh says 'jump', you say 'how high?'"

"Oh get stuffed, Molloy." Blood and snot were now bubbling in Parker's nose like soup. "You know me better than that! I won't allow the wharfies' lunatic action to destroy the Party. You think I've spent me whole life fighting for a fair go for the working man in labour camps and shearing sheds and factories and railway yards and wharves and hydro schemes and every other bloody thing way to buggery up the backa beyond, no plonk, no women, everything I owned in a swag or left-luggage, in and out of clink, battened by Specials and farmers and policemen and fascists of every stripe, you think I've done all that just to sit there and watch a mug like Barnes pour everything I've fought for since I was a little fella, *everything*, just pour it down the gurgler? Fuck that for a joke." He gently squeezed his bloody nose. "If giving Caitlin the boot was part of the price that had to be paid, then so flamin' what? In the schema of historical materialism, she's small potatoes."

"Go to hell," said Molloy.

"I'll see you there," said Parker, nostrils now stuck together, his voice taking on a nasal quality, like Michael Joseph Savage on the radio.

CHAPTER FIFTY-FOUR

It was mid-afternoon. Molloy hadn't eaten since breakfast. He stopped at the cake shop next to Progressive Books and bought two dried-out sausage rolls and ate them on the footpath, and then called in to the Shamrock for a glass of beer. His cheek burned from Parker's punch. Caitlin had been sacked from the *Star*. Furst had left the country. Parker and Walsh were collaborators. Collaborating on what? Where did O'Flynn fit in to all of this? Molloy finished his beer and walked to his office. He went up in the lift to the fourth floor and got out. There was a figure waiting in the shadows. Caitlin. She threw herself into his arms, bursting into tears.

"Oh, Johnny," she said. "Someone informed on me to the *Star*. I was given the sack this morning."

"I know. It was Parker."

Caitlin looked as though she'd been hit.

"Gets you, doesn't it?" he said, unlocking his office door.

"But why would he do that?" she said.

Molloy shrugged. "For the good of the Party," he said. "He's thrown his lot in with Walsh. A temporary and pragmatic reaction sorta thing." Molloy opened a drawer in his desk and took out a bottle of brandy. There was an inch left. He halved it and slid a glass across the desk to Caitlin.

"But Walsh barely knows me from Adam," said Caitlin.

"He knows you know about O'Flynn, though," said Molloy. "And that you're a reporter. Better to have you out of the picture." He shook two cigarettes from a pack and offered her one.

"You've talked to Vince?" said Caitlin, leaning into the match.

"I went round to his flat. We had a barney."

"Did you give him a hiding?"

"A bit of a one."

"Good. He was forever trying to put his grubby hands on me, now I think about it. Didn't seem terribly fraternal, I must say."

The telephone rang. Molloy picked up the receiver. "Are you there?"

There was a clanging sound as two pennies dropped into a slot.

"Is that bold Molloy, the private investigator?" said an echoing Irish voice.

"It is," said Molloy. "Who's this?"

"The name's Frank O'Flynn," said the voice. "Well, it is at the moment. I understand you've been looking for me."

"I understand you drowned."

"As your man said, miracles happen to those who believe. We need to have a wee talk, the two of us."

"Suits me," said Molloy. "When?"

"Tonight."

"Where?"

"Number 2 Shed in the Lighter Basin," said O'Flynn. "You know it?"

"I do," said Molloy. "Up from the Municipal Baths."

"Seven o'clock. Come by yourself."

The telephone went dead.

"Well, well," said Molloy, slowly returning the receiver to its cradle.

"O'Flynn?"

Molloy looked at his watch. "He wants to meet me on the waterfront tonight."

"Will those two hoodlums of Walsh's be there?"

"I hope so," said Molloy, standing.

There was a rectangle of worn carpet on the office floor. Molloy rolled it out of the way and opened his pocketknife. He prised up a short length of floorboard. In the gap between the joists was a shoebox. Molloy lifted it out and took off the lid. Wrapped in a faded Afrika Korps pennant eaten by silverfish and stained with gun oil was *Oberst i.G.* Egon Turtz's 9 mm semi-automatic Luger.

"Where did you get that?" said Caitlin.

"Italy." Molloy pressed the catch, took out the magazine, and removed the cover plate with a screwdriver he kept in a toolbag in the bottom drawer. He blew dust from the workings and gave them a squirt from a tiny can of sewing-machine oil. He reassembled the pistol and pushed the magazine into the grip with the heel of his hand until it clicked into place. He slid the toggle back as far as it would go and let it snap forward, locking the breech-block into place, and turned the safety lever down and to the rear. *Gesichert.* Made safe. He put on his jacket and put the Luger in the right-hand pocket.

"I'm coming with you," said Caitlin, standing.

"No. You could get in the way." Before she could say anything he added, "It really is no place for a girl. I mean it."

He gripped the pistol's textured stock. He hadn't thought about shooting anyone since 1945.

CHAPTER FIFTY-FIVE

Molloy turned into Packenham Street. There was a row of army trucks parked in the darkness, khaki-coloured three-ton Bedford QLDs, with the dear old fern leaf on the front mudguard, motors idling, headlights covered, canopies snapping in the unseasonal wind. The glow of cigarettes came from darkened cabs, and soldiers double-timed between vehicles, boots thumping on the bitumen.

Molloy stopped as a rooster in uniform — three stripes, a clipboard under his arm — marched towards him, his hand up in a stop motion, very pukka, beret just so, insurance agent's tiny moustache.

"Oi," said the NCO, a Pom. "This is a restricted area. On yer bike."

"What's the story?" said Molloy.

"Fook off," said the soldier, waving his arm. "That's the story."

Molloy almost saluted, knowing it would irritate the NCO, both for its sloppiness and its insolence, but even more so for its breach of etiquette. Only officers had the King's Commission, so when you saluted an officer you were actually saluting the King. But the King couldn't be a *non-commissioned* officer because, well, the very idea. Something along those ridiculous Pongo lines, anyway. Saluting Red Caps had been great fun in Cairo. The little bastards hated it. But Molloy controlled himself. This was not the time to have a bloke on, he thought to himself, not with a gun in my hand.

He turned and walked to Market Place and down an alley by the Municipal Baths. The fish market was closed, the timber yards and warehouses in darkness, the streets empty. Fishing boats were moored in the basin, bumping against the wharf piles, hawsers squeaking and groaning. Molloy could see the mechanical bridge in Halsey Street lifting for a late trawler and hear shouted instructions drifting faintly on the wind across the water.

No. 2 Shed was at the entrance to a boatyard. He took the Luger from his pocket and pushed the safety up and forward. Ready to fire. He went inside. He could make out the faint shape of a vessel on blocks. Other than that the space was pitch black.

He called out. "O'Flynn."

There was no reply.

He called again.

The click of a torch and everything went white. "Stay where you are," a voice said. "Keep your mitts where I can see them."

Molloy raised his hands.

"This your idea of a wee chat, is it, Frank?" he said, his eyes closed tight against the blinding glare.

O'Flynn moved forward slowly, his boots crunching on sand and broken glass. The torch beam moved slightly to one side. Molloy could make out his shape and the faint, moonlit gleam of a pistol.

The Irishman was tall and well-built, wearing a pea coat with the collar turned up, his gun hand steady. "So it's him himself," he said. "The private detective, neither tarnished nor afraid." He laughed. "You know how there's always that moment in the fillums," he said, "when the baddy's holding a gun on the hero and saying he's going to shoot him in a minute, right after he's sorted out a couple of things? And you're sitting there in the stalls with your ice and your sweeties and you're thinking why doesn't he just pull the trigger and be done with it because the hero's going to clobber him if he doesn't? But the baddy just keeps talking and talking, revelling in it like, getting himself deeper and deeper into the shite?"

"I don't go to the pictures much," said Molloy.

"No? Well it happens," said O'Flynn, thumbing the safety. "I suppose in the flicks it's a way of tying up the loose ends. Still, it's hard not to savour the moment. Right now, for example, there's a part of me saying Jaysus, you're courting fate with your delaying and your talking, just shoot the fucker and be done with it. But at the same time there's another part saying hold yer horses there, big fella! Before you put one in his guts and two in his head, take a moment to rub it in, to *clarify* the situation, you know?" He paused, enjoying the role of the happy-go-lucky gunman. "So, I may be an eejit of the first order, but—"

Molloy dived to his left and rolled on the floor, then up on his feet, taking the Luger from his pocket, banging against *something* in the gloom, pain shooting up his legs like being whacked on the shin with an iron bar. The pistol dropped onto the floor and into the darkness. O'Flynn fired twice. Molloy ran towards the moonlit door, knowing it would make him an easier target but thinking, if he was thinking at all, easier than *what*?

A woman's voice. "Stop! Or I'll shoot." Caitlin, backlit in the doorway, holding — oh, hell — a *piece of wood*! Molloy shouted, "Get down." O'Flynn fired once at her then back in the direction of where he thought Molloy might be — *bang, bang, bang* —

Click.

"Out of ammo," said Molloy. "I remember *that* from the pictures."

A cylinder snapped open, the tinkle of spent cases hitting the floor.

"Keep talking there, boyo!" said O'Flynn, reloading. "I'm all fockin' ears."

"Caitlin!" yelled Molloy.

"Here."

"Let's go."

They ran from the building. A car, its big six-cylinder engine roaring, turned into the alley from Fanshawe Street and caught them in its headlights.

"Is that the police?" said Caitlin.

"Not when you need them," said Molloy.

They turned and began running in the other direction. O'Flynn came out of the building and fired twice, the shots going wild. The car skidded to a halt and doors opened.

"Watch out. He's got a gun," said Sunny.

"Stop them, damn youse," said O'Flynn.

Molloy and Caitlin reached the edge of the wharf. They heard the sound of running feet.

Molloy looked at Caitlin and down at the dark, oily water.

He took her hand. "Hold your nose," he said, and they jumped.

CHAPTER FIFTY-SIX

Mrs Philpott put a shovelful of coal into the range, closed the door, and opened the damper. Caitlin was sitting on a chair, wrapped in a blanket, her hair in a towel. Molloy was wearing an old jersey that smelt of mothballs, and a dressing gown, part of the Philpott estate. Mrs Philpott took a bottle of whisky from a high shelf in the pantry, standing on a stool to reach.

"Normally I disapprove of alcohol, as you know, Mr Molloy," she said. "But under the circumstances." She poured a splash into two glasses and gave one each to Caitlin and Molloy. "Pre-war," she said. "A weakness of my late husband. One of a number."

"Would you mind if Miss O'Carolan slept here tonight, Dorothy?" said Molloy, disregarding convention.

"Of course not." Mrs Philpott squeezed Caitlin's hand. "I've made up a bed on the couch in the living room."

Caitlin smiled and put down her glass. "I may go there now. I'm feeling very tired all of a sudden."

"Get Miss O'Carolan a clean towel from the hall cupboard, John," said Mrs Philpott. "I'll bring you a washing bowl in the morning, dear, and a cup of tea."

Molloy led Caitlin from the kitchen. As they walked down the hallway the grandfather clock struck. Caitlin jumped. "Oh, gosh," she said, taking his arm. "That gave me a fright."

"It's ten o'clock," he said. "Been a big day."

A door opened and Miss Perkins put her head out. She was wearing rollers in her hair and there was cream on her face. "Everything all right?"

"Good as gold," said Molloy. "Oh. Miss Perkins, this is a friend of mine, Miss O'Carolan."

"How do you do," said Miss Perkins.

"Hello," said Caitlin.

Miss Perkins looked impassively at Molloy. "Good night," she said, closing her door.

Caitlin unwrapped the towel from her head and lay on the couch. She pulled up the blankets.

"Why did they want to shoot you?" she said, shivering.

"I don't think they did. Sunny Day said, 'Watch out, he's got a gun.' He was referring to O'Flynn, not me. I'm pretty sure shooting me was O'Flynn's plan, not theirs."

"What's their plan?" she said.

"I'll work it out." He kissed her damp hair. "Get a good night's sleep," he said. "It'll be clearer in the morning."

He returned to the kitchen.

"Everything all right?" said Mrs Philpott.

"Out like a light."

"I heard someone talking in the hallway," said Mrs Philpott.

"That was Miss Perkins."

"Was she upset?"

"Why would she be?"

"At seeing you with Miss O'Carolan?"

Molloy looked at her.

"I know where babies come from, John," said Mrs Philpott. She leaned forward and pushed the damper in an inch or so.

"Miss O'Carolan can look after herself, don't worry."

"It's Miss Perkins I'm worried about, poor soul," said Mrs Philpott.

They sat in silence. He picked up the whisky bottle. "May I?"

"Of course."

Molloy splashed some into his glass.

"How's your shin?" she said.

"It'll be all right."

"Are you in trouble, dear?"

He sipped. "Dorothy, if I told you someone tried to kill me tonight, what would you say?"

"Kill you?" She reached for the whisky bottle and poured some into her cocoa mug. "Oh, dear."

CHAPTER FIFTY-SEVEN

The Prime Minister, Sid Holland, stood in front of the bathroom mirror in his room at the Grand Hotel, wearing baggy underpants, black socks and a white shirt, his suit on a hanger behind the door, a tiny nodule of dried blood beneath one nostril where he had nicked himself with his cutthroat.

"The Government is alive to the danger that besets us," he said, shaking his finger at an imaginary audience on the edge of its seat. "And is determined to ensure that our enemy does not succeed."

He ran a blue tie under the collar of his shirt.

"We ..." he began, flipping the tie's wide end over the narrow end and back underneath. "We, um ..." He put on his reading glasses and looked at the sheet of paper balanced on the basin. "We are at war," he said. "Of course." He brought the wide end back over in front of the narrow end, making a loop. He cleared his throat. "We are at war. There is an enemy within which is just as unscrupulous, poisonous, treacherous and unyielding as the enemy without."

He pulled the wide end up and through the loop and brought it down in front. "He works night and day," he continued. "He never lets up." Holland paused. He unscrewed a pen from the inside pocket of his suit coat, scratched out "lets" and replaced it with "gives". He gently tugged on the narrow end of the tie. "He works night and

255

day. He never gives up." He slid the knot up towards his throat. "Our enemy gnaws away at the very vitals of our economy, just as the codling moth enters and gnaws away at the innards of an apple while everything on the outside looks shiny and rosy."

He looked at his reflection in the mirror and liked what he saw. Resolve. Determination. Leadership. Tie just so, a good, solid four-in-hand, unlike the Windsor favoured by some of the newer chaps in Cabinet, the Holyoakes and the Eyres. He didn't much care for the Windsor. There was something of the motor trade about it, Sid thought.

"We should be under way in five minutes, sir, if you wouldn't mind," said the bodyguard, from outside the door.

"Right you are," said Holland, picking up a hairbrush.

CHAPTER FIFTY-EIGHT

Lofty turned off State Highway 1 and drove up Patutohe Road West for five miles. He'd had the Plymouth up to seventy on the Great South Road and hardly even noticed. Those Yanks sure knew about motorcars.

There was a map spread out on the passenger seat and he had a quick look. There should be a turn-off coming up on the left. There was. No name, just a milk-run number nailed to a power pole. The road became gravel. Cows watched him blankly from a paddock. Out to his right he caught a quick glimpse of railway tracks. He came up a rise. The road went down the hill and under a bridge, veered left and disappeared round a corner. He tapped the brake and pulled off to the side, gradually slowing to a halt, keeping an eye on a steep ditch. He hated to think what Sunny would do to him if he pranged the car. Let alone Mr Walsh.

He turned off the engine and got out. The only sounds were the ticking of the manifold, and from somewhere in the distance, a sheep. Or sheep. Lofty had grown up in Freemans Bay. He checked his watch. The Limited, the only scheduled train between ten o'clock and five, was not due for at least two hours. The Limited was occasionally on time, but never early. He closed the door, opened the boot and took out a wooden beer crate containing gelignite, detonators and a rope, and walked delicately down the road to the bridge, the crate held out in front of him.

He climbed up the bank and onto the tracks, being careful not to look down because he was afraid of heights. Halfway across he stopped and put the crate on the gravel next to the line. He took out the rope and wrapped it loosely round a section of track between two sleepers, then placed half a dozen sticks of gelignite under the coils. Holding the bundle in place with one hand, he gently tightened the rope until it was secure, and tied it off. There were two lengths of fuse in case one went out. He squeezed the ends of both into the detonator, as O'Flynn had shown him, and walking backwards, fed them out along the line. He studied the set-up, checking in particular that the fuses were still connected. Everything seemed in order.

He struck a match and lit the first fuse and then the second. They fizzed and sparked and began to move slowly along the tracks towards the bundle. He had twelve minutes before the thing went off, according to O'Flynn, but he also felt that the Irishman didn't like him that much.

He scrambled down the bank to the road and ran to the Plymouth. You drongo! he suddenly thought. What if she doesn't start? But she did. He made a sweeping three-point turn and drove back up the hill. He stopped at the crest and got out, leaving the engine running this time, handbrake on, and waited. O'Flynn had doctored the gelly so that it would do no serious damage, but still, Lofty was curious.

The charge went off with a soft *poof* followed by an echoing *crack* and the clang of stones hitting the tracks and landing on the road below the bridge. The small amount of smoke and dust quickly dissipated. You'd barely call it an explosion but it would cause a hell of a stink.

He drove to Waiuku, made an anonymous call to the police from a phone box, read a short statement that Mr Walsh had written claiming responsibility for the bombing in the name of something called the Huntly Miners' Soviet, and then dropped into the Kentish Hotel for a jug.

CHAPTER FIFTY-NINE

Frank O'Flynn, wearing a boiler suit and carrying a canvas toolbag which contained a number of items including, as would be expected, saws, hammers, a plumb line and a measuring tape, but also rope, pliers, a torch, a knife, a box of matches, a clock, a paraffin lamp wrapped in a jersey, an auger, a two-inch masonry bit, a piece of chalk, several detonators, and twenty sticks of gelignite, strode into the foyer of the Auckland Town Hall. He passed, without pausing, policemen, NZBS technicians, government officials, uniformed ushers, excited members of the National Party, and young girls with wooden trays slung around their necks selling sweets and orange cordial and Eskimo Pies, and went through a door next to the Gentlemen's toilets marked BASEMENT. NO ADMITTANCE.

Behind the door the elegance of the Town Hall foyer gave way to the building's damp, utilitarian underbelly. There was a circular metal stairwell. He took out his torch, pointed the beam into the gloom, and began his descent.

CHAPTER SIXTY

Mrs Philpott came into the kitchen. She was wearing a pink suit and hat and white gloves.

"Good morning, everybody," she said, like Aunt Daisy. "Good morning, good morning, everybody." She smiled at Caitlin. "Did you sleep well, dear?"

"Very well, thank you," said Caitlin. "I feel so much better."

"You're dolled up today, Mrs Philpott," said Molloy, observing the old formalities. "Going to a wedding?"

The landlady took out a tram timetable from a kitchen drawer. "I'm going to the Town Hall," she said. "To hear the Prime Minister make an address. They say he's going to give the wharfies what for at long last and I want to be there to hear history made."

"Aren't you on the wharfies' side, Mrs Philpott?" said Caitlin, unable to help herself.

"I'm most certainly not!" said Mrs Philpott. "They're practically starving at Home and there's all this mutton just sitting there on the wharves because—"

Molloy put down his cup with a bang. "No you're not," he said.

"I *beg* your pardon?" said Mrs Philpott.

"You're not going anywhere near the Town Hall today, Mrs Philpott."

"Oh is that so?" said Mrs Philpott. "Well—"

"What did O'Flynn do in Ireland?" said Molloy to Caitlin, talking over Mrs Philpott.

"What?" said Caitlin, uncertain. "For a living, you mean?"

"He was in the IRA. He was a bomb maker."

"Yes," said Caitlin. "I'm not sure—"

"What did he *do*?" Molloy was standing now. "In 1938?"

"Um. Um. He tried to blow up the Earl of Galway."

"How?" said Molloy.

"How?" said Caitlin, confused. "With a bomb."

"What *are* you two talking about?" said Mrs Philpott.

"*Where*?" said Molloy, banging the table.

"Where?" said Caitlin. "In th—" Her eyes widened and her hand flew to her mouth. "Oh my God."

"Now, young lady, there's no call—" said Mrs Philpott.

"With a bomb," said Molloy, as though Mrs Philpott wasn't there. "In the Cork *Town Hall*."

CHAPTER SIXTY-ONE

Molloy backed his car out of the garage at speed, almost hitting a postman who swore at him, reckless driving being a constant danger in the swift completion of a postie's appointed rounds to this very day, and reached over to open the door for Caitlin.

"Have you got anything with you that says you're on the *Star*?" he said, skidding out onto Williamson Avenue.

"Not with me," said Caitlin. "It's in my purse at the bottom of the Lighter Basin. Why?"

"Have a look in the glovebox."

Caitlin poked around and found a school notebook and a fairly new 2 HB pencil. "These'll do."

Molloy pointed to the leather grip on the floor by her feet. "There's a camera in that bag. Do you reckon I could pass for a newspaperman if I followed you around? Wisecracking newshound and stolid shutterbug?"

She looked at him. "They tend to be tubbier."

"Nobody will be looking at me."

She opened the bag and took out the Voigtländer. "Where'd you get this?"

"Italy," said Molloy, checking the mirror.

"Italy was good to you, wasn't it?" she said, one hand gripping the door handle as Molloy overtook a tram.

"Bits of it weren't bad. Wouldn't want to live there though."

They double-parked at the bottom of Greys Avenue and ran down to Queen Street. There was a crowd in front of the Town Hall, filling the footpath. Buses from Helensville and Papakura and Thames and Whangarei were parked across the road, and cars crawled in both directions.

"Seriously," said Caitlin, after a moment, looking at the vehicles, the crowd, the police, her voice tightening. "Do you have a plan?"

"Look, it's probably better if you stay here," said Molloy. "This could get hairy."

"Not on your life, buster," she said, straightening her shoulders. "You would have been finished last night if I hadn't turned up."

"Too true." He squeezed her hand. "Come on. As a cobber of mine, John Newton, always says, momentum is everything."

CHAPTER SIXTY-TWO

O'Flynn thought of Oscar Guttman's 1892 text, *Blasting: A Handbook for the Use of Engineers and Others Engaged in Mining, Tunnelling, Quarrying, Etc.*, in religious terms, and he was not a religious man, nor was he an engineer, or one engaged in mining, tunnelling or quarrying. He fell into the broader category of *Etc.* and Guttman was his muse.

To blow up a masonry foundation the amount of gelignite needed is calculated, per Guttman, by using the formula $L = 0.1\ d^2$, where L is the charge in pounds, and d is the thickness in feet. So the destruction of a section of foundation wall two feet thick and twelve feet long requires 0.4 lb charges of gelignite in holes drilled four feet apart. O'Flynn had got the formula wrong in Cork. The bomb he planted in the basement of the Town Hall failed to collapse the building, despite doing considerable damage. The IRA's Director of Chemicals, Seamus O'Donovan, had given him a real bollocking.

He got out the paraffin lamp and the matches and put the lamp on a ledge. He pumped the primer. He raised the glass bowl and lit the flame, and when it took he lowered the glass and wound the wick back to a working height. He switched off his torch and put it in the toolbag. He measured the wall in four-foot lengths and marked each with a chalk cross. He wound up the tape measure and put it and the chalk back in the toolbox. For a man who in many ways led a chaotic life, O'Flynn was well organised when it mattered. He got out the auger, tightened the bit, lit a cigarette, and began drilling.

CHAPTER SIXTY-THREE

Sid Holland stood to loud applause, took his speech from his breast pocket, and walked to the lectern, his brogues squeaking on the wooden stage. The Town Hall was full. He unfolded his notes. The clapping died away, the only sounds a distant cough and the clacking of the prime ministerial reading glasses.

Sid loved moments like this. He felt like a conductor in one of the great concert halls of Europe, crowned heads and commoners alike poised for the tap of his baton. He cleared his throat to check the correct distance from the microphone, and began.

"Your Worship. Lady Allum." He inclined his head, fractionally and reluctantly, in the direction of Sir John Allum, the Mayor of Auckland, who looked, with his bristly moustache and Cheshire cat grin, exactly like the Minhinnick cartoon. He acknowledged the other dignitaries sitting in a row beside, but slightly behind, the mayoral presence. "Borough chairmen. Members of the Auckland City Council. Distinguished guests."

He turned to face the audience. "Ladies and gentlemen. The Government is alive to the danger that besets us, and is determined to ensure that our enemy does not succeed."

He paused. "We are at *war*."

CHAPTER SIXTY-FOUR

Molloy and Caitlin ran into the foyer of the Town Hall. A cleaner was sweeping cigarette butts and lolly wrappers off the floor.

"*Auckland Star*," said Molloy, indicating his camera. "Where's the basement entrance?"

The door was unlocked, the stairwell pitch black.

"Should have brought a torch," he said.

"Would a lighter be any good?" said Caitlin.

"Let's give it a try."

Caitlin opened her handbag and passed her lighter to Molloy. He flicked it on. It was better than nothing, but not much better.

"Hold onto the handrail and stay close," said Molloy.

They descended in silence, straining to hear, the atmosphere getting colder and damper with each step. The stairway gave out onto a corridor, with an uneven floor and rough brick walls, at the end of which weak yellow light spilled. They could hear the clinking of tools.

CHAPTER SIXTY-FIVE

O'Flynn tamped the last of the gelly into the holes, set the detonators and uncoiled the fuses. He looked at his watch. That big eejit Lofty should have set off the diversion on the Patutohe bridge by now, he thought, and the coppers would be all over it like a madwoman's shite. Unless Lofty had got lost, which was possible. Likely, even. Walsh's concern, not his.

Time for me to get lost too, he thought. The boat sailed for Sydney in two hours. Then where? South Africa? Mexico? The Orient maybe? He had a pal up that way. Siam, was it? Malaya? Rubber plantations. Growing tea. Native women of rare beauty who worshipped Europeans and would do anything for them. Somewhere a quid went a long way, anyway, and white men got away with murder.

He set the timer for fifteen minutes, then unbuttoned his boiler suit and dropped it on the ground. He was wearing grey trousers and a brown leather jacket. He'd watch the explosion from across the road. Noise and a bit of smoke, that's all. What the Director of Chemicals liked to call a "billy-do".

CHAPTER SIXTY-SIX

Walsh and Sunny were sitting at the back of the Town Hall. Holland was talking about codling moths. The audience was soaking it up. Sid was not unimpressive, Walsh thought.

Sunny looked at his watch and gently nudged his boss. They stood. Walsh did up his suit coat. Sunny left his jacket unbuttoned, better to conceal the Luger in his pocket. Walsh nodded to a uniformed constable standing by the door.

"Mr Walsh," said the policeman softly, straightening up and opening the door, the pneumatic hinges hissing.

They crossed the foyer and went through the door to the basement.

CHAPTER SIXTY-SEVEN

Molloy put up his hand and froze. Footsteps coming up the passage, someone holding a torch. With a straight arm he pressed Caitlin against the wall. "Shut your eyes," he whispered. O'Flynn came round the corner. Molloy brought up the camera and popped the flash, stepped forward and slammed O'Flynn full in the face.

The Irishman staggered back and lost his footing, but he was a tough bastard in a tough situation and he wasn't going to go down without a fight. His torch was on the ground, providing enough light to make out shapes. He came up and charged at Molloy, turning his head enough to slip a right and throwing a handful of dust and dirt into Molloy's eyes. O'Flynn punched him once, twice, three times, and picked up a broken brick to finish the job.

But Caitlin launched herself at him, her fingers raking his face, her knee slamming up into his groin. He yelled in anguish and threw her down. He brought the brick up like a club, turning his body for torque. "You fucking hooer!" he yelled.

"Frank. For Christ's sake!" said a voice, Walsh's, from the gloom.

"So it's a hooley now, is it?" said O'Flynn, his face contorted.

Walsh shone his torch at O'Flynn. Sunny stepped around from behind Walsh, Luger raised, and shot O'Flynn in the chest, an explosion in the tiny space, the force spinning the Irishman and leaving him face up on the ground.

"Why?" he said, utterly baffled, his chest rattling. Sunny stepped forward and shot him again, this time in the face.

"What about these two?" said Sunny.

"I'm thinking," said Walsh. "No. This is good. It's the gumshoe's Luger after all. Give it here. Go upstairs and fetch the police."

"You'll be all right on your own?"

"Oh, I should think so," said Walsh, putting the Luger in the pocket of his jacket, touched that Sunny cared. You never knew with people. "Oh, Sunny," he said.

"Mr Walsh?"

"Better disconnect the timer first. Wouldn't want the bloody thing to go off."

"Hell, that's right," said Sunny. "Borrow the torch?"

He moved down the passage.

Walsh hitched his trousers at the knee and squatted down by O'Flynn, lifting the Irishman's lifeless arm and placing the tips of two fingers between the bone and the tendon over the radial artery. Satisfied, he stood and regarded the body for a minute, silent and absorbed. He could have been praying for O'Flynn's immortal soul, or sending up a quick novena to St Jude, the patron saint of difficult causes. Unlikely, but not impossible. "Sad," he said. "Life's twists and turns." He gently pushed at the Irishman's shoulder with the tip of his brogue in a reflective manner. "This fella had quite a reputation in certain circles in the old country. 'Too long a sacrifice can make a stone of the heart'." He looked around. "Know your Yeats? Should do, name like Molloy."

"I thought he was a rat," said Molloy, his arms around Caitlin, who was shaking, her teeth chattering.

"Sometimes circumstances will force a fella to act in a way that he might never have imagined he would," said Walsh, his voice soft. "And he carries that knowledge with him always."

"You set him up for this and then you had him killed," said Molloy. "Why?"

Walsh flicked a handkerchief open and bent down to wipe the toe of his shoe. "Why?" He stood and began to fold the handkerchief, taking his time, holding the corners together, shaking out the creases, putting his thoughts in order. "They say you'll find that word scratched on the walls of every cell in the Soviet Union. *Pochemy*? In Russian it means sort of, 'Why *me*? After everything *I've* done for the Revolution? For the Party? For Uncle Joe?'" He pulled back a cuff and checked the time. "But you know what? I'll tell you why."

Molloy thought of O'Flynn's comments from the previous night about the baddy's foolish insistence on tying up a plot's loose ends.

Walsh read his mind. "Don't flatter yourself, son," he said. "I always blab after a killing. It's the penitent in me, buried away."

He put the folded handkerchief back in his pocket. "I've never been a bible basher or a street-corner man of any kind — I've got no use for God or any of that malarkey — but a lot of the places I've bunked in over the years — flops, jails, People's Palaces, what-have-you — a lot of those places the Bible was the only way to pass the time. The occasional almanac or lingerie catalogue or political tract of one sort or another, a deck of cards sometimes, but always the Bible. So I know it pretty well. Take the religion out and it's a good read. And I can quote it at length. Hell's bells, show me a Wobbly who can't."

He turned and nodded towards O'Flynn. "Timothy 6:10. 'The root of all these evils is the love of money and there are some who have desired it and have erred from the faith and have brought themselves many miseries.'"

He clapped dirt off his hands and brushed it from his strides. "Banal as it might seem here in this dank corridor with a dead

Irishman and a German gun and enough explosives to blow up Parliament — well, that last one's a stretch — but there's your why. Plain old money. The root of everything. It's brought *me* many miseries, God knows. I've fought inequity in all its evil guises me whole life. And now I find I'm asking *myself* why? Because this thing I've been fighting for so long, it's just so flamin'" — he stretched out his hands — "*big*. And you can't touch it! It's like the blimmin' Vatican or the Rothschilds or, I dunno, Black Lodge Masonry. It can't be changed from the outside, I doubt it could be changed from within."

He took off his hat and ran a hand through his hair. "The very things I despised in my father, always worrying about *money* and *tomorrow* — in *Poverty Bay* for Christ's sake, was ever a place better named? — those very things are happening to me! I look around. What have I achieved? And I'm getting old and I have bugger all to show for it. Farms in the Wairarapa? Bunkum. A few acres and a couple of cows." He put his hat back on and squared it. "So if an opportunity comes along I have to act upon it. And an opportunity came along. Simple as that. Fortuitously, on this occasion, I happen to agree with the outcome."

He shrugged. "See what I mean? Just pours out. Am I dreading the loss of heaven? Could well be."

He hooked a thumb in the direction of Queen Street. "And we're on the verge of chaos, let's not forget. Anarchists. Bombs. Innocent civilians. The country held by the throat. Those stories seeping out of Russia? Is that how it will end? Is that why so many bombs were thrown and so many good men and women died? I'm just doing what I can to tilt things in the right direction." He pointed to the late O'Flynn. "Hard on Frank, but he was a fella who lived by the sword, so in his heart he'd understand."

He looked at his watch. "Anyway, son. You foiled an attempt on the life of our beloved Prime Minister. By a wild-eyed Red, what's more. The country's in your debt. You'll be working with a better class of divorcée from now on, I'd think."

CHAPTER SIXTY-EIGHT

Sid Holland's bodyguard escorted him to the scene of the crime. An electric cable had been fed down the stairwell and lighting strung along the beams.

"Brace yourself, Prime Minister," said Walsh, as he took hold of the sheet covering O'Flynn. "This is fairly ghoulish."

"I was on the Western Front, Walsh," said Holland. "I've seen plenty of dead bodies, don't you worry."

Walsh pulled back the sheet, tugging slightly where the blood was sticking in the area of the head and chest. Half of O'Flynn's face had collapsed. His dead eyes stared at the ceiling.

"Do we know who the bastard is?" said Holland.

Walsh stood. "A wharfie," he said. "Frank O'Flynn. Known wrecker and malingerer." Walsh took a note from his suit pocket and handed it to the Prime Minister. "This was on him."

"'Thus always to tyrants!'" said Holland, translating. "*Tyrannis* with one 'n'. Can't even spell, the ignorant beggar." He looked at O'Flynn's bloodied face. "He's a Red, I suppose?"

"As pigeon's blood," said Walsh.

"I want this kept under wraps," said Holland. "No use scaring the horses."

"Understood," said Walsh.

"They set a charge on a railway bridge near Huntly this morning," said Holland. "God alone knows how many people might have perished. Fortunately, the police were tipped off." He shook his head. "The whole show's starting to feel like St Petersburg in 1917, don't you think?"

"Identical, Sid," said Walsh. "What now?"

"Oh I know what now," said Holland. "Don't you worry about that." He looked around. "By the way, where's the fella who shot him?" he said. "Like to express my appreciation."

"Upstairs," said Walsh. "Giving statements."

"Excellent," said Holland. "Police taking charge. We're going to see a lot more of that, mark my words."

The Prime Minister and his party left.

A young constable cleared his throat. "Excuse me, Mr Walsh," he said. "Would you mind having a look at something for me."

Walsh followed the constable's torch beam into O'Flynn's work area.

"What is it, son?"

"I'm probably speaking out of turn, but when I left school and before I joined the police I was a pit boy at the Blackpool Mine in Westport," said the policeman. "So I've had experience around explosives. Not a lot, but some."

"Is this area safe?" said Walsh, putting one hand into his pocket, feeling the Luger.

"It is," said the policeman. "As houses. That's what I'm trying to say, Mr Walsh. That's what's funny."

"What's your point, son?"

The young policeman shone his torch on the timer. "Well, this whole set-up looks a bit queer to me. Only one of the fuses was plugged into a detonator. And look at the size of the stick?" He shook his head. "You'd get a bigger explosion from a string of Double Happies. I can't, sorta, work out what he was, y'know, what he was hoping to do."

Walsh relaxed. He took a notebook from his breast pocket and thumbed for a clean page. "What's your name, lad?" he said.

"Robbins, sir."

Walsh licked his pencil and wrote down the name. "Christian name?"

"Kerry, Mr Walsh."

"Enjoy police work, do you, Robbins?"

"I do, sir, yes," said Robbins.

"Intend sticking with it?"

"I do, Mr Walsh, yes."

"I like your stamp, Constable," said Walsh. "I'm going to keep an eye on you. I think you'll go far."

"Oh, thanks, Mr Walsh," said Robbins.

"But my advice, and I say this to all young blokes starting out in life, whatever their position — it's not an original observation but it's a sound one — I say to them, for your first couple of years breathe through your nose. You know what I mean by that?"

Robbins thought hard. "Um, not really, no, sir."

"No," said Walsh. He closed his notebook. "No, I bet you don't. I'm saying keep your blasted trap shut. I'm saying there are things going on here that will be dealt with at a level beyond your comprehension. Ordnance examiners and Special Branch and God-knows-what. Not some country bumpkin who thinks he smells a rat because he spent a couple of days in the pit when he was a lad." Walsh put his hand on Robbins' shoulder and pulled him in close. "I'm saying that if you voice your misguided and ill-informed concerns to anyone, *anyone* mind, you'll be checking padlocks in Eketahuna till 1970. You foller?"

"Jesus," said the young constable in a small voice.

"And there's no call for profanity, either," said Walsh, hooking a thumb in O'Flynn's direction. "A man's warm body lying just down the hallway, his poor soul still in transition."

"I'm sorry, Mr Walsh," said Robbins.

"Good," said Walsh.

CHAPTER SIXTY-NINE

Molloy and Caitlin were waiting in a room next to the Town Hall manager's office. A constable had brought in tea and biscuits. Caitlin had a spray of blood on her blouse. She was very quiet, hand shaking when she lifted her cup.

The door opened and a man entered. He was wearing a white shirt with the sleeves rolled up and had policeman written all over him. He sat down and put a folder on the floor by his chair.

"How d'you do," he said. "Detective Sergeant Howard."

"What's going on?" said Molloy.

Howard looked at him. "A looney tried to blow up the Town Hall and kill the Prime Minister and several hundred of the good people of Auckland," he said. "Then he was shot and killed by a private detective. Doesn't happen that often. Raises a few questions, sorta thing." He took a packet of cigarettes from his shirt pocket. "Smoke?"

"Good on you," said Molloy, taking two and handing one to Caitlin. The policeman put a box of matches on the table. "Okay," he said. "Want to tell me what happened?"

"Miss O'Carolan had nothing to do with all this," said Molloy. "She was an innocent bystander."

"Funny place to be a bystander," said Howard. "Two floors under the Town Hall."

"She's a reporter."

"Even so."

"The dead bloke's name is O'Flynn," said Molloy. "That's the name he uses, anyway. Used to use. I think his real name's O'Phelan. He's an Irishman. I didn't shoot him. Maori called Sunny Day did. Works for F.P. Walsh, the union big wig. Shot him with a Luger that belonged to me."

"Where'd you get the Luger?" said Howard.

"Italy."

"I thought your mug was familiar," said Howard, looking up. "22nd?"

"That's right."

"23rd," said Howard, tapping his chest. "Just at the end. Fiji for two years. Then a year's jungle training in Queensland in preparation for the Japs. Once we were ready for that they sent us to Italy."

"Situation normal," said Molloy.

"You're telling me," said Howard.

There was a knock on the door.

"Got a mo', Craig?"

There was whispering.

"Back in a tick," said the policeman, closing the door.

"What's going on?" said Caitlin, still in shock.

"Not sure. Are you all right?"

"Not really. I can feel his blood on my clothes."

They waited for what could have been an hour. The door would open and people would look in and change their minds and go out. At one point Walsh's laughter could be heard. Molloy went to check in the corridor but a constable prevented him from leaving. Eventually, Howard returned, accompanied by a tall, stooped man in a well-cut suit, with a wrinkled face, a suggestion of white hair, and dark eyes that could cut steel. "Two days in a row, Caitlin," he said. "Your father will be putting me on a commission."

"Johnny, this is Mr Haigh," said Caitlin.

"We've met," said Molloy. "How are you, Frank?"

"I'm well, Johnny," said the lawyer. "Yourself?" He took two sheets of paper from his briefcase. "This is a suppression order. You're not to discuss or write or in any way pass on details of what happened in the basement of this building earlier today, on pain of prosecution under section 161 of the Emergency Powers Act. An Act which has yet to be passed, incidentally, but that doesn't seem to worry these clowns." He unscrewed a fountain pen and offered it to Caitlin. "Once you've both signed you're free to go. My motorcar is outside. Shall we?"

"What about Johnny?" said Caitlin.

"He can take off too," said Howard.

"How come?" said Molloy.

Howard shrugged and held a hand way above his head. "I'm just the flunky," he said.

CHAPTER SEVENTY

Sid Holland took a seat in 1YA's Studio C. There was a jug of water and a glass on a table in front of him, and a microphone covered with a sock.

"Some of our speakers like to have a gargle beforehand, Mr Holland," said the nervous studio manager.

"Done this sort of thing plenty of times," said Holland. "Let's get started, shall we?" He pulled the heavy microphone towards him. "Testing, testing. One, two, three, four."

"Sorry, sir," said a voice from the control room. "Caught us by surprise there, Mr Holland."

"Well, hurry it up," said Holland. "I've got an aeroplane to catch." He took notes from his breast pocket and unfolded his reading glasses.

"We're ready now, sir," said the voice.

"Excellent," said Holland. "Count me down."

He waited for the pips to finish and began speaking.

"Good evening, everyone," he began, reading slowly, his voice rising and falling. "I have not previously approached the task of making a broadcast to the people of New Zealand with a greater sense of responsibility, or with a deeper sense of public duty, than I do at this very moment. When I took the oath of my office I swore on my honour that I should do my duty to my country and to the people who put me where I am. Tonight, I honour my pledge to my King and my country, and difficult though the task may be, I feel that my colleagues and I have the backing and goodwill of the people to whom I address myself."

He turned a page. "The industrial crisis in which New Zealand has been gripped has taken a dramatic and grave turn. A very determined and dramatic effort has been made to overthrow orderly government by force."

Oh this is good, he thought. This is rousing stuff.

CHAPTER SEVENTY-ONE

Through connections Caitlin was offered a position on the *Birmingham Post*. It wasn't the *Manchester Guardian*, but it was getting there. She stood with a cluster of family and friends as all around her excited passengers walked awkwardly up the wooden gangway to the *Rangitata*, bound for London. Cranes swung bales of wool into the *Rangitata*'s hold. Soldiers and sailors, shirts off, loaded wool, butter and frozen mutton onto pallets. Caitlin kissed her mother and shook her father's hand. He took an envelope from his inside pocket and gave it to her, ignoring her protestations.

She picked up an overnight case, adjusted her scarf, looked around for Molloy one last time, and saw him, leaning against the wall of a cargo shed.

She dropped her bag and ran to him.

"I don't want to go," she said.

"It's where you belong," he said. "The big wide world."

Her eyes filled with tears. "You're just saying that to make me leave."

"I'm saying it because it's true," he said, passing her a handkerchief. "If that boat leaves and you're not on it, you'll always regret it."

"I thought you didn't go to the pictures," she said, blowing her nose.

"The USO had a projector at our embarkation camp in Venice," he said. "And two flicks. A John Wayne and that one. There was nothing else to do."

"Italy," said Caitlin. "Of course."

The *Rangitata*'s foghorn blew. A tugboat's propeller churned the water. A cheer went up from the crowd on the wharf, followed by a ragged chorus of "Now is the Hour".

Eyes glistening, she turned and walked up the gangway. At the top she found room and leaned over the rail. She blew him a passionate kiss.

He reached up and caught it in mid-air, closed his fist and brought it in, thumb facing out, hand angled towards his cheek, the salute of the Left Opposition.

CHAPTER SEVENTY-TWO

Molloy spoke to Tom O'Driscoll, the *Star*'s police roundsman, about the situation with Tom's younger brother Bruce, and their mother June, who was staying on Bruce's farm just out of Morrinsville, and looking after his children following the death of his wife from polio. Bruce's boys were a handful. Molloy told Tom that he knew someone who might be looking for work as a housekeeper and was used to big families. Tom spoke to Bruce, who said that that sounded good. June came up on the train and met Brigid Toomey at Farmers. They got along. Brigid was respectful, and June knew about men like Pat Toomey.

They drove to Arch Hill. June waited in the car while Molloy and Brigid went inside. Brigid packed a suitcase. Molloy climbed up into the ceiling and had a poke round. He drove both women to the station and bought Brigid a ticket to Hamilton with a bus connection to Morrinsville. He gave her a hundred pounds in a sealed envelope, and a kiss on the cheek.

Later that evening Molloy parked outside Toomey's house. There were lights on inside. He approached the house and knocked.

"Who is it?" said Toomey.

"Johnny Molloy."

The door opened. Toomey was wearing braces over an unbuttoned white shirt, and holding a glass of beer. He brewed his own from a set-up under the house.

"The man of the hour," said Toomey, standing back. "Long time no see, as the Chinaman said. Come in. I'm just sampling a new brew."

Molloy held a glass at an angle as Toomey slowly poured. The policeman put the flagon on the bench. "Cheers."

"Good luck."

They drank. It was a lively brew with a good head and a hoppy flavour.

"Not bad," said Molloy, putting his glass down.

"Tell me," said Toomey. "And this is the beer talking, probably. Loose lips sink ships, sorta thing? But what's it feel like to shoot a bloke? Never had the pleasure, myself."

Molloy put his glass on the kitchen table. "Depends on the bloke," he said, looking Toomey in the eye. "Some ratbags I wouldn't think twice about."

Toomey straightened slightly. "What's on your mind, John?" he said.

"I want to talk to you about Brigid."

Toomey looked at him. "What about Brigid?"

"About that shiner you gave her."

"The effrontery," said Toomey, putting down his glass. "It's none of your blasted business. What goes on between a married couple in the—"

Molloy spun off his right leg, sending a hook smashing into Toomey's ribcage, the false ribs at the bottom, the ones easiest to break.

The policeman doubled over, gasping, one hand on the bench for support, the other wrapped around his middle. Molloy stepped in and hit him again.

"The first one was for Brigid. The second was for setting me up with Sunny Day outside the RSC that night, you gutless bastard."

"Are you mad?" Toomey said eventually, his eyes watering, face contorted. "Battery on a member of the police? You'll swing for this, you fucking Communist."

"Brigid's gone away," said Molloy. "She won't be back. I've stashed four hundred quid in a paper bag somewhere round this section. Bloodhounds couldn't find it. But if I hear Brigid's so much as stubbed a toe you're for the high jump, Pat. I've got mates on *Truth*. They won't ignore open corruption, even in the gaming squad." He washed his glass and put it upside down on the bench by the sink. "Thanks for the beer."

Molloy drove to the Municipal Baths and stood under a hot shower for a long time. He was hungry. He drove to Greys Avenue and parked outside the Golden Dragon. The dining room was empty apart from a waiter making notes with a pencil on a copy of *Best Bets*, and a woman sitting alone in the corner, smoking. He sat down by the door. The waiter padded over with a plate of bread and butter. Molloy asked for chow mein and a pot of tea. There was a brief outburst of shouting between the waiter and the kitchen, which Molloy assumed had something to do with the lateness of the hour. A pot crashed onto a stovetop. The woman, who had red lipstick and a tight dress, gave the private detective what Sister Colleen would have described as a brazen look. But Molloy didn't feel like it. He shook his head and the woman went back to her cigarette. He ate dinner, and went home.

THE END

to

MAURICE CULLINANE

and

REX LAWRENCE

with love and respect

Everything that was good from that small, remote country had gone
into them — sunshine and strength, good sense, patience, the
versatility of practical men.

— John Mulgan, *Report on Experience*

ACKNOWLEDGMENTS

Red Herring is fiction, "pure bunkum from end to end", as Jock Barnes might have said, with historical events reordered to suit the demands of the plot. I've read a number of books and articles written during and about the period, not so much for their factual content as for their colour. "Pure bunkum from end to end", for example, is a quote from Barry Gustafson's history of the National Party, *The First 50 Years* (with its ominous implication that there will be 50 more), as was Sid Holland's response to the suggestion that he get some flunky to shine his shoes. Bones Harrington's line to Molloy, "get that down your rotten guts", is from the late Gordon Slatter's account of the Italian Campaign, *One More River*. "You pansies never knew what a real war was" is from Slatter's wonderful novel, *A Gun In My Hand*.

The material about F.P. Walsh was suggested by Dean Parker's 1988 *Metro* article, "The Black Prince", and Graeme Hunt's 2004 Walsh biography, *Black Prince: The Story of Fintan Patrick Walsh*. V.G. Parker is a salute to Dean's legendary uncle, Uncle Vic, "the Dzerzhinsky of Grafton Gully."

Material about the Maori Battalion is based on Monty Souter's magnificent and moving *Nga Tama Toa*, the reading of which has been one of the delights of this whole exercise. The Thomas Cook heist was suggested by a passing remark in Peter Winter's vivid account of the Crete Campaign, *Expendable*.

I came across the line, "His last radio message was 'Japanese coming. Regards to all'" in Michael Field's memoir, *Swimming with Sharks*. The message was sent by Coastwatcher Arthur Heenan, a farmer's son from Middlemarch, executed by the Japanese in October 1942, on Tarawa in what is now Kiribat.

The description of the colour of the earth on Chunuk Bair — "I would say it was a dull, browny red. And that was blood" — was recounted by Vic Nicholson, a veteran of the Wellington Battalion, in the 1984 TVNZ documentary, *Gallipoli: The New Zealand Story*.

Both Michael Bassett and R.C.J. Stone have written about the Kelly Gang, described by the pre-war American Consul-General in Auckland, Walter Boyle, as "dissatisfied conservatives naively endeavouring to run affairs of state from their deep leather armchairs in Princes Street." Conrad Bollinger, in *Grog's Own Country*, says that the gang got its name "not because it shared any of the Robin Hood qualities of Ned Kelly's cohorts but merely because of the similarity of their business methods to those of bushrangers". *Grog's Own Country* is also the source of Sid Holland's remark about the complexity of the Emergency Regulations, "It would take a Philadelphia lawyer to understand them."

The term "stonking" — described by *The Official History of New Zealand in the Second World War* as "the terrifying concentration of the fire of all the divisional artillery upon a single crucial point" — is from Haddon Donald's *In Peace and War: A Civilian Soldier's Story*. Donald was CO of the 22nd Battalion and the epitome of the long-service soldier — "22 right through" — from Greece to Trieste.

"The New Zealand Division's first combined exercise was a battle and they did pretty well" is a reworking of a line from *The Official History of New Zealand in the Second World War*. The original is, "Instead of being a training run, our first combined exercise was to become a battle." Material on the Greek Campaign is from Christopher Pugsley's utterly engaging *A Bloody Road Home* and Monty Souter's *Nga Tama Toa*. My version would not stand a historian's scrutiny but I think the tone is true.

I read or was told or overheard *somewhere* the description of a young and pregnant woman waiting with her mother for the Limited at Taihape while her father remained in the car, but have been unable to find the source. My apologies. The original is very moving and much better.

"He was a strange bugger, old Peter. Loved funerals." This line was suggested by material in Gavin McLean's biography of Peter Fraser on the nzhistory.net.nz site. I have spent many happy hours on both nzhistory.net.nz and TeAra.govt.nz, both of which took me down endless and thoroughly enjoyable rabbit holes of diversion and speculation.

"Landed as Pat Tuohy, left as Pat Walsh." One of the few unquestionably true things in this book is the fact that why Walsh changed his name and the circumstances of his stay in Ireland has never been satisfactorily explained. There is a caption beneath a photograph of Walsh on page 123 of Redmer Yska's history, *Truth: The Rise and Fall of the People's Paper*, that reads, "In 1959 feared union strongman F.P. Walsh threatened to hire a Sydney hitman to shoot *Truth*'s leading lights Cliff Plimmer and J.H. Dunn." And on the following page, "In a legendary exchange in Wellington's supreme court Dunn [*Truth*'s publisher] got Walsh to provide his real name and to confess to having once been a communist."

"Paul Jeffrey, a seagull and part-time music teacher at Seddon Tech, who occasionally sat in for Crombie Murdoch with Ted Croad's big band at the Orange Ballroom on a Saturday night ..." This over-egged detail is an opportunity to salute Chris Bourke's

Blue Smoke: The Lost Dawn of New Zealand Popular Music 1918–1964 about which Gordon Campbell wrote in *Metro*, "If there is any justice *Blue Smoke* will become the *Edmonds Cookbook* of New Zealand popular culture — because truly, every home in the country should own a copy of this impeccably researched, spectacularly illustrated history of how popular music evolved here." I picked it up initially in the hope of finding where you might get a good cup of coffee in Auckland in 1951.

"The bomber who leaned his armed bicycle against the wall …" In trying to work out why O'Flynn might have left Ireland I read about the IRA and came across a number of references to the Mainland Campaign. In a site called *Historic Coventry* run by Robert Orland I read an article on the Broadgate bombing — the low point of the campaign — written by Simon Shaw. The article included this line: "The unknown bomb maker completed his task the following morning." Unknown bomb maker, eh? I wrote to Simon who said he had got that detail from Tim Pat Coogan's rollicking history of the IRA (called, prosaically, *The IRA*), which I read for details about the Broadgate bombing and the wider campaign. The bomber's identity is still unconfirmed although in 1969 a Cork man named Joby O'Sullivan told a journalist with Ireland's RTÉ, Mike Burns, that he was the perpetrator but that the carnage was accidental. "The intention was to bomb the Broadgate police station but the bicycle wheels kept getting stuck in the tram tracks so O'Sullivan abandoned it and took off." My nephew, Ed White, told me about the "Twelve Apostles", Michael Connelly's squad of IRA assassins.

Marching Through Georgia really did win the Irish Greyhound Derby in 1939. Has there ever been a more magnificent name for a dog?

"Walsh, that Freemanite, I knew it!" A reference to Frederick Engels (yes!) Freeman, who trained at the Comintern's Lenin School in Moscow and became General Secretary of the CPNZ in 1933. He was expelled from the Party in 1937 for coming down on the wrong side of the Popular Front line. He spent the rest of his working life in the Hutt Railway workshops, was active in the Amalgamated Society of Railway Servants, President of the Wellington branch of the NZUSSR Society, and an enthusiastic ballroom dancer and keen amateur photographer. He died of a heart attack after collapsing on the gangway of a Soviet research vessel in Wellington harbour in 1969. These details are from Maureen Birchfield's *Looking for Answers: A Life of Elsie Locke*, and from Elsie's son, Keith Locke.

"The Black Death came to Sydney in January 1900 ..." This description of the arrival of the bubonic plague in Sydney is based on material in the catalogue which accompanied *Plague! Rats in the Realm*, an exhibition held at the University of Sydney, Faculty of Medicine, in 2009.

In Anna Green's history *British Capital, Antipodean Labour. Working the New Zealand Waterfront 1915–1951*, "One member of the Auckland executive recalled that fostering social and cultural activities had been a deliberate union policy after the war to 'combat a long, continuous, vicious media campaign against us' and to build up the union into an organisation that would gain the respect of the community as a whole." Wharfies had sports teams, boxing competitions, pipe bands and chess clubs. Their debating team won the Athenaeum Challenge Cup — the senior debating trophy of the Auckland Debating Association — in 1948 and 1950. So the existence of a Watersiders' Chorale, like a lot of other stuff in this story, is not *out of the question.*

I'd like to thank the following: Johnny Fay, all the Molloys, Geoff Walker, Sue Reidy, Finlay Macdonald, the late Gordon Slatter, Dean Parker, Andrew Maben, Graeme Hunt, Monty Souter, Christopher Pugsley, Stuart Hoar, John Newton, Christine Winter, Susan Butterworth, Gwion Thornley, Bill Rosenberg, Jim McAloon, Pat Booth, Barry Gustafson, Redmer Yska, Anna Green, David Tossman, Murray Horton, Keith Locke, Andrew Laben, Jane Elliott.Elliott, Mick Sinclair, Robert Orland, Simon Shaw, Tim Hunkin, Sara Vui-Talitu, Margie Thomson, Jim Welch, Julia Knapman, Dianne Blacklock, Sandra Noakes, Penguin Books for permission to use Michael King's quote from *The Penguin History of New Zealand*, Victoria University Press for permission to use John Mulgan's quote from *Report on Experience*, Frances and Pete, Nick and Kate.

Errors, willful and otherwise, are my own.

Jonothan Cullinane was born in Palmerston North in 1951. Having established his proletarian bona fides as a roughneck on oil rigs in Canada and the North Sea and as a proofreader and bartender in New York City during the 1970s, he began working in the New Zealand film industry in 1981. In 2007 he wrote and directed *We're Here to Help*, about the Christchurch businessman Dave Henderson's titanic run-in with the IRD. The unprecedented success of that film led to a job as a postie in Mt Roskill, Auckland, a position he still holds.

Red Herring is his first novel.